After
Obsession

Also by Carrie Jones

Need
Captivate
Entice

After
Obsession

Carrie Jones
& Steven E. Wedel

BLOOMSBURY

LONDON BERLIN NEW YORK SYDNEY

Bloomsbury Publishing, London, Berlin, New York and Sydney

First published in Great Britain in September 2011
by Bloomsbury Publishing Plc
50 Bedford Square, London, WC1B 3DP

First published in the USA in September 2011
by Bloomsbury Books for Young Readers
175 Fifth Avenue, New York, NY 10010

A CIP catalogue record for this book is available from the British Library

ISBN 978 1 4088 1827 5

Printed in Great Britain by Clays Ltd, St Ives plc, Bungay, Suffolk

1 3 5 7 9 10 8 6 4 2

www.bloomsbury.com

*To Emily Ciciotte, Rena Morse, and
Shaun Farrar for always showing me
how to face the scary*

—C. J.

*To my wife, Kim, and the kids.
Thanks for your patience*

—S. E. W.

You are mine.
You all will be mine.

These are the words I hear every single freaking morning since my friend Courtney's dad died. They slither around inside my brain all day until I think I'm going crazy, and today is no exception. Even hanging out half-naked on the grass in the backyard with my boyfriend, Blake, I hear them. We're supposed to be looking up at the sky, enjoying the lazy post-make-out feeling, but no . . .

"You, Aimee, are the best," Blake says. "You are the best girlfriend in the universe and you are mine forever. Got it?"

The words remind me of that dream voice, and even though my head rests on Blake's chest, I don't feel calm like I normally do when we're together. Queasiness settles into my stomach. Blake's heart thumps away like the drum beat to a blood song I can't hear. Blake's a singer. He always has a song going on in his head, and I imagine that song fills him all the way, pumping into his blood, spreading throughout his capillaries, going into every inch of him, the way the words go into me. I sigh over his heartbeat.

"Gramps and Benji will be home pretty soon," I say.

"Hint, hint?" he asks, reaching for his shirt and smiling his rock-star smile that makes everyone swoon.

"Sort of," I apologize.

All around us is just woods and river and the house; it feels like they're watching, telling us it's okay to be young and happy. But it's not okay to be young and happy, not today. Not now. Not when Courtney's dad is dead. It isn't right for me to be happy when everything inside of her is a big, big ache. I know that ache personally. The ocean took Courtney's dad; the river took my mom. It was a long time ago, but my ache is still there.

Blake leans me against the biggest pine tree, but I'm not really feeling it anymore. In the last few weeks, I've been feeling it less and less with Blake, and that worries me so much because we are perfect for each other; everyone says that.

Blake groans. "We have to write a paper in psych about our deepest fears."

"Yeah?" His eyes are so gray. They are ocean eyes; that's what I like to think. Although, the ocean isn't so great an image anymore. Still, I take the bait and ask, "So what's yours?"

He moves his hands down from my shoulders to my arms, all the way to my wrists, and grabs me there while he shrugs. "I don't know. I'm not really scared of much. Fire, maybe. Not getting into Stanford."

Something inside me sloshes around like old coffee, stale and nauseating. A crow takes off from the tree, black wings beating against the air, with the air, of the air.

"What are you afraid of?" he asks.

I think about it, then just tell the truth. "I'm afraid of myself."

His eyebrows wrinkle, confused.

I push out a big breath and say, "Me. The thing I'm afraid of the most is me."

There are some things about myself that I can't explain. Sometimes, I see things in my dreams before they happen—just like my mom used to, which makes me think there's some sort of genetic component to the whole "psychic" thing. Yes, I know this is weird, and yes, I saw things about Courtney, and yes, I am seeing things about some rugged boy I've never met, a boy who has the kind of skin that looks perpetually tanned. And yes, weeks ago I had a dream about men drowning, but the fog was so intense and the lighting was so bad that I couldn't make out who they were, didn't know how to stop it. I didn't realize one of them was Courtney's dad.

The dreams suck like that.

It's not just dreams. Sometimes when people are sick or hurt, I can touch them and somehow they are better or they start healing. Sometimes you can see their wounds start to close. I don't know if my mom could do that, too; she didn't live long enough for me to ask her.

I am not crazy.

Right before Blake leaves, we kiss good-bye, long, slow, him pressing me into the edge of his old Volvo station wagon.

"I wish you didn't have to go," I say.

He pulls his head away, moves some hair out of my face. His words touch my cheek, soft. "Me, too."

I step backward. The wind blows my hair back into my face. Blake stares up at my house, a big, wood-shingled cape with a front porch, attached garage, all that. "Your house is so cozy looking," he says.

"*Cozy* looking?"

"It just looks nice. I like to imagine you in there sleeping at night."

I turn around to look at the house and lean back against his car with him. "It *is* cozy looking. It's so different from Courtney's house now. Sometimes it feels awful there, you know?"

"I think it's a common feeling." He tugs my wrist, pulling me closer to him. "Call Courtney, have her come over. Then maybe you'll both feel better."

So, right after Blake leaves, I text Courtney to come kayaking with me, and Gramps texts me that it'll be another hour before he and Benji get home.

As soon as Courtney gets to my house, we grab life jackets and paddles and head to the long, wooden dock that juts out into the river. It's about a half a mile to the bay and the ocean where Courtney's dad died. It's the same distance back to town, farther by car. The river is the quick way in and out. For a second, Courtney looks out to sea, and I know she's got to be thinking about her dad because her eyes dull and her mouth droops down. She shakes it off, though, and it's like I can actually witness her rearrange her features into something happy.

"You would not believe what happened to me today," she says. Her dark hair lifts up off of her face with the wind. She shakes her head like the memory is too much.

"What?" I hold our tandem kayak steady as she slides into the front compartment.

"It is so super horrible," she says, leaning forward to hang on to the dock while I get in the back of the kayak. "Seriously. Like it's horrible on the level of women's magazine 'true life horror stories.'"

We grab our paddles and push sideways, scooting across the top of the water. I try not to think about Courtney's dad being dead or my mom being dead, either. At least we knew where she died—right here. Those are bad thoughts. I push them out of my head.

"Tell me what happened," I beg and smile. It's so good to see Courtney acting like her old self, not too sad, talking again.

"Okay. So, Justin Willis needed a pen in Honors Bio, and I pulled out a pen from my purse, right?" Our kayak slices through the water as she talks, a steady up and down rhythm.

"Right," I say, because she has paused for acknowledgment.

"So, I take the pen out and hold it up and he's still like, 'I need a pen. Anyone got a pen?' And I'm like, 'Dude, here!' And I'm waving my pen in front of his face now, because I'm super annoyed that he's ignoring me, and I'm thinking, *What? Is my pen not good enough for you, Justin Willis?*"

"Of course it is!" I'm getting all offended on Courtney's behalf.

"No. No. Wait for it . . ." She stops paddling and starts laughing, twisting around so I can see her face as she tells the rest of the story. She squeezes her eyes shut like it's just too much. "So then I actually look at the pen in my hand, and it's not a pen."

"It's not a pen?" I ask into the silence. Courtney is really good at telling stories. She should be a comedian, I swear.

5

"It's not a pen! It's a tampon! I'm waving a *tampon* in Justin Willis's face!" Her head tilts back and she laughs so hard the kayak wiggles. Or maybe that's because I'm laughing, too.

"That's soooo terrible!" I say.

"I know! I know!"

We both give up on paddling and just float there for a minute, because life is way too funny sometimes.

"I love you, Court," I tell her. "You are the biggest goofball in the world and I love you."

"Ha!" she laughs. "I know!"

A cloud passes over the sun, making shadows on the river. We're too close to the bay where her dad died, and she says, her voice all full of sadness again, "Let's go back toward town, okay?"

My grandfather and Benji come back just a couple of minutes after Courtney leaves. I'm browsing through the fridge for food when they burst in. The moment they both step inside, a potato from the far end of the kitchen counter plops off the marble and bangs onto the floor. It rolls and rolls. I grab it. Potatoes smell so earthy, just like dirt, and normally I like that smell, but this time it makes me shudder. I don't know why. It's moments like these when I kind of doubt that I'm sane at all.

Gramps kisses me on the forehead. "How was soccer?"

"Good," I say. "How was Cub Scouts?"

"Boring," Benji says as he throws his wet swim stuff on the floor. It lands in a heap of squishiness, the wet making the blue of his swimsuit dark, almost like a seal head poking up out of the ocean water. For a second I shift into this weird zone that always happens when I get my vision things. I see a seal—a real seal. She stares at me. Her eyes are full of loss and . . . something else. Warning? I shake my head, make it go away.

"Pick that up, Benji. It will mold. Scouts was fine. We swam at the Y," Gramps says. His forehead crinkles. "Pick it up *now*, Benji."

Benji trots back and picks up his wet stuff. "Gramps was flirting again."

"Really?" I grab an apple off the counter and bite into it. "Gramps never flirts."

"No, I don't," he says, but his eyes get a wicked-old-man twinkle.

"Never. The least flirty man I know," I tease, moving away.

"Where you going?" Gramps asks me, then yells down toward the laundry room, "Put those wet things in the washer, not the hamper, Benji!"

"Whatever," Benji yells back.

Gramps raises his eyebrows into his grandfather-not-pleased look. He plucks his own apple from the bowl. "He's getting an attitude."

"I'm going upstairs to paint," I tell him.

Gramps likes to know what we're doing. It makes him feel like he's competent and in control. The perfect surrogate mom. "I'm in charge of dinner tonight. Steaks sound good?"

"Yep." I've started up the stairs but stop to ask, "Is Dad coming home?"

"Late meeting with the physicians."

"Again?"

He sighs. "Again. How is Courtney doing?"

7

"She seemed a bit better today." Sadness settles over me. "But she thinks her dad might still be—"

"Alive?" Gramps shakes his head. "Maine water is too cold for anyone to last long, even those men. It's best to accept the facts."

"I know." I swallow hard, trying not to remember the vision where the men in the water were reaching up, trying to find something to hold on to, but finding only fog.

Gramps is suddenly next to me, grabbing my arm. "Steady there, camper."

"Sorry. It's just so . . . it's so sad."

"I know. *Life* is sad sometimes."

"Her cousin came today," I say, "and her aunt. They're from somewhere in the Midwest, I think. They're going to try to help them keep the house."

Gramps lets me go. "Good. God knows they need all the help they can get."

Just an hour later I'm through my homework and painting when Gramps starts yelling our names up the stairs. "Aimee! Benji! Dinner!"

Benji rushes out of his room, sticks his tongue out at me, and thunders down the staircase. I follow him, yelling, "I'm going to beat you. You are sooooo slow!"

This is a total lie, because I'm not even trying.

"Winner!" He slams down at the table and announces, "I love steak!"

"Dead cow. Yummy," I say, sitting down. I imagine the poor cow's life, stuck at the factory farm, diseased, lonely. I can see it perfectly. I try to reassign my thoughts because this isn't mentally healthy and I check out my grandfather. He looks a bit tired. He does so much around here because my dad has sixty-hour workweeks. "I would have set the table, Gramps."

"I know, but you were busy. Plus, an old man needs to feel useful." He forks a steak onto my plate. "Did I tell you about the little venture Benji and I have got going?" he asks.

I shake my head and cut my meat. "Nope."

"Benji." Gramps points toward the fridge.

Benji puts his fork down, pops up and rushes over to the counter, vaults on top of it, reaches to the top of the fridge, and grabs something in a Ziploc bag, then leaps off the counter and waves the bag in my face. I inspect the orange contents.

"It's a Cheeto?"

"Not just any Cheeto, right, Gramps?" Benji says.

Gramps rubs his hands together. "That's for sure."

I examine the processed-food orangeness and try to figure out what to say. "Okay. It's, um, it's . . ."

"Marilyn Monroe!" Benji announces.

"What?" I look to Gramps for help.

"Marilyn Monroe. She was one of the big-time movie stars back in the day. She had blond hair and—"

"Massive hooters!" Benji interrupts.

"Benji!" I yell at him.

He plops down in his seat, giggling. Gramps is chuckling.

"Men suck," I say.

"We do not say 'suck' in this family," Gramps says sternly.

I point my fork at him. Some steak falls off. "No, but we say 'hooters.' That's fair. Anyway, I know who Marilyn Monroe is. I just don't understand what she has to do with the Cheeto."

Benji rolls his eyes. "She *is* the Cheeto."

"Reincarnated?" I stab a piece of steak.

"No." Gramps swipes the bag from Benji and puts it in front of my face again. "Look closely. Doesn't it look like Marilyn?"

I chew this over. "Um. Well, there are some bumps there."

Benji points at the top of the Cheeto. "See, that's her hair. You can see it, can't you, Aimee? It looks just like her."

He is all eager cuteness. There's a big thump upstairs, which makes us jump. I drop my fork. It clanks against the dish.

"Just a book falling down," Gramps says, which doesn't get rid of my goose bumps. "Do you see her in the Cheeto?"

"Sure," I say, picking up my fork. "I see it."

"*Her*," he corrects.

"Her. I see her. Wow." I nod really big. "That's super cool. What are you going to do with your Marilyn Monroe Cheeto?"

Benji jumps up and down, excited. "Sell her on eBay."

I choke and manage to somehow say, "eBay?"

"It's an Internet auction site," Gramps explains. "Benji, eat your dinner."

"I know what eBay is." I put my fork down on purpose this time and say it again just to make sure I understand. "You're selling her on eBay."

"Yep!" Benji says. "People are already bidding."

"Does Dad know about this?" I ask.

"He would if he ever actually came home," Benji says. His smile is gone. He stuffs more potato into his face. His teeth slam together and he swallows. "I bet we could get a thousand dollars."

My heart hurts for him.

"What do you think, Aim? How much could we get?" Gramps asks.

"Oh," I lie, "probably at least two thousand dollars."

Benji's eyes light up.

I lay it on harder, like another layer of paint, making it thicker. "Maybe more."

After dinner I'm in the upstairs bathroom wiping the paint thinner off my size 2 fan brush. There are still tiny flecks of yellow on the handle, but I'm okay with that. It makes it look well used. There's the faintest sound of footsteps, like Benji's slipping around or something.

Slowly, I put the brush down and peek out the open bathroom door into the hallway, clutching my paint scraper. There's nothing there, of course.

My mom taught me a prayer when I was little. She made me swear to say it every night.

"It won't get rid of the dreams, not completely, but it will help make them better," she said. "It's worked for others."

O God, who made the heav'n and earth,
From dreams this night protect me.
Destroy each succubus at birth,
No incubus infect me.

I say it in bed, but it doesn't keep the dreams from coming. In them, I'm trapped below water and something evil and bad is sucking my life away. It's dark. The water weighs on me, heavier and heavier, and in the distance is a wicked, ghostly laugh and a wail that's me screaming, screaming, screaming. Something reaches for me, lifting me up. At first it's scary and

11

furry and strong, all muscles and claws and it looks like a cougar, but then it changes into a guy, a huge guy. His dark eyes stare into mine, dark and frightened and wet, but strong somehow, too, determined.

"We have to save her," he says.

"Who?" I ask him. "Who?"

He goes cougar again and snarls. He is all teeth and noise. I wake up cranky and scared because I know that someone is in danger, but I don't know who or how to save them, just that I have to find out before it's too late. Wow, I hate dreams.

· 2 ·
ALAN

"What do you mean you don't have football here?" I ask.

Mrs. Wood, the counselor, is speechless for a moment.

"This is high school. You have to have football." I look to my mom in the chair beside me. "How can they *not* have football? Did you know about this?"

"I'm sorry, Alan," the counselor says. She really seems upset. She keeps glancing at my mom. "I thought I'd mentioned that."

"Mom? You knew, didn't you? You knew they didn't have football and you made me move up here anyway. Didn't you?"

"I'm sorry, Alan," she says, crossing her legs. "I did."

Back home, in Oklahoma City, a lot of my friends would have cussed out their moms right then and there. As mad as I am, I still can't do that. I just slump into the chair like a balloon suddenly emptied of air.

"Alan was second-team all-state in Class 5A last year," Mom explains. "He's really good at football. He's a running back."

"Is there another school that has football?" I ask.

"Not within fifty miles. We have soccer, cross-country, and wrestling," Mrs. Wood offers.

"Soccer? I can't get a football scholarship to OU playing soccer."

"Alan has wanted to play football for the University of Oklahoma forever," Mom explains before turning her attention back to me. "Alan, let's make the best of this."

It wasn't my idea to come to Maine. *Maine?* Really, who moves to Maine? Besides my mom, who brought us up here to live with my aunt and cousin now that they are husband- and fatherless. Nobody came to live with us just because I was fatherless, and I've been that way all my life.

"Whatever." It's the best concession I can offer. "Put me in cross-country. Do you at least have track in the spring?"

"Yes." Mrs. Wood almost fist-pumps, she's so happy. She puts me in cross-country and track as the computer vomits out the page that is my schedule of classes.

"Thank you." Mom is all consolatory smiles. "We just got here over the weekend. My sister's husband was recently killed— well, lost at sea, I guess. He owned a fishing boat and . . ."

"Oh, the *Dawn Greeter*." Realization fills Mrs. Wood's dark eyes. She looks at me and asks, "So, you're Courtney's cousin?"

"Yeah."

"She's a sweet girl," Mrs. Wood promises. I don't really know if she is or not. I saw Courtney for a few minutes last night, but other than that we've only met twice in our lives. "It was a city-wide tragedy when the boat was lost. All the crew was from here in town. Three of our students, including Courtney, lost fathers."

14

"That's horrible," Mom says. "I never understood how Lisa dealt with Mike going out to sea every day."

"Well, it's a lifestyle here." Mrs. Wood's eyes slide around her office for a moment, looking at pictures of ships and a brass bell mounted above the office door. "I'm sure working men face some kind of danger every day back there in Oklahoma, too."

"Yes, but at least there's usually a body to bury if something happens."

"True." Mrs. Wood starts to say more, but a bell rings and the hallway outside her office fills with teenagers. "First hour's over. As soon as things settle down, Alan, I'll have our office aide show you your locker and give you a quick tour of the school. Then he'll take you to biology."

I watch the flow of students but try not to be obvious about it. I see that a lot of them are looking through the glass window at me. The differences are pretty obvious and I know they're taking it in. My dusky skin and long black hair are very different from anything I see in the stream of humanity outside the office. The father I've never known is Navajo. I steel myself for the usual crap that comes with my emphasis on my Navajo heritage. They'll call me "chief," make reservation jokes, ask for cigars and wooden nickels until I lose my temper and kick some ass. After that there might be some grudging respect.

Another bell rings and the last couple of students in the hall run for open doors where teachers wait. A tall guy with short black hair comes into the counselor's office and drops some books on a small desk set off to the side.

"Blake?" Mrs. Wood calls. "This is Alan Parson. Today's his first day. Will you show him around?"

"Sure," Blake says. I watch him look me over, then nod at me. I nod back.

I follow him out of the office. Mom calls "Bye" behind me but I only wave, still mad about the football issue. Blake is a little taller than me, and he walks fast. He's wearing a blue T-shirt with GOFFSTOWN HIGH SCHOOL CROSS-COUNTRY printed on the back.

"You're in cross-country?" I ask.

"Yeah. Do you run?"

"I guess I do now," I say. "I can't believe you guys don't have a football team. In Oklahoma, every high school has a football team, even the little country schools."

"Football just isn't a big thing here," Blake says as he leads me up a hallway. "Plus, it's an expensive sport, and, in case you haven't noticed, this isn't a rich school. We have sports that don't cost much."

"Oh." I hadn't thought about the cost. "Is the cross-country team good?"

"Pretty good," he answers. "I was all-state last year. We had two guys and three girls make all-state individuals. We'll get the whole team in this year."

"That's cool." At least it was something.

"Here's your locker," he says as we round a corner. He points to a tall yellow door. "Give the lock a try." As I spin the dial to the numbers I've been given, he asks, "So, you're from Oklahoma?"

"Yeah."

"Why'd you come to Maine?"

While I tell him why I left Oklahoma, I close the door and face Blake again. "Oh, Courtney. Yeah, that sucked about her dad," he says.

I follow Blake up and down hallways while he points out restrooms, the auditorium, classrooms, and the cafeteria. He offers commentary about various teachers as we walk, and I soon realize he's one of the kids teachers love. Any negative thing he says about a teacher is followed with a positive. "Mrs. Bailey's classes are hard, but she's really cool. She brings cookies on Fridays."

Finally we come to a classroom door where Blake knocks. A guy sitting near the door jumps up and looks out at us through the narrow window before opening the door. He and Blake bump fists in greeting, and then Blake turns his attention to the teacher.

"Mr. Swanson," Blake says, "this is Alan Parson. He's new here. He's in your class for second hour."

More than a dozen pairs of eyes bore into me, watching, judging, making up stories about why I'm here. Mr. Swanson is a tall man with a thin white goatee and whitening blond hair. His eyes seem to sag, and he moves at a very leisurely pace as he comes to stand before me.

"Hello, Alan," he says. "Why don't you take a seat right over here? I was about to give an assignment. Once I get everyone else working, I'll get you caught up."

I go to the desk and sit behind a guy who needs a diet and in front of a redheaded girl who's vigorously chewing gum. I settle into the desk and wait, forcing my hand to stay off the medicine pouch I wear under my shirt. Usually I wear it outside my shirt, but that's back home. For now, the medicine pouch stays hidden.

Back home I'd be in Coach Baldwin's Street Law class right

now. I suppress a sigh and try to pretend people aren't staring at me instead of their books.

I survive an awkward bus ride home and get off at the stop when Courtney does.

"Sorry I didn't sit with you," Courtney says as we walk up the driveway. "Mom says I need to make you feel welcome."

"Don't worry about it." I look her over for the first time, really, since getting to Maine late Saturday evening. She's short, maybe four feet ten inches tall, and very thin and pale. Her brown hair hangs straight and limp and she lets it fall mostly over her face. Behind her glasses, she wears too much eyeliner. She has on a black AFI hoodie and faded blue jeans. I guess she's trying to be emo. I wonder if she cuts herself.

"Did Mom give you a key to the house yet?" she asks. I shake my head. It's a nice house. I have my own bedroom. "She will."

There are no vehicles in the driveway. I wonder if my mom is inside. She was supposed to have a job interview at the mill where Aunt Lisa works.

"Mom says you're going to live with us for a while," Courtney says. I can't tell if she thinks that's good or bad, or if she even cares.

"I guess so. You okay with that?"

"Yeah. I don't know," she says. "It's been really strange since Dad left. Mom was afraid she'd lose the house until Aunt Holly said you guys would come live with us and help out." We step onto the porch and Courtney pulls a key from her pocket to unlock the door. "I'm glad we won't lose it."

"Me, too," I say. Sure, I'm probably losing my future as an Oklahoma Sooner running back, then going pro, but at least Aunt Lisa and Courtney will get to keep their house. "Why didn't you guys just move to Oklahoma? Your mom grew up there."

Courtney gives me a look that says I must be the stupidest creature to ever stand on two legs. "My dad is lost, get it? *Lost*. He might be on some island waiting for help. He could get rescued and come home tomorrow. What if we weren't here? What if he came home and we were gone?"

I feel myself blink at her a couple of times as I try to comprehend that she really believes this. Could it be true?

"Does that happen?" I ask. "Do people get lost in storms, then turn up later?"

"It could happen," Courtney says, her voice suddenly shrill. She spins away from me and runs through the living room to the stairs, leaving me holding the front door open.

A sudden wind blows across the porch. It's cold, but gone as fast as it came. I look at the old leaves it blows past me as they scatter off the edge of the porch. There's a shadow racing with the wind. Strange. I hear a bedroom door slam upstairs.

Above me, something seems to scratch in the space between the inside and outside walls of the house. I don't bother to look up. Mice are mice, whether they live in the Great Plains or on the East Coast.

I do my homework because there's nothing else to do and Aunt Lisa only has basic cable. I'm just finishing up my science reading when Aunt Lisa's car rumbles into the driveway.

"I got the job," Mom yells as she enters the house. There

are yellowish wood shavings still clinging to her sandy-blond hair and her face is glowing as she pushes past her sister and comes to me for a hug.

I hug her back, but not with a lot of enthusiasm.

"You could have let us know," I say in a teasing tone.

"I left a message on the machine," she says, pointing behind me to the telephone. A red light on the answering machine is blinking.

"Oh, I didn't think I should listen." Never mind that I hadn't even noticed.

"Don't be silly, Alan," Aunt Lisa says. "You live here now. Mia casa is you-a casa."

This is the first thing I've heard Aunt Lisa say that wasn't tinged with sorrow, so I force a chuckle at her butchering of Spanish.

"Okay, I'll remember that. Congrats on the job, Mom. I guess you started today, huh?" I pluck a curly shaving from her hair. It looks like pine.

Mom laughs and puts her hands in her hair to shake it. "You told me I got it all out, Lisa."

"You're such a rookie, Holly," my aunt says as she walks by Mom and snatches another shaving from her hair. She asks me, "Did Courtney make dinner?"

I hesitate, wondering if I'll be getting my cousin in trouble if I tell the truth. They're going to find out anyway. "No. She went upstairs as soon as we got home. I haven't seen her since. They gave me a ton of homework."

"You can handle it," Mom says. "Is Courtney okay?"

"I think so." I'm no shrink, but believing your dead father

20

may return after his boat was lost in the North Atlantic doesn't seem okay to me. I saw *Titanic*. I know people can't survive for long in cold water, especially during a storm.

"Well, I think we should go out to dinner to celebrate your mom's new job and you guys moving to Maine," Aunt Lisa says.

Celebrate moving to Maine? Yeah, right. Mom claps her hands and says that's the best idea she's heard in weeks, that she's dying to try some fresh seafood.

"Sure," I say. "Why not? I'll go up and get Courtney."

Courtney's bedroom is at the end of the hall, just past my new room. The hallway seems very dark, even though the overhead light is on. I know there's something wrong. The hair on my arms prickles as I come to Courtney's closed door, and I feel cold, like I'm standing in front of a freezer with a leak.

"Courtney?" I knock on the door. The scratching noise comes again, right beneath my feet. I consider stamping my foot to silence the mice, but don't. Why point out to Aunt Lisa that I know she has rodents in her house?

"Courtney?" I knock again, louder.

The cold air around me vanishes. It's been sucked back under Courtney's door. She still doesn't answer, so I turn the knob and push. For an instant, there is resistance, then the door opens easily.

Courtney's lying on the bed, her eyes open, her arms rigid at her sides, her palms pressed against her thighs. It looks very weird.

"Courtney? You okay?"

Slowly, she turns her head to look at me. Behind her glasses, her eyes seem strange, magnified and too bright.

21

"We're going out for dinner. You ready?"

"Sure. I'll be right down," she says in a dazed voice.

I close the door and back away a step. Behind the door I can hear her moving, the rustle of her clothes as she sits up on the bed. Deciding she must be okay, just emo-weird, I go back downstairs. Aunt Lisa is picking the last of the wood shavings from Mom's hair and talking about somebody at the mill.

A couple of minutes later Courtney bops down the stairs. Her eyes seem normal again and she hugs her mom, asking, "Where are we going? Charlie's?"

"Sounds good to me," Aunt Lisa says. "You guys ready?"

Mom and I follow them out to their SUV, where I sit in the back with Courtney.

"You're in class with my best friend," Courtney says as we hit the road.

"Oh yeah? Who's that?"

"Aimee Avery."

I shake my head and shrug. "I haven't learned many names yet. What class?"

"She didn't say."

"What does she look like?"

"She's gorgeous, but she thinks she looks like a Muppet. She has red hair."

I remember the gum-smacker in Swanson's biology class. "I think I know who you're talking about."

"She's nice," Courtney adds. "Check out the cop car."

I watch as a tall officer pushes some guy over the hood of a truck and cuffs him. The guy fights it all the way. "I wonder what he did."

"Probably drunk," Aunt Lisa says. "More people have been

getting drunk and disorderly lately. You hear about another fight almost every day. Must be the weather."

That night I wake up from a dream and sit up straight in bed. My eyes are open wide and staring in front of me but not seeing anything. It was a totem dream, a vision. Onawa, my totem cougar, was trying to tell me something. I lay back in the bed, my eyes still open. Reaching to the table beside the bed I find the leather thong of my medicine pouch and pull it to me, clutching it in both hands over my chest.

My heart continues to race.

Onawa was afraid. We were in a forest. I remember that. She stood on a rock so that her beautiful tawny head was level with my face. Behind her, though . . . it was all black, like the forest was being swallowed in a black fog. Shapes moved in the darkness.

Onawa had been saying something. Something important. I clutch the medicine bag harder, thinking, trying to remember.

I was distracted. There was somebody else in the dream. A girl? Yes, it was a girl. She was holding a torch, or some kind of red light. Or maybe she had red hair? Maybe. But there'd been something about light, too. She brought light. Onawa, though, told me something, and now I can't remember what it was.

Then the mice start scratching under the floor again. Moonlight filters in through the thin curtain over my window. I feel sure there wasn't that much light in the room a few minutes ago. It was pitch-black when I woke up. It was dark when the mice were scratching. Clouds? Maybe.

I must have fallen asleep, because my alarm clock starts beeping way too early, jarring me back into consciousness. I turn it off and roll out of bed. The bare wood is cold under my feet. This is crazy. It's never this cold in Oklahoma this early in the school year. I slip the leather string of my medicine pouch around my head and let go of the bag. My left hand cramps from holding it so tightly for . . . what? Four hours? Five? I flex my hand as I paw through a box of clothes with my right, choosing a black Metallica *Kill 'Em All* T-shirt for the day. It's a little wrinkled, but so what? I slip it on, hesitate, then pull the medicine pouch out to wear over the shirt. I yank out the rest of my uniform for the day: black jeans, black socks, and my Army-surplus combat boots.

I am not good at math. My transfer grade in algebra is a C minus, and it looks like it has nowhere to go but down as I sit in first hour staring at Mrs. Bailey while she scrawls numbers and letters across the chalkboard. She's a short woman, late thirties, and not ugly for someone her age, but what she's doing with those numbers and letters seems unholy. She tells us to work the problems on page 42, then goes to her desk.

Finally the bell rings and books snap closed, feet shuffle, backpacks are hefted, and the teenage Pavlovian dogs move to the next kennel. I move with them, trying to remember my way to biology class.

"There he is."

I look over my shoulder and see three girls standing beside an open locker, all of them making sure they're not looking at me. I turn away and keep walking. The bell is ringing as I walk through the classroom door.

It's her.

Red.

Courtney's friend. The pretty girl with red hair. The dream rushes back to me. We were falling, clutching at each other, with twisting darkness all around us. Onawa had been there, too. The girl looks up at me and I realize I've stopped walking and am staring at her. I get my feet moving again but can't stop staring. I see something in her eyes, something like recognition.

I take my seat, finally breaking the gaze we've been holding as I face the front of the room.

"Hey."

It's her. What's her real name? Angel? Agnes? Something with an A. I turn around and say, "Hi."

"How was your first day?" she asks.

"Pretty good."

"Yeah? You're Courtney's cousin."

It doesn't sound like a question, but I nod. "Yeah."

"She's my best friend."

"She told me. I forgot your name, though."

"Aimee," she says. "Aimee Avery."

"Right."

"People call me Aim, or—"

"Red," I say. "They call you Red."

She looks surprised. "Yeah. They do. Did Courtney tell you that?"

I'm not about to start telling some girl I've just met about my visions. Definitely not about Onawa. No matter how hot she is or how good she smells this close.

"Yeah, Courtney told me," I lie.

"Miss Avery, are you about finished entertaining our new

25

student?" Mr. Swanson asks from the front of the room. I didn't even realize he'd come into the class. I give Aimee a quick wink and turn around.

"Yes, sir, Mr. Swanson," Aimee says behind me. "He's all yours now. Please teach us."

Biology isn't much easier than algebra, but at least it's a little bit more interesting. Every time Aimee shifts in her desk behind me, though, I get a distracting whiff of her perfume. I can feel her foot tapping out some rhythm on the back leg of my desk. The bell rings and the ritual of shuffling toward the door begins again.

"See you later, Alan," Aimee says, pushing past me at the front of the room and waving with her fingers. They look like one wing of a butterfly flitting away. She's out of range before I think to say anything.

One thing is consistent: School lunches are school lunches, whether you're in Oklahoma or Maine. The hamburger tastes like flavored cardboard and the Tater Tots have no taste at all until I cover them with salt. I'm sitting alone, chewing the crud, when I'm suddenly surrounded by girls. Four of them put their trays on the table around me.

"Can we sit with you?" one of them asks. She's a blonde with big blue eyes and a tiny nose.

"You looked so lonely," a brunette in a cheerleader jacket says as she sits across from me.

"Yeah, I guess," I say. A cheerleader? Do I look like a guy who'd be interested in talking to a cheerleader? They all sit down and start firing questions at me.

"You're from Texas?"

"Oklahoma," I say.

"That's where the Dust Bowl happened, right?"

"Uh, yeah, like eighty years ago."

"Did you have a horse there?"

"No."

"I heard you played football."

"Uh-huh."

"We don't have football here," the cheerleader says.

"I heard," I say.

"Do you like Li'l Wayne, or do you just listen to that head-banging stuff?"

"Just the head-banging stuff."

"Why? I so can't see the point in that."

"Well, Li'l Wayne, Little Boosey, and all those other Little guys cornered the market on synthesized pop," I say. A-ha! They can be quiet. Eight eyes stare at me, blink, blink, blink. Reboot. Then they start again like nothing happened.

"Did you live on a farm or ranch?"

"Is Oklahoma really just a big wheat field?"

"Alan? You're supposed to come sit with us, man. Remember?" I look up from the hamburger I'd been studying to see Blake, the counselor's aide, standing beside me. "Come on. Cross-country sits together."

"Oh. Yeah. I forgot," I say. "Excuse me, ladies." I grab my tray and follow Blake.

"You're quite the sensation," he says as we cross the cafeteria.

"I don't mean to be."

"You're new. You're different. We don't get many different

27

people around here," he says. "Aimee sent me to rescue you. We watched for a while, but when you were obviously zoning out on them she sent me to get you."

There she is. Blake leads me right up to the table where Aimee is sitting with Courtney and three other people. I put my tray down and watch as Blake slides into the seat next to Aimee, puts an arm around her shoulders, and hugs her quickly.

"Blake to the rescue," he says.

Something inside me deflates.

· 3 ·
AIMEE

School happens. Eventually it's lunch. Blake goes and rescues Courtney's cousin Alan from the girls who always try to hook up with everyone.

"I hate school," Blake is telling Alan when they come back over. "I mean, I act like I like school because I'd never get into National Honor Society without that. There's this stupid character component, which basically means you have to suck up to teachers. That's rule number one."

Courtney nods and looks at me. She knows that I really can't stand any negativity about anything. She calls me her little peacemaker. She means it nicely, really. Anyway, just so Blake won't get more cranky about the rules of National Honor Society, I try to make him laugh by pretending to be my father, all serious and acting like a "model father" from ancient 1950s TV shows even though he wasn't even alive then. "You know, Blake, *hate* is a serious word with serious connotations."

He makes like he's going to chuck his bagel at my cleavage. I mock shriek, which makes the monitor, Mrs. Los Santos, point at me with a daggerlike black-nailed finger. I smile and she softens. I turn back to Blake.

"Are you threatening me with that?" I say in a Mafia-man tone. "Because let me tell you, I do not take kindly to threatening. Particularly threatening with bagels. I mean, do you know who you're dealing with here?"

Alan cracks up, and I can't help but notice that he's so cute when he smiles. He mimics the voice back. "I think we do. I think we are dealing with a definite hard-ass here."

And in that second I know, absolutely *know*, that something in my life has changed irrevocably. This is the guy from my dreams. Right here. And we are going to have to do something, save something, together. I just don't know what.

"Aimee is beautifully weird today," Blake says, biting into his bagel. He talks like I'm not here. "And she has paint on her hands."

I do. "It's hard to get paint off."

"You paint?" Alan asks.

It is the first thing at lunch that he says to me directly. I look up into his eyes. This is such a mistake. "Yeah."

I can't look away. He doesn't look away either. He was in my dream. He was the one pulling me out. It was him. And even though I don't tell anyone about my dreams, I want to tell him. I want to tell him everything, which is a very wrong way to feel about some random guy I've just met when I have a boyfriend!

Courtney uses her dolphin-decal fingernail and scrapes at

the paint on my skin. She does it so hard it hurts. "I don't know why we put up with her."

"Attention, people talking about me: I. Am. Right. Here," I say, pulling my hand away. I decide to go somewhere safe and conflict-free. "Look, Alan, I'm not going to ask about Oklahoma and moving because—no offense—I'm sure it sucks and you're sick of it, so I'm just going to bring you slam-bang into my life, unless you want me to ask the required questions, because I will, because I care, but I don't want to be . . . I don't know. I don't want to bore you with the same old–same old."

His lips quiver. He leans back and starts laughing again.

"Aimee!" Blake scolds.

"No." Alan flattens one of his super-big hands out across the table. "No. I'd love it. I am so tired of people asking about me."

I nod. It's like we're the only people here. There's all this activity around us but none of it matters. I start, "So, anyway, my gramps—"

"Gramps," Blake interrupts knowingly. He possessively puts his arm around my shoulder. He keeps doing that today, which is not really normal Blake behavior. Lately, it's been like every bad quirk in everyone is taking them over. Blake's possessiveness. My own insecure-ness. Courtney's bitchiness. Blake continues mocking me in that cloying-boyfriend way. "So sweet."

"He is mean to me," I tell Alan, and continue. "Anyway, he and my brother, Benji, found a Cheeto they claim looks just like Marilyn Monroe."

This makes everyone quiet for a second, and then Alan goes, "Marilyn Monroe?"

"She's this old, dead movie star, you know. She was all curvy and probably slept with the Kennedys and sang 'Diamonds Are a Girl's Best Friend,'" Courtney explains. "And that 'Happy Birthday, Mr. President' thing, and there's this poster of her standing over some sewer thing in a city and trying to keep her white skirt from going over her head."

"I know who she is. I just don't understand the Cheeto." Alan looks at me for help. My heart goes all crazy again.

"They think the Cheeto looks just like her," I say. I've decided this is not the kind of story that makes a good impression and suddenly I don't want to tell it at all.

"Does it?" Courtney asks.

I sigh. "No. It's kind of bumpy like her breasts and everything, but I mean, it could be any female form."

Courtney snorts water out her nose, which makes me shriek while Courtney pushes her hands to her face, laughing hysterically.

Blake thrusts napkins into my hand. Alan reaches for some, too. We both start wiping at the table. I dab at Courtney's nose while he calmly asks, "Did they eat it?"

"That's what I'm trying to explain. They did not eat it. Gramps took a picture of it and posted it on eBay."

Courtney slams her fist onto the table. "Oh my freaking—DUDE!"

"Shut up. Shut up, shut up!" Blake starts laughing so hard he sputters and dribbles. I hand him a soggy napkin.

"They put it in a Ziploc bag and Gramps is hiding it on top of the fridge so nobody accidentally eats her," I explain.

"That's so wrong," Blake says.

"It's insane." Courtney rubs her hand where she smacked the table.

"I know." I smile at them because for a second it's like it was before Courtney's dad died. Blake's not grumpy. Courtney's not sad. We're laughing.

"Has anyone bid on it?" Hayley asks, leaning over. Her beautiful brown hair swings dangerously close to my cream cheese, so I move my bagel. She blushes. "Sorry. I totally started eavesdropping."

"It's very eavesdroppable stuff," Courtney agrees as everyone waits for my answer: Courtney, Alan, Blake, Hayley, Hayley's boyfriend, Eric, and Eric's and Blake's best friend, Toby.

"Someone's bid five hundred dollars."

Everyone squeals and starts imagining a franchise of Cheeto look-alikes. We could do Elvis, or Jesus, or Barack Obama.

"Britney Spears!" Courtney says. "*I'd* pay a hundred dollars for a Cheeto that looks like Britney."

It's all good and happy and we laugh, then break off into two groups again and settle into our lunchtime routine of Courtney reciting sex facts from *Cosmo*. Blake rubs his foot up and down my leg in a sexified way, which for some reason just makes me feel a little restless and not at all sexified. Alan and Courtney argue about lobsters looking at you while you eat them and I play all peacemaker and then scoot a glance at Alan. He's the guy from my dream, I know it. And that means he's in some kind of danger, I think.

Blake passes me some new lyrics he's written on notebook paper. He's totally turned on by this New Hampshire–based hip-hop trio. We all say they're brilliant, except Alan.

Court stares really hard at us and then looks at her cousin, who is focusing on the remains of his hamburger. "What do you think, Alan?"

There's a massive pause.

Courtney injects into it, "Our metal-head cowboy action hero here doesn't like hip-hop or rap or country or lobster or anything in the entire state of Maine."

Wow, she's snarky. It's like this whole different person, I swear. Something inside me shivers. The bell rings.

"Saved by the bell." Blake laughs, but it's really obvious that he's faking it. He's hurt or something. Poor sweet Blake requires a lot of praise. He leans over, kisses my cheek, and is off to class with Courtney.

Alan and I stand there. The table separates us. He comes around to my side. "They ditched us pretty fast."

"Their class is all the way in the foreign-language wing. They're always late. I'm in the opposite direction," I explain. I blush. I pull out some gum. "Want any?"

He seems to have a hard time deciding. "Sure."

He reaches for the gum. His fingers touch my fingers and all of a sudden it's my dream again. I'm falling downward. Something is pulling me. Water is everywhere and my lungs are ready to explode.

"Whoa . . . Aimee . . ." His hands are around my arms, jolting me back. My knees are shaking and it takes a second before I can focus on him. His face is right in front of me. I want to touch his skin with my fingers. Why? God. *Do not touch him!* He's squinting hard like he's trying to see inside my head. He can*not* see inside my head. I won't let him.

"Sorry." I straighten up, making sure I don't touch him. I lie, because to tell the truth would make him think I was crazy. "Little woozy there."

He cocks his head.

"Woozy?" he asks. "Do you get woozy a lot?"

He knows. He knows I'm lying.

"I'm going to be late. Um, thanks," I say, still resisting the whole touching urge. His long hair swings a little in front of his face.

He drops his hands. I start fast-walking toward the cafeteria door, the one that goes toward social studies and language arts.

"I'm going that way, too," he says. His voice is low and slower than a Maine voice, which is really saying something. It resonates a lot. He's wearing a black metal band shirt. I hate black shirts. I hate metal bands.

We're the stragglers, heading out of the cafeteria late. The sweet show-choir girl in front of us, Amber, doesn't see us and the door starts to close in my face. Alan pushes it open for me, just reaches over my head and extends his arm, which is kind of Superman of him. I can see why the cheerleaders were moving in so fast.

I want to tell him. I want to tell him about my dream. I want to tell him about my visions. I want to tell him everything, but that's not who I am. I do *not* tell people things—ever. I am not Aimee the Freak anymore. I am Aimee who goes out with Blake and plays sports and paints.

"Thanks," I say, remembering my manners. "I'm sorry Court was so . . . so weird to you. She was kind of mean."

He shrugs. "She isn't always like that?"

"No." We head up the hallway. I almost have to jog to keep up with him. He seems to notice and slows his pace. "She's usually really nice, beyond nice. This whole thing with her dad . . . it's kind of messed with her head a little bit."

He nods. He swallows hard. It's like he's trying to figure out something to say.

I blurt ahead, somehow afraid of whatever it is he wants to tell me. "Blake and I have been going out forever."

"Oh."

I cringe. I can actually feel myself cringe. "Sorry. I mean . . . I think she feels like a third wheel sometimes, you know, so that can't help. And . . . it's just hard on her. I mean, it must be hard on you, too, moving here with no football, no actual mall or anything."

"I'm okay with no mall. Football? Yeah, it's not easy," he admits. His shoulders are wide. He ducks his head down when he talks to me, like he's worried his voice won't carry down so low, like I won't be able to hear him.

"Yeah . . . yeah . . . I bet. It's really good of you, really brave. Most people would have a fit."

"I'm not most people, I guess." He looks at me full on. The right side of his mouth turns up in a smile. The left side just stays put.

"No, guess not." I smile back.

Court sends me a text while we're in Advanced English, which is totally against school rules.

She knows that's not something I want to remember.

Everyone left my house after this seventh-grade séance. They ran to their moms' cars and rushed off thinking I was a total freak. Everyone except Courtney and Chuck. Right after the séance I had this vision thing where Chuck died on his way home, but that was after the other freaky thing that happened, after everyone left.

In my vision, I saw a Saab smash into his mom's Subaru as she was waiting to turn left into the Tideway Market. I saw her car jump into the path of the box truck carrying lobsters. I saw Chuck's body smashed up in the backseat, his mom sobbing, blood running down her white shirt. Her arm was broken but she was still trying to push away the Emergency Medical Technicians, still trying to hold on to Chuck.

I must have gasped because Chuck, the still-living, still-breathing Chuck, bounced away from me, hitting the coffee table with his leg. "What? What did you see?"

I shook my head and stared at him and Courtney before finally lying. "Nothing."

He died. Of course he died. He died just the way I saw. He died on his way home that day. I shake the memory away. What is wrong with Court? She knows I can't deal with this at all.

I sit at my desk and trace the graffiti on it: EVERYTHING SUCKS. Juvenile, yet profound.

Somehow it does not make me feel better that some other person sat at this desk and felt the same way. I eyeball Blake and Court, who are stuck across the room. Assigned seats in

37

here, which is very fourth grade considering it's Advanced Placement. But our teacher, Mrs. Bloom, is like that, all yip-yap peppy like she's a cheerleader for the classics.

Court makes a face that tells me I should check out Mrs. Bloom's ensemble. I do. It's a sweater that's way too matchy-matchy with a big plaid skirt, and what looks like her husband's brown trouser socks, pulled up, but not quite to the hem of her skirt.

"Bea-u-ti-ful," I mouth to Court.

Court mouths back, "I want it."

Briley Flood glares at me. She's sitting in front of Blake and he snaps his finger into her shoulder, telling her to turn around. Briley's always nice. I don't know why she's glaring. People are all on edge lately, even Blake.

Mrs. Bloom claps her hands together and chirps, "Class! I am so excited. Today we continue our discussion about William Shakespeare's classic play *Hamlet*."

I slump down in my chair, because I might as well die right now.

"Miss Avery! Sit up!" Mrs. Bloom says. "Why don't you read the part of Ophelia?"

I fake smile. Great. The crazy female. Perfect, given the way I'm feeling.

Mrs. Bloom pulls at her bra beneath her armpit like it's chafing her and starts preaching. "Let's talk about Ophelia first. Who do you think is the most boring, one-dimensional character in *Hamlet*?"

That's a tough one. I raise my hand because I need bonus points after slouching. Mrs. Bloom points at me with the super enthusiasm that only a bra-adjusting English teacher can summon. "Miss Avery?"

"Ophelia," I say, feeling pretty brilliant because this should be enough to show her that I am listening and that she doesn't need to call on me ever again in this class despite my slouchy posture.

Mrs. Bloom keeps chirping along. "That's right. Now why? Aimee?"

Crap. I have the follow-up answer responsibility, too, unless some butt-kisser jumps in. Countdown to butt-kisser. *Three . . . Two . . . One . . .* It's Court. Only she's butt-saving instead of butt-kissing. She tries to be casual, leaning back, legs out straight like a girl jock. She taps her pen on her desk and says, "Ophelia is really boring because she has all this potential, right? Like she could be the whole tragic heroine deal, but instead she just lets herself become crazy and she loses all the heroine potential and just becomes tragic."

"Right!" Mrs. Bloom beams.

"But . . ." The word is out of my mouth before I can stop it.

"What is it, Miss Avery? Is there something you want to add?"

I swallow and my stomach flops into itself. "I just . . . I just don't think you *let* yourself become crazy. Mental illness is usually some kind of chemical imbalance, or a disorder. There's genetic predisposition. It's not just about giving up."

"Genetic predisposition?" Court mock whispers. "She should know."

I swear the whole room hears her except for Mrs. Bloom, who has gone deaf on purpose. Something inside me explodes and hollows out. *What is with her?* I close my eyes and will everyone to go away. Instead, an image of my mother flashes into my head. Her hands reach out to me from the black river water. Her voice says my name, begging me to save . . . who? I open my eyes to witness Blake giving Court the glare-down, which I totally appreciate. He gets good boyfriend points for that one.

"That's true, Miss Avery!" Mrs. Bloom is going after me full force now. Her blue eyes are bland excitement. I have entered the land of teacher's pet. "Why do you think Shakespeare did this?" She turns away from me. She trots to the front of the room, happy as a poodle at a big dog show, smiling, prancing, tail up in the air. She doesn't give anyone a chance to answer. "Shakespeare does this because Ophelia's choice mirrors Hamlet's. Shakespeare uses insanity to prove a thematic point."

Mrs. Bloom is oblivious to how upset I am, and she just keeps teaching. It's amazing how teachers have no clue about what's going on inside us. I mean, Courtney's giving Blake the finger and everything. Blake grabs her finger and whispers in her ear.

We start reading *Hamlet* out loud, but I zone out in the parts Ophelia's not in and think about my mom, which is dangerous.

When I was a real little kid and my mom was still with us, I woke up one night and got out of my bed. I'd had a dream that my mom was floating in the river, facedown, her long brown hair streaming out around her and fish nibbling on her toes. Her body was puffed up like there were balloons beneath her skin, and she was a funny color.

40

It scared me so much that I left my bed just to make sure she was okay. I tiptoed down the stairs and past my dad, who was passed out on the couch. I looked in my parents' room, but the bed was empty.

In class everyone turns the page. I turn my page, too. I read my lines. Another page. I skim ahead. No Ophelia for a little while, so I go back to remembering looking in my parents' bedroom. I go back to remembering things that are probably completely Ophelia-style unhealthy to remember.

"Mommy?" I whispered into the empty bedroom. "Mommy?"

But I knew where she was.

I knew because of my dream.

I ran past my dad this time, not caring about noise. I raced out the door and went as fast as I could across the backyard, through the woods, and to the river. You could see the river from the house, and the moon was high and full in the middle of the sky.

There was a lady standing by the river, right between the trees. I was sure it was a lady; I knew it from the shape. Her shape was a darkness that deepened the night. And standing in the river was a man. He was beckoning for her to come to him. Water flowed out of his mouth. His eyes were nothing eyes, charcoal pits. And he wanted her.

"Mommy?"

She didn't answer.

I ran as fast as I could, but it was hard in my nightie, which was too narrow to allow my legs to stretch out into full stride. The pine needles and branches hurt my feet, pricking into them, cutting them. I kept running.

"Mommy?" I whispered as I got closer to the darkness of the river and the man, closer to her, and I stopped running. "Mommy?"

The whole world smelled rotten, like old cucumbers in the fridge that had gone mooshy.

I took a step toward her. I reached out my hand and my fingers touched her fingers, even though for a second hers didn't move. Her face was blank like the moon; it had already started to withdraw. Already. Way back then. She was far away, across the sky, into the moon, maybe the stars, or just the blackness between.

"Mommy?" My fingers felt warm and glowing and power-ful. I clenched her hand as hard as I could and tried to send all the love I had into her. That was the first time I ever tried to heal anybody.

Nothing. And then her fingers moved to grasp mine, hold-ing, holding, holding me tightly, too tightly. I knew then that she wasn't really like other mothers. Something was going on. I just didn't know what.

"Aimee?" Her voice was wind-whisper sweet. "Did you come to get me? To make sure he didn't get me?"

"Uh-huh," I said, because I figured I did.

She lifted me in her arms. "Let's carry each other home."

When I looked back in the river the man was gone, disap-peared under the surface.

That was the only time any of my visions did any good. Just that once. That one time I actually saved her.

· 4 ·
ALAN

I try to focus on Act II of *Macbeth*, but all I can think about is Aimee Avery. My English teacher, Mrs. Carey, is trying her best to make Shakespeare interesting, and I have to admit that what I've read is okay, for Shakespeare. I like the witches and the conspiracy, but Shakespeare requires a lot of work, a lot of mental focus, and right now I just don't have it. Not for Bill Shakespeare, anyway.

Aimee said she'd see me later. It's not like it's a date or anything. It wasn't even really saying she wouldn't avoid me later. It was just a common parting. Not a promise. Shakespeare would have written it as "Fare thee well" or something like that.

She has a boyfriend. Blake. A bell rings and I move on to my art class. Instead of reading, I'm holding a paint brush and staring at a piece of canvas. There's red paint on my brush and it makes me think of the red paint on Aimee's hand. She's an artist. She has red hair.

. . . Red . . .

The damn dream. It hasn't gone away. Maybe because I know now that the girl is Aimee. Usually, however, when a dream lingers like this one has—when Onawa is in the dream—it's more than just a mental picture show.

My hand is moving. I let it go. I don't really think about what I'm doing. It's like I'm on autopilot. I paint and think, keeping the two things separate. I don't paint often. I'm not very good at it, but I do like it. I have incredible images in my head, but my hands aren't very good translators.

A Cheeto that looks like Marilyn Monroe? I smile at that memory. Aimee's gramps and her little brother sound pretty cool. Who the hell would bid $500 for a Cheeto?

I freeze, my paintbrush poised over my one-foot canvas square. I've painted my vision. There is Aimee looking back at me, her red hair flying around her face, her green eyes wide, and her mouth open. Behind her are the green eyes of Onawa, and surrounding them both is blackness filled with swirling shapes. This is crazy. Probably nobody else would see the shapes in the black paint. Nobody would realize who I'd painted. Would they?

"Alan, that's very nice."

Oh crap. Mr. Burnham stands behind me, his hand on his chin, his eyes fixed on my handiwork. He's probably in his late twenties, with short black hair gelled to stand up over his forehead. He has a tribal tattoo on his left wrist, which makes me think he's probably the coolest teacher in this school. Still, I just want him to go away.

"You realize the bell rang a few minutes ago, right?" he asks.

No wonder it's so quiet. I look around. There are no students in the art room.

"I guess I didn't hear it," I say.

"You were pretty intense there. I can write you a note to your next teacher, but you need to put this away. I'll clean your brushes for you today," he says, and now I'm sure he's the coolest. "Tell me, are these spirits swirled in the black of the underworld?"

"Yeah, I guess so," I say.

"And the green eyes?"

"Cougar."

"Personal totem?"

I'm not sure what to say. I look at his tattoo. Those things are so generic. Every poser who wants to feel primitive gets one. It doesn't mean anything. "You know about totems?" I ask.

"A little."

"Yeah. It is."

"We should all have a spirit guide. It'd make life easier."

"Do you?" I ask.

"No. Somewhere back up the line, on my mom's side, there's some Penobscot blood, but it's too thin in me. I'm just a run-of-the-mill pagan. Not that I tell too many people about that. Folks around here are pretty conservative, in case you hadn't figured it out."

I nod. I want to skip woodworking and stay here and talk to him, but Mr. Burnham takes the brush from my hand.

"Wash up," he says. "This is my planning period. I'll put

45

Aimee and your cougar away and clean the brushes after I write your note to class."

"You know who it is?"

"Aimee Avery is the best artist in this school. Naturally she's one of my favorites. You are aware that she has a boyfriend. Blake Stanley."

I give him a sheepish look that a blind man could interpret. "She's the only person who really talks to me."

"She's a nice girl," he says as he writes a note on the back of a scrap of paper. "Who's your teacher?"

After woodworking, it's off to the locker room to suit up for cross-country. At home, the Jets are on the field practicing for Friday's game against the Chickasha Fighting Chicks. Beating the Chicks would earn the Jets a playoff berth. Will they win without me? Maybe. I decide I don't want to think about it.

The cross-country team gathers outside the field house and Coach Treat, a thin woman with mousy hair and pale freckles, outlines the route we'll be running for the day. I don't recognize the street names, of course, which means I have to stay with someone who knows where they're going. It turns out that someone is Blake, who quickly jumps out ahead of the pack. I catch up and run along beside him.

"I don't know the route," I explain. "The street names."

"It's easy to remember once you've done it a few times," he says. He's not breathing hard. His words are punctuated by the fall of his feet on the pavement. Despite the chill, we're all wearing shorts. I glance down at Blake's pumping legs. They're toned, but skinny. No real muscle mass. I can see the muscles of his calves flexing, but there's almost no definition in his thighs. He's all cardio and no resistance training. No squats.

We run side-by-side for about forty minutes with no more conversation. We come around one last corner. There is a little convenience store with gas pumps on one side and a drug store on the other. The school's field house is about two blocks away.

"Let's see what you've got," I challenge. Blake gives me a look that says I'm stupid to challenge him.

"Go!" He leans into it and sprints forward. I do the same. Behind us, the rest of the team shouts encouragement. It's mostly generic, but every now and then I hear, "Go Blake!"

I pass him easily, and now I can hear him panting. Then I can't. He's falling behind. Ten yards. Twenty. I race past the fence around the soccer field and see Coach Treat standing in front of the field house with the stopwatch in her hand. I think of the last yards between me and a touchdown that would send the Jets to the playoffs and find another burst of speed. I blow by the coach as she clicks the watch, her eyes following me as I start to slow down.

Blake finishes a good four seconds behind me. I go back and reach out to shake his hand. He hesitates for a moment, then grips my hand. His breath puffs out in vapor clouds. I'm breathing a little hard, but not like him. The rest of the team trickles in. Coach Treat calls times and her student assistant records them. When everyone's in, she calls me over to her.

"Are you always that fast?" she asks.

I shrug. "I don't know. I guess."

"Alan, you've got a good chance of making the all-state team if you keep that up," she says. "Good job." She looks over the whole team, then calls, "Hit the showers."

Once we're in the locker room, people who hadn't talked to me before are now congratulating me and talking about how fast I am. I know I'm a pretty good athlete, but all this praise makes me kind of uncomfortable. It's not like I'm Adrian Peterson or Barry Sanders. I'm standing there by the middle bench that is stuck between two long lines of maroon lockers, listening and trying to take it all in. I bend over and start unlacing my shoe, staring at the cold concrete floor, hiding a smile.

"It's because he's an Indian. He's used to stealing those scalps and running before he gets caught."

The boys' locker room is deathly quiet except for the static sound of one shower running behind the lockers. The air turns icy cold and then hot, as if hate itself is running through it. Somebody's towel drops to the floor with a wicked splat. The few boys in front of me part. A short, scrawny kid stands near Blake. I don't know the kid's name, but it's obvious he's the one who said it. He stares back at me. He can't be more than five foot six, a hundred thirty pounds. I've got seven inches and forty pounds on him.

"What'd you say?" I ask. It's a bad thing to do, but I take a step toward him. It's a really bad thing. I take another step. Guys move farther away from me. The kid looks toward Blake, but Blake ignores him. Another step. "You say something about scalps?"

"Hey, man, I was just playing around," he offers, lifting a

hand in supplication. He backs toward an open locker. Someone's jock dangles from a hook.

"Playing around? You say I steal scalps, then run like a coward, and that's playing around?"

"Yeah, man. You know, like in the movies. *Native Americans* are always scalping people . . . you know . . ."

"Yeah. I *know*," I say. I'm standing right in front of him now, and his face is level with my chest. He has to look up at me while I talk down to him. He's not a threat. Maybe he thought Blake would back him up. "I know all about the old movie Indians. Now I'm gonna tell you something. I don't know how you boys in Maine do things, but in Oklahoma, when someone insults someone else, we don't stand around and talk about it. We just start kicking ass."

"Hey, man, really, I was just playing around." He steps back, but I stay with him.

"Alan, man, Matt's a douche. Just ignore him," someone behind me says.

"He's always saying crap he can't back up," someone else says.

Matt's eyes show fear. That's good enough. This time. "Listen to me, little paleface. I'll only warn you once. You make another 'Indian' joke and I just might take the hair off your head after I kick your ass. Got it?"

"Yeah, man. We're cool?" He offers a hand.

I look slowly from the hand to his eyes. His eyes are pleading. You can tell a lot by a person's eyes. Matt's weak. He thinks he's funny. I nod, but don't shake his hand.

"We're cool."

The tension breaks and guys go back to changing clothes. Mom would have killed me if I'd gotten into a fight my second day at a new school. I shower and dress as fast as I can without seeming obvious, then head for the late bus.

· 5 ·

AIMEE

The entire way home from practice, Blake is a total jerk, which is so unlike him. I'm gross and sweaty and he's complaining. "You're dripping on the car, Aim."

"And you aren't?" I shift in the seat, leaning toward the door.

"It's different."

"Why's it different?"

He pauses. "Because I'm a guy."

"No," I say in what I hope is a peppy, upbeat way. "What you are is a Cranky McCrankerson."

Chris Paquette is in the backseat, sitting with Eric. "Truce, children. Let's admit that Blake is sexist *and* cranky and move on from there."

"What I am is pissed off," Blake admits. He turns down the music so nobody has to yell over the hard slow beats of it. He twists his head to glare at me instead of the road. "Aren't you going to ask me why?"

I bite even though I don't want to. Part of what I like about Blake is that he's a pretty positive person. I tend to shy away from the negatives. Still, I ask, "Why?"

"Courtney's stupid cousin trounced me today. He was like some sort of superhero," Blake says.

"He killed him." Eric leans forward between the seats. "He'll be first man. Blake'll be second. I'll be third. Toby and Dalton? Four and five. We have a definite chance for state as a team this year, not just individuals."

"I hate losing to someone like him," Blake mutters.

Eric and I exchange looks.

"Someone like him?" I repeat, turning back forward in my seat. Does he mean because he's Native American? Or because he's poor? Or a metalhead? None are good. Anger creeps into my throat and shame hits me hard right in the middle of the chest. "What do you mean?"

"Nothing," Blake grunts.

Nothing? I wipe at my forehead, trying to figure out what's happened lately to sweet, nice, overachiever Blake, trying to figure out how someone's entire personality can change. He's not the only one, though. Everyone is getting crankier, meaner somehow. You can feel it in the air. We pass the Congregational Church and head down the Bucksport Road.

"Let me out first," I say.

As soon as I get in the door, Gramps hands me an oatmeal raisin cookie and says, "Your brother's being temperamental."

I bite the cookie. It's still warm. "How come?"

"Some brat beat him up at school today." Gramps throws a

dish towel over his bony shoulder. "The principal said there have been fights every damn day. She doesn't know what's going on. She sounded just about ready to throw up her hands on the lot of them. Anyway, I told your brother he had to fight back. He told me he was a pacifist. I told him there are no pacifists allowed in this house. Go talk to him, Aimee."

"Me?"

"He needs a woman's touch, and you're so good at making people calmer." Gramps tries to smile in a charming way. "I'll make you more cookies."

"Fine."

Maybe thinking about Benji will keep me from thinking about Alan. Maybe it'll keep me sane. Who knows? Maybe it'll keep me from remembering my dreams.

Poor Benji's climbed up into the tree house we made him last year for his birthday. It's an A-frame and has a ladder, a deck, and a pretty awesome view of the river. You can smell the salt of the ocean on the wind today. I like that smell.

He's not all curled up and fetal, not sobbing his heart out or anything, which is what I was worried about. Instead, he's chucking twigs off the tiny deck, throwing as hard and as far as he can. As I haul myself up, a twig smashes into a tall fir tree. A squirrel gets spastic about it.

"You are such a boy," I say, sitting on the plywood.

He grunts.

"You are."

He shrugs, but something in his face shifts. He snaps a twig in half and kicks some pine needles off the deck. They tumble to the ground. He starts sweeping all the needles off the wood, cleaning house.

"So, what's going on at school?" I ask him.

"You don't care."

"Right, that's why I'm up here in your tree house watching you kick pine needles instead of getting a snack, or doing my homework, or painting."

"You're just avoiding Gramps."

I drop my butt down on the deck and pull my knees up to my chest. "Sometimes Gramps is a pain."

"At least he's here," Benji says. He reaches into the back pocket of his jeans, pulls out a very used tissue, and blows his nose.

"What do you mean?"

"Mom's not here."

"She *can't* be here anymore, Benj. You know that. She died."

He scrapes at the corner of his eye like he's getting out those sleep crud things that are there in the morning, only it's not morning. Then he says, "Dad's never here."

"He has to work." It sounds like a lame excuse, just like when Dad says it, but it's true. Dad's not a bad dad. He's just a dad with a busy job. I switch tactics. "That's an awesome goose egg on your forehead. Did you get in a fight?"

"This kid said Mom was mental."

I pull in a big breath. "Mom had a disease, a disorder. Bipolar disorder. Right? You know that."

He shrugs.

"She wasn't crazy," I tell Benji, the same way Gramps told me a million times right after she died. "She wasn't crazy. She was ill. She was still beautiful and good and kind, but she sometimes couldn't control how she felt."

"What's the difference between crazy and sick?" Benji asks.

I think about how sweet our mom was most of the time; how she'd put her hand on my forehead when I didn't feel good; how she'd hug me and I'd feel so safe; how she could sing lullabies that were softer than bird wings. She just got lost sometimes.

But I don't say anything about any of that. I just say, "I'm not sure."

The squirrel rattles off a list of our crimes at us. He jumps up and down on a branch, shaking his paws—hands—at us.

"That squirrel's got a serious problem," I tell Benji.

There's this huge pause and it's like the entire world is waiting for what Benji's going to say next. He says, "I think our house is haunted."

"Me, too."

His face lights up. "Really?"

"Yeah. I was thinking maybe it's Mom, just visiting us, checking in, you know? I can almost smell her vanilla soap sometimes. Do *not* look at me like I'm crazy, Benji." And I start to say more, but then the freaking squirrel throws an acorn at me. An acorn! It hits the side of my shoulder. "What the heck!"

Benji's eyes get huge. "He attacked you!"

Another acorn comes pelting down. It hits the deck between us and skitters over the side.

"Don't attack my sister!" Benji screams. He starts throwing twigs at the squirrel.

"I thought you were a pacifist," I say.

Benji raises an eyebrow at me. "Not when it's my sister. Duh. I was just trying to make Gramps mad."

"Look! He's got backup," I say, pointing at two other squirrels.

"Attack!" Benji yells.

I grab a pinecone and throw it. "Leave us alone!"

"Loser squirrels!"

"Jerks!"

We keep throwing things at the squirrels. I don't know what we'd do if we actually hit them or anything, but it feels good, somehow, me and Benji battling off the world. Squirrels scurry up higher into branches, leap from one to the other, away.

"They're retreating!" Benji jumps up and down, pumping his fist in the air.

"Dude, we rock." I give him a glam rock-'n'-roller hand signal, and he hugs me. I don't ask him if he feels better about the bully boy now. I don't say anything stupid and parenty and chirpy, because I don't have to. I just know. "Does your head hurt?"

"A little." He scrapes the toe of his shoe against the plywood, sweeping off a few last pine needles. "You want to touch it?"

"You want me to?"

"Sometimes you make things feel better."

He says it very matter-of-factly. My palm presses lightly against the bump on his head. My hand starts to tingle in a circle right where I'm touching him. His face relaxes. I pull my hand away. "Better?"

"Way better." He reaches up to touch it and asks, "Is it smaller?"

"Half the size." I smile.

"I wish I could do that. Gramps said Mom could do that. I tried to ask Dad about it, but he got all mad."

"It's nothing."

"It's not nothing. You always say everything you do is nothing. Painting is nothing. Soccer is nothing. It drives me crazy!" He glares at me.

"Sorry," I offer.

"Hmph. Why does Dad get mad about stuff like that?"

"I think it makes him miss Mom too much," I say, and don't add that I think he worries that if I've inherited her healing traits, then I've probably inherited her bipolar disorder, too. Instead, I check out the plywood of the tree house and say, "You want to paint this?"

His eyes widen. "Really?"

"Yeah."

"Can it be like a mural with dragons and knights and stuff?"

I imagine the scenes on the slanted plywood, knights defending ladies' honor. Dragons screaming fiery threats. "That would be cool."

"I can help, right?"

"Of course you can help." I tussle his hair like any good American McSister would do. And for a second we are it: the American McDream.

But we aren't any McDream. Our mother is dead. Our dad is MIA most of the time. My boyfriend is maybe a closet racist, which means he can*not* be my boyfriend anymore. My best friend is so sad.

And me?

Sometimes lately it feels like everything in the world is so heavy, just pulling me down, and I wonder if that's how my mom felt when she was in a depressed place, when she would stare at that river, just stare and stare.

Something splashes in the water. A cloud shades the sunlight.

"Aimee?" Benji's voice comes out in a scared little squeak.

I grab his hand and squeeze it. "What, sweetie?"

"Ghosts can't hurt you, can they?"

I make my voice as serious and calm as I can. "Not if I can help it. Okay?"

He pulls his lips in and then lets go. "Okay. And if they did, you'd heal me all up, right?"

"Right."

When I hear the minivan start rumbling up the driveway, I hop out of the tree house and corner my dad by the garage.

"Hey, kiddo," he says, pulling his long legs out of the car. He opens his arms for a hug. I step into them.

"You had spaghetti for lunch?" I ask, pulling away a bit.

"Leftovers. How'd you know that?"

"Your tie smells like spaghetti sauce."

He grabs this leather satchel thing out of the car. He uses it like a briefcase. I take some mail and his travel coffee mug. He turns to go into the house.

"How was school?"

"Okay." I block his way. I swallow. He stares at me, waiting. He's not a stupid guy, my dad; he knows something is up.

"What is it, sweetie?"

An eagle circles over us, higher and higher circles. "Benji misses you."

He squints. "What do you mean?"

"He just needs you, you know. You've been working a lot lately."

He steps back. "Things have been hard at work . . ."

I won't let him get away with that. "Dad."

"You're right, no excuses." The briefcase dangles from his fingers. "I'll try to do a better job, okay?"

My breath flies out. "It's just, Gramps has been super cranky lately and everything, and I've been at soccer a lot, and there's some bully jerk beating on Benji at school, and he just needs you; he's a little vulnerable right now."

This stops him.

"Aimee," he says. "When are we not vulnerable?"

6

ALAN

At home I grab a granola bar from the kitchen cabinet and change into sweatpants and running shoes. Courtney goes straight to her room and slams the door. I leave my room and call out, "I'm going for a walk."

She doesn't answer, so I gallop down the stairs and out the front door, leaving it unlocked because I still don't have a key. There are woods behind the house and I want to explore them. I go to the end of the block, turn, and follow a trail toward the tree line.

Woods are something we don't have in Oklahoma. Not like this. Not where I lived in the city. When I turned sixteen and got my driver's license I had to drive from Oklahoma City to Thunderbird Lake out past Norman to find real forest. I told Mom I was sleeping over at Chance Botkin's house for a couple of nights, then went to the state park for my vision quest.

I read what I can about American Indians in general, but focus mostly on the nations of the Southwest, specifically the Navajo. At puberty, I learned, boys would go on a vision quest, where they'd find their totem guide, and sometimes even learn their purpose in life. I fasted for two days before my trip to Lake Thunderbird. When I got there I gutted the floor out of my canvas tent and created a little sweat lodge—as best I could—inside the tent. I sat in it for the first morning, still not eating. After the sweat lodge experience, which was really intense, I read all the prayers to the Great Spirit I'd found in books and on the Internet.

That night I chewed a small piece of the peyote I'd also bought on the Internet. Three days without food, a morning in a sweat lodge, then chewing peyote. Yeah, who wouldn't have visions? If it wasn't for the things now in my medicine pouch, I might have believed what I saw were only hallucinations.

That's where Onawa came to me. Different totem animals represent different things. The cougar is supposed to be a leader, conscious of its own strength, and a messenger between humans and gods or spirits. People with a cougar totem are supposed to have those traits, too. I'm not sure I do.

My medicine pouch bumps my chest as I climb a short rise into thicker trees. It is so quiet here. Very still. The ground is soft and springy with old pine needles. The air is moist and heavy. The only sound is my own feet moving me forward. I top the rise and look down a gentle slope filled with more trees. At the bottom I can see the sparkle of water. It has to be a river. I make my way down the hill until I come out of the trees onto the bank of the river. It's slow here, but looks pretty deep. I've seen the ocean when we were driving around; this must feed into it.

"What I wouldn't give for a canoe right now," I mutter. My voice seems alien here, just like I seem alien here, but the thing is, I really like the river and the trees. Still, it wasn't just the football issue that made me angry about moving here. It was also my dad. I know that he's never tried to find me, but moving here? It makes it seem like I'll never find him, either.

I make my way back up the hill, out of the woods and onto the street. The evening is getting dark. Lights are on in the houses between the end of the road and Aunt Lisa's. As I get closer, I see that Courtney has turned on her bedroom light. Then I stop. There's a shape silhouetted in her window.

It's a man.

A big man.

All I can see is a tall, broad-shouldered black shape on the other side of her thin pink curtains. The shape seems to be looking out the window. Looking at me.

I sprint for the house, throw open the door, and fly up the stairs. I hesitate at Courtney's door, then grab the knob and fling it open. It smells like roadkill baked in the sun. Courtney's on her bed. She jumps up when I rush in. She tries to hide a book behind her as she starts screaming at me.

"What the hell are you doing? Get out! Get out of my room!"

She's completely alone.

"I thought I saw somebody in here," I say. "A man. I thought—"

"Get! Out! Now!"

I leave. I close the door and go to my own room, where I throw myself on the bed. "Psycho bitch from hell," I tell the ceiling.

There was no man in her room. Just her, the smell of decay, her girly stuff, and some book she didn't want me to see.

I get off the bed and go to my stacks of boxes and start unpacking the things I brought with me from home. My real home. A few minutes later my cell phone rings. It's the first call I've had since moving up here. I still have an Oklahoma number, of course. The ringtone is Danzig's "Mother," which means it's Mom calling me.

"Come outside," she says when I answer.

Headlights flash through the windows as a vehicle turns into the driveway. They're followed by a second set. I could look out, but I don't. I just go downstairs and out the front door, and there's Mom and Aunt Lisa beaming at me in front of a sweet 1972 Ford F-150 pickup that appears to be in cherry condition.

"If you like it, he said I can bring your money tomorrow," Mom says. She's almost bouncing. "Lisa called and he e-mailed us some pictures and I knew it was perfect for you."

I make myself stop and give her a hard and tight hug before I open the door and slide into the cab. Finally, I am mobile again. Independent. Sweet!

"I'm going to take it for a spin," I announce, my hands gently stroking the big old steering wheel, then the gear shift, down to the ignition.

"I don't know, Alan," Mom says. "You don't have insurance on it. You don't even have a Maine driver's license."

"Oh, Holly, leave him alone," Aunt Lisa argues. "Alan, stay

63

in the city limits. If Nathan Wainscott pulls you over, you just tell him who you are and that you bought this truck from John Farley tonight."

"Nathan Wainscott?" I ask.

"He's the night cop," Aunt Lisa says. "Don't do anything wrong and he won't bother you."

"I won't," I promise. I turn the key and the engine roars to life, then idles as smooth as silk. I know I'm grinning like an idiot.

I close the door and drop the gearshift into reverse. The truck rolls out of the driveway. The brakes feel firm. I put it in drive and tap the accelerator. The old Ford eases forward, and we're off. There are no misses, no knocks, no odd sounds at all, and no lights on that shouldn't be. The heater blows hot. The radio works. The wipers work. No air-conditioning, but maybe they don't need that in Maine.

I soon realize just how small Goffstown is. This town would be jealous of a speck on the map. I drive through neighborhoods, past a grocery store, around the high school, along a bumpy back road, and finally end up back at Aunt Lisa's house. I park behind her SUV and kill the engine.

No more school bus!

I pocket the keys and go into the house. Everybody's huddled around the table.

"Alan!" Aunt Lisa motions for me to sit down.

"I'll eat in my room." Courtney glares at me before grabbing her plate and heading up the stairs. I watch her go as I make my way toward the table.

"Alan, did you go in her room without knocking?" Mom

asks. Both her and Aunt Lisa are looking at me, waiting for an answer.

I nod, guilty. "Yeah."

"Why?" Mom asks.

"I . . ." *I thought I saw the boogeyman in her window.* Can't say that. "I went for a walk after school. When I was coming back I thought I saw something in the window. I was worried about her."

My mom repeats what I said like she's trying to convince herself to believe me. "You were worried about her."

"Aimee called while you were gone," Aunt Lisa says, changing the topic. "She wants you to call her back, Alan." She pauses and her eyebrows kind of come together and a deep line forms over her nose. She's trying to think of something to say.

Aimee called and wanted to talk to me. Why?

Mom drops her gaze to the table and I do, too. There are hamburger fixings laid out on plates. I reach for a bun.

"Wash up, Alan, and sit down to eat," Mom says. "I want you to be extra nice to Courtney, okay?"

I wash my hands and sit back down to eat my second hamburger of the day. I let a few minutes go by before I ask, "Did you say Aimee called for me?"

"She's been dating Blake Stanley for a long time," Aunt Lisa says. "Personally, I think all his brains are in his muscles."

I think of how I beat him in the seven-mile today and how, if his brains are in his muscles, he still isn't very well off. I force myself not to gobble down the burger in two bites. I can feel the two women watching me and I know they know I'm much more excited than I'm letting on. They pretend to talk about things at the mill, but their eyes keep sliding back to me and tiny smiles play around their mouths. I can't take it anymore. I cram the last quarter of the burger into my mouth and wash it down with a swig of Coke.

"I guess I'll call her back," I say, getting up from the table.

"Gonna talk about her boyfriend?" Mom teases.

Aunt Lisa points me toward the wireless phone and recites a number for me. The phone starts buzzing in my ear.

"That's her cell number, in case you're interested," she adds. "And the phone gets reception upstairs, if you want some privacy."

I think about staying downstairs just to prove there's nothing going on, but I can't. I take the stairs two at a time and Aimee answers when I'm about halfway up.

"Hey, Aimee. It's Alan," I say. "Alan Parson. The new guy at school."

"I know who you are, Alan." It sounds like she's smiling. Is she smiling? I hope she's smiling. I make it to the top of the stairs and into my room.

"I heard you called looking for me."

"I did."

"What's up?"

"I was just checking to make sure you were okay. We were talking on the way home. I can't believe you outran Blake."

She really *did* call to talk about her boyfriend? Crap! Does she want me to let him beat me? I keep my voice as neutral as I can. "Well, I guess. He's good. I just got the jump on him there the last hundred yards or so."

"He was so furious. He drove home at like ninety miles per hour. He's super competitive, you know. Nobody's bested him since middle school."

"Oh."

"Competition is good for him, but he . . . he took it hard or something. He wasn't himself," she says, and then there's a silence, like maybe the words have more meaning than cross-country. No, that's stupid. I'm putting connotations to her words. Connotations. That's one of those words we had to learn in English class.

"Competition is good for any athlete," I say, because it feels like I have to say something. There's another long pause that feels really awkward. "So, you okay? No more woozy spells like at lunch?"

"No, I'm fine. Sorry. I hope I didn't freak you out. It was just so weird. I'm good, really. Thanks for helping me."

"That's cool. I was worried about you for a second there."

She pauses. "Um. That's really nice of you, but I'm okay. I'm so sorry I made you worry."

"Yeah. Well . . ." There has to be something to say. Why'd she really call? I carry on talking just to keep her on the line. "How about biology? Is Swanson always so boring?"

She laughs a little, but it sounds like it's just a polite laugh. "Mr. Monotone," she says. "There's no inflection to his voice, unless you can make him mad. Then he's like a volcano. His eyes get all red. If he's just minor-league mad, he'll yell at the class. If he's super-insane mad he storms out of the room and slams the door, then comes back for a while and sends somebody to the office for sniffing or slouching or whatever. He's not bad, though. Kind of funny sometimes. They say he smokes pot during his planning period to stay mellow."

Long silence.

I break it. "So, did you call to tell me Blake's mad at me?"

"Oh, I didn't mean it like that. He's not mad at you, specifically, you know, as an individual. He's just mad that somebody beat him." She hesitates. "But no, that's not why I called."

"Okay."

She pauses again. "Okay. Um . . . Well, basically, I saw your painting in Mr. Burnham's class."

Holy crap! I forgot about that. I can feel the blood rushing to the surface of my face. "You did?"

"Yeah."

Did she recognize herself? Stupid question. Of course she did. She wouldn't be calling if she hadn't.

"I'm sorry," I say. "I was thinking about . . . something else and just painting. You know, just letting my hands work, and then Burnham told me I'd missed the bell. I didn't even realize I was painting that. Well, you know, that I was painting *you*."

"You didn't know you were painting me?" She sounds like she doesn't believe it.

"No."

"So, you're saying you subconsciously painted me screaming while ghosts are swirling around behind me and a cougar is watching it all?"

"A cougar?" Could she really have recognized Onawa's eyes? That would be too freaky.

"It wasn't a cougar? Those weren't cougar eyes?"

"Yeah," I admit. "I just didn't think you'd recognize them."

"Alan, I want to ask you something. You'll probably think I'm crazy for asking, but when I saw your painting it really freaked me out." She pauses for a long time. "Oh . . . I can't do it. I'm sorry. I can't do it. I should go."

"I won't think you're crazy," I say really fast.

"Okay . . . You have to promise not to think I'm a freak or anything. I know freak is a bad word, but, um . . . can you just promise?"

"I promise." I think she's a lot of things, but freak is not one of them.

She pulls in her breath so hard I can hear it over the phone, then she blurts out, "Do you have dreams that, you know, come true?"

"Not really." My hand goes to the medicine bundle at my chest. How do I tell her about Onawa?

Her voice gets really tiny. "Oh. I do."

Neither of us speaks for a minute. Then I say, "I don't think you're a freak."

"Oh. Thanks. That's really nice of you to say . . . I don't . . . I don't think you're one, either." She makes this tiny hiccup noise. "Listen, Alan, I don't want to talk about this on the phone, but I think we have to talk because my dream is really not good and I don't want to sound like a wimp, but it's scaring me. We should meet somewhere. Not at school. Too many people might hear."

Blake would get jealous. I don't say it. Instead I say, "Okay. Where and when?"

"Tomorrow," she says. "I'll figure it out. Peace, Alan."

Peace?

★　★　★

I promised Mom I'd never go to sleep wearing my medicine bundle. Since I came home from Lake Thunderbird with it, she'd reluctantly allowed me to keep it, but wouldn't let me wear it to bed. "You'll get it wrapped around your throat while you're asleep," she argued. I wasn't sure that would happen, but I'd promised. Still, I'm holding the bundle in a tight fist against my chest right now.

And I'm praying. That's something I don't do very often. Sure, I have conversations with Onawa in my head all the time, but that's different. Onawa isn't the Great Spirit. The Great Spirit intimidates me, I guess. I mean, who am I to pray to a Navajo god, even if it is the same deity anyone else prays to, just with a different name? I don't even know who my father is. I can't apply for the tribal roll because Mom isn't 100 percent sure my dad is Navajo or if the partial name he gave her is really his name. It makes me feel like I'm trying to claim something that isn't really mine.

I lie awake in bed. Everyone else in the house is sleeping. The house should be quiet, but the scratching noise goes on beneath the floor of the upstairs bedrooms. Is it just mice? I'm not so sure anymore.

Mom met my father at a party. They had sex. Apparently the condom failed, and I was the result. All Mom can tell me about him is that he was very good looking, tall and muscular with long hair and fierce eyes. "Bad-boy eyes," she calls them. She says I have his eyes. She says she was a little drunk, but she felt it when he locked his eyes on her at this party. They barely talked before sneaking off to a bedroom of the house where the party was going on. He told her his name was White Deer, that he was

Navajo and didn't live in Oklahoma City. That's it. Mom screwed him, they went back to the party, then he was gone. She's never seen him since. She doesn't even have a picture of him.

She stopped partying when she found out I was growing in her womb. She hasn't told me everything she used to do, but she's told me enough that I know she led a pretty rough life. She sobered up and got a job at a tire factory right after I was born, and she worked there until we moved to Maine.

She named me after my father. Alan Whitedeer Parson. She says she wanted my birth records to show that my father is Indian, but without knowing his last name she couldn't do it.

"We don't need their casino money," she said when she told the story. I don't care about the money. White Deer, whoever he is, probably saved her life by knocking her up. When I was little I liked to think that the Great Spirit sent him to save her and help create me, but I guess that's pretty conceited.

Only Onawa tells me different. If not for the vision quest, I'd think I'd just made her up out of my desire to know something about where I came from. Mom's dead parents were both the grandchildren of German immigrants. Fine. Okay. I'm half German. That's not the half I'm interested in.

I don't know many of the prayers. The ones I know I got off the Internet. Still, it's the best I can do. I recite a Cherokee prayer over and over as I lie awake, listening to the scratching.

"As I walk the trail of life in the fear of the wind and rain, grant me, oh Great Spirit, that I may always walk like a man."

Walking like a man in the face of fear. Sometimes it's the best we can do.

★   ★   ★

71

I'm in that state between being asleep and being awake. That's when Onawa usually finds me. I can only think of Aimee. Aimee screaming something at me as the black spirit world closes around her. Is she being possessed or something? I don't know. Aimee's red hair is flying around her face, like in my painting.

Remembering the painting breaks the vision apart. Onawa calls to me. She has more to say, but I can't hear it. My eyes open as I feel my face flushing again over the thought of Aimee finding my crude painting of her in the art room.

"I'm such a dumb-ass," I tell the ceiling. Still, it *had* gotten her to call me, and she didn't seem mad that I'd painted her.

It's early morning. I dress and go downstairs. I start the coffeepot, then put some water on the stove for oatmeal. Aunt Lisa is in the kitchen when I turn away from the stove.

"You're quite the handyman around the kitchen, Alan." She gives me an early-morning smile before adding, "Not in a girly way, you understand."

"It's the least I can do for the aunt who found that awesome truck for me," I say. "Want some oatmeal?"

Eventually, Mom and Courtney make their way to the kitchen, too. I run up to my room to get my books, and as I'm coming out of my room I hear a commotion downstairs.

"No, I'm not riding with him. I'll take the bus like I always do," Courtney says loud enough that I can hear her on the upstairs landing. "I don't like him."

"Why?" Aunt Lisa asks. "Alan is a nice boy."

"He's an asshole. He came into my room!"

"Courtney Rae Tucker! You will *not* use that kind of language or tone in this house, and especially not about our family."

Aunt Lisa is furious. I wonder what Mom is doing during this exchange. As far as I know, she's still in the kitchen. I feel awkward even hearing the conversation from up here.

"Fuck you!" Courtney screams. Even I'm shocked by this, and I'm pretty used to hearing kids cuss at their parents. She runs through the dining room and out of the house. She doesn't bother to close the door.

Below me, Aunt Lisa starts crying. Mom is saying something to her, but I don't get to hear what because something sharp slams into my back. The pain is sudden, completely unexpected, and right on my spine. I can't help but let out a girly little yelp, like a dog that's been stepped on or something. Whatever hit me falls to the floor and I hear glass breaking.

God, it hurts!

I look down and see a framed picture of Courtney. It looks like it's from early grade school. The glass is broken and one corner of the frame is busted. Her face stares up at me with a happy little gap-toothed smile. She doesn't look like a girl who'd yell curses at her mother.

My back hurts. The pain isn't quite as sharp as it was, but it's still there, in a spot just out of reach so I can't even rub at it.

What caused that?

I look around the hallway and find a rectangle of space on the wall that's whiter than the rest. The spot is a good twenty feet away from where I was when the picture hit me. My arm hair prickles up again. No way that was a coincidence. No. Freaking. Way.

7

AIMEE

You are mine. You are all mine.

Despite the stupid dream voice that's echoing in my head, I go kayaking when I wake up, same as always.

Last night it wasn't just the voice. I dreamed of boys beneath the water and a seal with seeing eyes. But things are normal on the river. It's so quiet as the kayak glides over the water that I almost think I can hear my mom there, feel her breath when she kisses me good night, hear her say my name. Ospreys glide in ever-widening circles above me, catching up winds. I would like to stay out here forever, but there's school. There's always school.

I get ready to go, kissing all the men in my life good morning, which causes Benji to make fake puking noises. I bop him lightly on the arm, but it's like I'm just going through the motions. In the shower I make a list of things I have to do today, but the first one makes me stumble, slip in the stall, and hit the tiled wall. Today I have to dump Blake.

He picks me up in his Volvo. I slide inside, put my bag on my lap. He leans over to kiss me. It's all I can do not to cringe. I turn my head so he gets my cheek.

"So, how's my favorite beautiful groupie this fine morning?" he asks, pulling out of the driveway, acting like nothing at all is wrong. He turns the music back up. He always turns it down when he gets me so that Gramps won't lecture us about our precious eardrums.

"I'm okay," I answer.

It's like all my courage washed down the drain in the bathroom. Blake keeps talking about his tunes and cross-country and more about his tunes. Then he suddenly throws out, "Him beating me was just a fluke."

"Yeah? Who?" I have this disconnect, can't figure out what he's talking about.

"That Indian. Courtney's cousin."

My heart beats once. It beats twice. We head down a hill toward Schoolhouse Corner. "Did you just refer to him as 'that Indian'?" I shift around, trying to find a way to get comfortable. My foot lands on the top of some ancient Glue CD cover.

Blake reaches over and yanks it from under my foot, then straightens up again. "Jesus. You cracked the cover. What's wrong with you?"

Somehow he manages to stay on the road.

I decide to not be the peacemaker this time.

"What's wrong with *me*?" I say. "You're the one who just referred to someone by their race like it's their one defining character trait or something. I'm not the one who just did that. Plus, you took the Lord's name in vain."

"Aimee, calm down." His face sort of gets normal again, like his anger is seeping out of him. "I didn't mean it that way."

"You said it, Blake. Lately you've been acting differently."

"I could say the same about you."

I stare at him. "What's that supposed to mean?"

"Whatever, Aimee."

"Whatever?"

He grabs the steering wheel so tightly his knuckles whiten. "Whatever."

All my insides tighten up. I switch off the music, trying to calm myself for what I have to say to Blake, who I thought I knew, who I thought was nice, but somehow isn't all of a sudden. I just say it. "We can't go out anymore."

"What?"

I repeat it. "We can't go out anymore."

He gets his I'm-humoring-her voice. "Okay. Why can't we go out anymore?"

"Because you're a racist."

He stops the car. "What? Saying 'that Indian' does not make me a racist. You're acting crazy."

"I'm not crazy."

"No. You're just looking for excuses to break up with me." His voice is full-on angry, tight, compressed. A muscle twitches under his eye.

"You're a racist, Blake. I mean, that's not all you are, obviously. You're funny and you're a great singer and stuff, but you— you—" I can't find the words. "I just can't go out with you."

"It's because of him, isn't it? Because of that Indian?"

"You said it again!"

"Whatever. You like him. He's faster than me, so you want to go out with him now, right? He's just this giant stud." His jaw clenches and all the happy-fun-singing Blake is gone. It's just gone. It's like something else is looking out of his eyes. He glares at me and spits out the words. "You are freaking insane."

"I'm not crazy!" I push myself farther away from him and lean against the car door, trying to stay calm. He's hurting inside. That's all. That's why he's saying these sorts of things that he's never said before. That's why his face is a twisted mask of rage. "What is wrong with you? You aren't acting like you."

"Right. *I'm* the one who's acting like a freak." He snorts. For a second he's silent. For a second nothing happens. For a second cars just pass on the street. Then he roars—literally roars—"It's that kid! It's that stupid Indian kid!" He slams himself out the driver's side door. Two seconds pass and he's on my side. My door flies open before I can figure out what's happening. He's yanking me out. "Out of my car. Out of my goddamn car."

My bag falls on the ground. "My seat belt."

It's still attached. I'm tangled up. I'm a mess. I'm stuck in the car. He's grabbing both my arms, yanking. I manage to reach over and unclick the belt. The moment I do, I'm tumbling out of the car sideways. I land on my hip and my elbow and my bag. Blake is standing above me and I'm sobbing out, "Don't you kick me. Don't you dare kick me."

His face suddenly changes. It loses its anger, just snaps into his normal face. His lips quiver for a second. His eyes widen and he says, "Oh my God. Oh . . . Aimee . . . I'm . . . I'm sorry. I don't know why I did that. Aimee, I'm so—"

He reaches his hand down to help me up. I've held that hand a million times, but I know I won't ever again.

"Don't touch me," I snap, holding on to my anger so I can stop crying. "Don't."

The bus goes by. I swear eight hundred million people look out the windows at us. The one face I recognize for sure is Courtney's. She smiles. They are all smiling.

I cringe and haul myself up. My knee barely holds my weight, wiggling, trying to find its place. Dirt marks my jeans, smeared across the side of my leg.

"Aimee. I'm sorry. I was just so mad—" Blake starts. "I don't know what I was doing. I—I can't believe I just did that. Aim— I'm—I'm so—I don't know what's wrong with me lately—"

I raise my hand to stop him talking. My shoulder aches. "Don't."

I haul my bag up and start walking. Each step sends a knife of sorrow-pain through my leg and right into the core of me. I go around him, putting one foot in front of the other, ignoring the trash that's on the shoulder of the road, the old McDonald's bag, the Ziploc sandwich bag, the newspaper, wet and moldy and discarded. I keep walking to school, limping, hurting, but that's all. It's over. I'm okay. I am perfectly okay.

Blake has never been like this before. He's always been a tiny bit competitive, but he's never been jealous, never been racist or sexist. He's the kind of guy who wants to succeed, win some running awards, go to college, sing, be happy. He was nice. He was good. Everyone knows that. In a town like this every-one knows everything, really, and . . . I swear, I'm just walk-ing down the hall before first period and people are already whispering about what happened with Blake and me on the side of the road. Their voices come at me from all sides, girls, guys, high, low, worried, know-it-all.

"He just hauled off on her . . . totally not like Blake. Everyone's so freaking pissy lately—"

"She and Blake broke up."

"Her mom was totally psycho. I heard she—"

"What crap. You know it's a rumor. They'd never break up. They're perfect. They put like a hundred hearts on each other's status updates."

The two-minute walk to Spanish seems to take hours. All I want is the safety of my desk and conjugated verbs. I manage to hold it together before I remember that I'll see Alan in bio next period and I need to have some kind of plan for us to talk— like I'm in any condition to talk right now. But I have to be, don't I?

Courtney corners me after Spanish. She's got her ancient orange textbook under her arm. With her free arm she grabs my elbow and pulls me closer. She speaks softly. "Aim, are you sure about this?"

I want to say, "About what?" but instead I just nod.

"He told me. Wow, Aimee, you and Blake. You've been going out forever and . . ." She struggles for the words. Her dark brown eyes close and then open again. "I don't think you should just dump him like that. He's really sorry."

"I know . . ." I remember her face smiling in the bus while I was on the ground. "It doesn't matter. How about you? Are you okay?"

"Me?" She stops walking. Her voice goes shrill. "Oh, yeah.

79

I'm brilliant. You know, it's not like my dad *is missing* and everyone insists he's dead."

"Court . . ." I don't know what to say.

"And, my stupid-ass cousin barged into my room without knocking."

"He did?" My brain shudders. Alan's supposed to be the good one. Why would he do that?

"Yes." She shakes her head, lets go of my elbow, and wraps her arms around her rib cage. "Everyone is acting funny lately. Have you noticed? It's like all the bad in them, all the bad qualities are getting pumped up more often, like everyone's losing their temper, like everyone's getting more insecure or mean or jerky or something. I don't know . . . I don't know. I can't believe you dumped him."

I start to say something, but I'm having a hard time figuring out what to respond to. She's all over the place.

She talks before I have a chance, letting go of her ribs and running both hands through her hair really quickly. "That's not what matters. What matters is . . . do you remember what happened at that séance?"

I swallow. I don't answer. Our feet move us forward through people weighed down with backpacks and book bags and secrets.

Court keeps going. "Do you remember what happened to you?"

"Yeah," I say, flat and hard. How can I not remember the pencil catching on fire? The way my hair was suddenly wet and how I'd screamed and screamed because it felt like someone was ripping my arms off, and how I'd freaked everyone out. "Why? What's this about?"

"It's just . . . There are certain things, Aimee, things that you can't do anything about, you know? Certain things are totally beyond you."

I adjust my bag, which is slipping. Everything smells stale, like old-lady houses and nursing homes, or clothes that haven't been washed in a while. "And you believe that?"

She smiles, a slow half smile that is far from happy. We're at the place in the hall where she goes left and I go right. Some people wave and say hi. We all jostle forward into the middle of the intersection.

I head to the wall and open my locker, shoving my Spanish book onto the top shelf.

"Aim . . ." Court's voice tugs at me.

I shut the locker.

"I just want to make sure you know what you're risking. Going out with Blake made you seem more normal."

"What? So everyone will think I'm a freak again if we stay broken up?" I angry-whisper at her. And for a second I almost think that I made the wrong decision when I broke up with Blake, but it isn't just because of what happened today. He's been getting progressively jerkier and I've been getting less and less happy with him. You shouldn't make do when you're dating, should you? You shouldn't date just because dating makes you seem less crazy.

Courtney shakes her head. "No. That's not what I'm afraid of."

"What, then?"

She swallows. "I'm worried something bad will happen to you, like at the séance, and with Chuck. I'm worried that he'll notice you again."

My heart stops beating, but my mouth still works and I whisper, "Who?"

"The River Man."

Everything stills. Shivers seem to creep around my hair. "He could be a figment of my imagination."

"Aimee. We both know that's not true." Her face is a crashed-apart painting. Her eyes and mouth are rigid-scared because she knows how bad things can be. "I think he's doing some-thing, right now, to the town, making people mean."

"So you're saying Blake isn't a jerk because he's a jerk. He's being a jerk because of the River Man."

"Yes," she whispers. "Yes."

About a week after that seventh-grade séance, Court and I tried this Ouija board thing. It's supposed to connect you to the spirit world. We wanted to find out why Chuck died. The Ouija board has this little pointer that you place your finger-tips on. Then it spells out words by moving to letters of the alphabet.

"Why did Chuck die?" Court had asked the board, because we'd agreed that I was not the person to communicate with the spirits anymore.

The pointer spelled out, "Because I wanted him to."

I took my fingers off the pointer and hugged my arms around myself, terrified.

Court battled on. "One more question, Aimee. Okay?"

"I don't want to do this," I'd said, my voice edging into hys-teria. "I don't want to."

"Aim. One more," Court said, and like an idiot I put my

fingers back on the pointer thing. Then she asked, all strong and calm, "Who are you?"

And it answered: "The River Man."

Hayley finds me outside the door to bio. Her hair is all crazy because she has PE first period. She grabs my hands. "You're limping."

I shrug.

"You broke up with Blake this morning." She makes it a statement.

"Yeah . . ." I start and stop because Alan's super-big self is suddenly there. Something flutters in my stomach. His eyes meet my eyes. He takes in the dirt on my jeans and his mouth starts to form a question, but then he clamps it shut again. Instead, he just nods and ducks his head, fast-walking into bio like he's embarrassed to see me or something.

"Did he hit you?" Hayley says.

I have to do a double take. "What?"

She gets insistent. "Did Blake hit you? You're walking funny. Your jeans are dirty. And people are, well, talking. Did he hit you?"

"He dragged me out of the car," I whisper, because I can't hold it inside anymore.

Hayley's mouth drops open. Then she grabs me, crushing me to her chest. "Oh, baby . . . I am so sorry. Oh, that asshole. I never thought he'd be like that—not ever. Oh, Aimee."

"It's okay." I sniff. She smells like rain.

"No, it's not. It's not okay," she whispers as people move by us into class. "It is never okay. You know we all have times where we freak out a little, get moody, whatever, but throwing you out of the car is not okay, Aimee."

"I know. That's not what I mean. It's just . . . I'm okay."

She pushes me away to look into my eyes. "You're crying. You are not okay."

I have no answer.

"Girls. Class." Mr. Swanson is totally ignoring my teary face, which is nice of him, I guess, or else that's just a symptom of what Courtney was talking about.

We walk into the classroom. I'm still limping. Hayley goes to her seat by the window. I slide into my desk behind Alan. He turns to look at me. His eyes are huge and deep and questioning. I try to smile but can't quite do it.

"You okay?" he mouths.

I do this fast nod. His eyes narrow the tiniest bit. I can tell he doesn't believe me. Opening my bag, I grab some gum and put it in my mouth. Then I take out my notebook and a pen and write: *Five minutes. I'll pretend to faint. You take me to nurse's office. Okay?*

When Mr. Swanson turns to the wipe board I reach forward and slide the note over Alan's shoulder. He catches it.

There. Step one, done.

· 8 ·
ALAN

I read the note one more time, then fold it once, twice, and stick it between some middle pages of my biology book before I check out the clock. Five minutes. I try to focus on Swanson, but I'm really just staring blankly at him, thinking about Aimee.

There's something wrong with her. Her jeans are covered in dirt that looks ground in, and she limped when she came into class. There'd been talk in first hour, talk about her and Blake. Someone said they'd seen him hit her. Someone else said that would never happen. I wondered. Granted, I barely know the guy, but he—

I sense Aimee standing up behind me.

"Mr. Swanson," she says, "I don't feel—"

She's taken a step forward and is beside me when she crumples sideways. I catch her as I'm standing up. Dead silence. All eyes are on us as I hold her up, clamped against my chest, her cheek pressed hard against my medicine bag. The world shimmers and slams just like the last time I touched her. Images swarm into my mind, a river, being pulled deep into the water, a man's voice . . . It's not quite as powerful as last time, but it freezes me for a second. Then I shake myself out of it.

"I'll take her to the nurse," I announce, then put an arm behind her knees and scoop her up. She's so light! I hold her high enough that her feet won't kick anyone in the face and head for the door.

"Across from the front office," Mr. Swanson calls as I push through the door. I guess he's telling me where the nurse's station is. I don't know.

The classroom door closes and Aimee whispers, "Go left to the end of the hall and out the door."

I move fast, passing closed doors with those little slits for windows. I can't tell if anyone sees us. No one confronts us, and I keep moving until I get to the blue steel door at the end of the hall. I push it open with my hip and step into the cool morning air.

"Okay, you can put me down," Aimee says.

I look down into her face and think about that. Her skin is so white and flawless, her eyes so green and bright and full of life. A little breeze ruffles her magnificent red hair. I don't really want to put her down.

"You *were* limping," I say. "Maybe I shouldn't make you walk."

She smiles up at me. What a smile! I mean, it sounds all mushy, I know, but damn, that girl has a smile that makes you want to smile right back at her.

"I'm good. Really," she says, but she doesn't wiggle or try to get out of my arms.

"Me, too." Okay, I have to admit that I'm not usually so bold with girls. Looking into Aimee's eyes, though, I know there is depth here. There's already some kind of connection. "Where are we going?"

"You are so not going to carry me all the way," she argues, but still, she's not trying to get down. "You'll get hurt."

I lower her feet to the ground and let her go, then realize how warm she'd been against me. She crosses her arms over her chest and hunkers against the cool breeze.

"All right, but you start limping and I'm carrying you again."

"Are you always so gallant, so knight-in-shining-armor?" she asks.

"Just bossy," I answer, and I'm still smiling because she is.

"Come on," she says. "Behind the field house."

We dash across a short stretch of lawn and into the parking lot. I follow her lead, staying low between the parked vehicles. She's limping, but managing to move pretty fast anyway. We get to the side of the field house and scooch along the wall like SWAT cops until we slide around to the back, where she collapses to the ground, her back against the cinderblock wall.

"You were limping," I accuse.

"Yeah, but you couldn't catch me."

All I can do is laugh.

"What's in the bag?" she asks, nodding toward my chest.

I touch the leather. "It's a medicine bag. It's kind of like a good-luck charm."

"What's in it? I mean, you don't have to tell me. I'm sorry. I guess I'm just nosy. It smelled—" She stops, like she's embarrassed to finish.

"Probably smelled like sweat," I finish.

"Well, it smelled like you, but there was more. Kind of . . . earthy."

I finger the bag, watching Aimee, but thinking back to Lake Thunderbird. Her eyes, so clear and green, promise me I can trust her.

"A rock," I say, and my throat is surprisingly dry. I've never told anyone, not even Mom, what's in the bag. "A white rock about as big as a robin's egg. Some hair. And some dirt."

Her eyes ask a question, but her mouth doesn't. She nods.

I change the subject. "First off, Courtney wasn't good this morning. She told her mom to fuck off and ran out of the house. She doesn't like me."

"That's not normal. She's not acting like Courtney, you know." Aimee's tone is very serious. "She would never say that to her mom . . . this thing with her dad has really changed her."

"Tell me," I urge. A bruise has formed on my spine from the picture hitting me and it hurts as I sit with my back against the wall.

"They were pretty close," Aimee says. "You could tell he really loved her, like she was everything to him, and she loved him soooo much. Sometimes she'd even skip out on going to the movies or hanging out with us to go for a walk or play Monopoly with her dad. She was a total daddy's girl."

I'm listening, but I'm also thinking about my own father. I'm a little jealous. At least Courtney had her dad for fifteen years.

"She hasn't accepted that he's not going to come home," Aimee says.

I nod.

"There's more, though. Now she's . . ." Aimee stops. I'd looked away. I was looking at the grass between my shoes, actually, just taking in what she was saying. Now I look up at her face again and I can see the confusion. Her voice is a whisper. It's very, very sad. She's really struggling with something big, struggling to say what she wants. I figure she's wondering if I'll think she's weird.

"Do you know what a vision quest is?" I ask.

She smiles a little and admits she doesn't, so I make myself man up and tell her about my vision quest and Onawa.

"Oh." Her bright green eyes are clouded now, confused. I know that look. Usually that comes right before the girl says, "I have to go home and wash the dog, Alan. See ya." But Aimee doesn't say anything.

"Onawa showed me things. She showed me the spirit world. It was all dark, with ghosts moving in it. The ghosts were just kind of swirling around, like bubbles in boiling water. I don't know. That sounds dumb, but that's what I thought. Then she . . ." I pause and look away for a minute.

"What?" Aimee asks. "You can tell me. If you want to."

"She told me someday I would be called Spirit Warrior. She doesn't usually actually speak to me. She just shows me things, or, I don't know, puts out a vibe? That sounds lame, but it's kind of right. She gives me a feeling that sort of means something. That's the only time she's actually spoken. She said, 'Someday they will call you Spirit Warrior.' I've never admitted that to anyone. Why would I have a name like that?"

The clouds are gone from Aimee's eyes and she is looking at me, steady and clear again. "Spirit Warrior."

"Yeah. I—I can't believe I just told you that . . . Anyway, I would have thought it was all just a dream, or just the peyote and hunger, you know. I'm not stupid. I know you can hallucinate just from being hungry enough. Add the drugs in there and, yeah, you could see anything, especially if . . ." I pause, but those big green eyes won't let me stop. "You know, if it's something you really, really want."

"I understand," she says, and I think she really does.

"Well, I would have just written the whole thing off as a weird trip and wishful thinking, but in the vision Onawa gave me a rock. A stone that looked like an egg. She said it was a symbol of me being reborn. When I woke up, I had this little white rock in my hand. It's all smooth and white, just like a little egg."

Aimee nods.

"Still, I thought it was a coincidence. You know, I was stumbling around, completely stoned, and found the rock and somehow added it to my hallucination. But then I saw the brown fur on a big rock. It was stuck there, like an animal had been scratching its back against the rock. And there in the mud beside the rock was one animal footprint. A big cat. A cougar. I knew it was a cougar."

"So you put the hair, rock, and mud in your bag," Aimee says, finishing my story.

"Yeah. That's what I did. Most people would think that's really weird."

"I don't," she says, and I know she's telling me the truth.

"I know you don't. And that's why you can tell me anything. Tell me about your dreams. I won't think you're weird."

"You'll be my spirit warrior?" She smiles, but it's a small, hesitant smile.

I have to drop my eyes for a moment. I look back at her and try to smile but fail. "I don't know. I'll try."

"Okay. If Court or anyone hasn't told you already . . . my mom died a few years ago." She swallows. "She was sick. It was a . . . a mental illness. Bipolar disorder. Everyone says she killed herself."

I'd heard that. "I'm sorry."

"Afterward, me and Court and some other friends had a séance in my house because I missed her so much, you know, and I just wanted to see if she was okay. I don't think any of us actually expected it to work or anything, you know? My dreams, or 'psychic visions,' started for real after that. It got really freaky. I mean, really freaky."

"Your mom talked to you?"

"No! It wasn't her. It was . . . something else. Something dark. I'd seen it before, at the river. It's shaped like a man, but looks like it's just a shadow. You know, a shadow that's thick, like a man, but just shadow. And everyone freaked out. I know that makes no sense."

I think back to what I saw in Courtney's bedroom window last night. "He's tall, with broad shoulders. Just kind of stands there looking at you and makes you feel cold."

"You've seen him?" Her voice is hushed.

A cloud moves through the sky and covers us in shade for a few seconds. She jumps and clutches at my arm. I take her tiny hands in one of mine and squeeze gently.

"I saw him last night in Courtney's bedroom window."

"Oh . . . whoa!" Her hands in mine are suddenly rigid. "She talked about him today. She said I should be careful, so that he wouldn't notice me again. He . . . I saw him before my mom died. She was at the river, and I saw him standing with her. Then at the séance . . ." She pauses and her eyes darken, like a cloud has crossed between them and the life-light that makes them shine. "Alan, I'm scared. I know that sounds really wussy, but I am. I'm scared."

"It'll be okay." I'm not sure what to do. I squeeze her hands and say, "You know the bell's gonna ring in a few minutes, right?"

"Really?" She slowly pulls her left hand away from me and looks at her watch. "We have to get back inside."

I get up first and then haul her up beside me. As we walk back to school, I can't wait any longer. "Is what they're saying true?"

"What?" Those eyes tell me she knows exactly what I'm talking about. She tries to hide them from me. Her hair flops in front of her face.

"They said in first hour you broke up with Blake. That he beat you up."

"I broke up with him," she says. "He didn't beat me up."

"Why are you limping then?"

She swallows real hard. "He pulled me out of his car, which is not technically beating me up. Although, it's probably assault or something and it is not cool. I was not cool with it."

Her hands move to her forearms unconsciously but I notice. I take her left arm and carefully push the sleeve up to her elbow. When I touch her, there are tiny sparks of something that passes between us, but no visions.

She flinches but doesn't pull away. The bruises are fresh and finger shaped. "That son of a bitch," I say.

"He's never been like this, been so angry or possessive. I think he'd get deranged if he even knew we were talking. It's weird. I don't even know who he is anymore. Courtney says that it's not just him. She thinks everyone is acting strangely, more nasty, and I kind of think she's right. That doesn't excuse what he did at all. It just feels like something bigger is going on." She reaches for the door handle but it's locked. She gives me a terrified look.

"Crap. Does this mean we have to go in through the front door?" I ask.

Before she can answer, the door flies open, missing us by inches. Courtney stands in the doorway, glaring at us, a smirk on her face. There's something odd. It takes me a moment to realize she's broken out in a pretty nasty case of oozing acne.

"Court, what happened?" Aimee asks. "Your f—"

"You've been talking about me," Courtney accuses.

Aimee starts to say something, but Courtney's eyes roll up into her head and she collapses. She's like a marionette whose strings just got cut. She sags to her knees, then flops forward, her head smacking the concrete in front of our feet.

"Court!" Aimee screams and drops to her knees. Inside the school a bell rings and people come spilling into the hallway. I crouch beside Courtney and roll her over. There's blood pouring from a gash in her forehead. The skin around the wound is swelling fast. I grab her up.

"I guess I really am carrying someone to the nurse," I say.

Aimee jumps in front of me and tries to clear people out

of the way as we hurry through the hall, around a corner, and finally to the nurse's station. The nurse isn't in and has to be paged. Aimee and I stay with Courtney, who's still unconscious. I find an icepack in a little refrigerator and put it over the bump after Aimee cleans away the blood. The bleeding has almost stopped by now.

"The halls are going to look like something out of a horror movie," Aimee says. "She was bleeding so bad. Oh man, poor Court."

"Head wounds are the worst for that," I say. "She probably has a concussion. Where is that nurse?"

"She's behind you." It isn't Aimee. Aimee is looking at me and covering her mouth.

"Hi, Mrs. Higgins," she says, looking past my shoulder. I turn around to see a short lady with tidy brown hair and a serious face.

"My cousin's hurt. She fell and busted her head open."

Mrs. Higgins pushes past me, lifts the icepack, and looks at the wound.

"She'll need stitches," she says. She looks to Aimee and says, "Hold this on her head while I call her mom."

Mrs. Higgins calls Aunt Lisa at work. The conversation is brief. Aunt Lisa tells the nurse to call the ambulance, but she's on her way, too. Mrs. Higgins hangs up and looks at us. "You two go on to class."

We leave the nurse's station, but don't make it to class. A tall, sunburned man with a gray beard is waiting for us. I swear he looks like a bear. His arms are thick and I can only think he must have been a lumberjack at some point.

"Who's your friend, Miss Avery?" he asks. No, he demands the answer.

"Alan," she says. "He's new."

"What's your name, young man?" His eyes are blue and steely.

"Alan Parson," I say.

"Come with me. Both of you." He turns around and walks away. He walks in kind of a bowlegged fashion, those thick arms swinging at his sides. He takes us to a corner office and motions us into a couple of padded leather chairs while he goes around and sits behind a cluttered desk. His office walls are covered in pictures of buffalo and University of Colorado pennants. He glares at us. "Aimee, have you ever been in my office before?"

"No," she says. A carved nameplate tells me we're facing John Everson, vice principal.

"This young man comes to school and in his first week you're both in my office for skipping class," he says. "That doesn't say much for him."

"It was my fault, Mr. Everson," Aimee says. "I've been super worried about Courtney after . . . you know. They're cousins. And I thought he might be able to help but I didn't want to talk about it in front of her or in class or at lunch when everybody could hear. I'm babbling. I'm sorry. I'm babbling, aren't I?"

He nods for her to go on.

"And I just thought it would be better if we snuck away for a second and the only place I could think of going was outside and Alan was so nice. He just did it because he's kind like that. And now Court's all hurt anyway." Her voice breaks a little bit.

His icy blue eyes flick to me and I nod. "Yes, sir. Courtney Tucker is my cousin. She's with the nurse now."

"She wasn't with the nurse when you snuck out of school, though," he says.

We're both quiet for a moment; then Aimee says, "No, but we could tell she's sick. Ever since her dad, you know, she's been acting really strange."

"I see," he says, then focuses more fully on me. "You're the kid that beat Blake Stanley yesterday in cross-country."

"Yeah."

"From where? Oklahoma, isn't it?"

"Yeah. OKC. Does everyone know about me and Blake?"

"This is a small school, Mr. Parson." His beard splits in a grin for a moment, then he suppresses it. Maybe he's not always the hard-ass he acts like. "Somebody outrunning Blake is a big deal. You're the one who got worked up because we don't have football."

"Yeah. Man, does *everyone* know *everything* around here?"

"Get used to it," Everson says. "I used to play football."

"Colorado?" I guess.

"That's right," he says.

"I planned to go to OU."

"Ah, the Sooners," he says, and shakes his head. "We used to play them back when it was the Big Eight conference."

"I know," I say. I consider saying something about how Oklahoma was always whipping Colorado, but the sound of sirens saves me from doing anything that stupid.

"You two get to class," Everson says. "I don't want to see you back in here. Understand?"

* * *

96

At lunch, I sit alone because it just seems like the right thing to do. Aimee sits with Hayley and Eric while Blake hangs out with the cross-country guys. Halfway through, someone plops a note written on a napkin in front of my face.

"Don't get involved with her," it reads.

It's so melodramatic. I crumple it up and throw it away, then put my ear buds in and rock out, all alone in my own little world. Aimee catches my eye and waves. I can't help it. I wave back.

Coach Treat has heard about the friction on her team. Her hair's pulled back in a high ponytail and she's wearing shorts despite the cold. Her legs are pale enough to glow in the dark.

"Same course as yesterday," Coach calls. "Seven miles. Line up! Alan, you stay with me."

Coach Treat runs alongside me, taking long, easy strides. She's good at this. Her upper body seems to glide, while I bounce up and down, my feet pounding the pavement much harder than hers.

"You're fast, Alan, but not steady," she says. "Cross-country is about endurance. You'll wear yourself out if you don't learn to be lighter. You're losing energy every time you stomp the ground. Take longer strides. Keep your torso straight up and down. Nobody's going to tackle you. You don't have to lean over a goal line."

I try taking her advice, but it feels like I'm trying to gallop. For a school without football, these people seem to know a lot about it.

"One thing at a time, Alan. Focus on keeping your torso straight," she says.

I try it. It messes with my stride, but I keep it up.

"That's it," she says. "Head straight above your waist. Focus on keeping that posture most of the run. If it's close at the end, then you can lean into it and smoke the competition."

We run. She doesn't let me cut loose at the end, instead making me keep pace with her while the other boys race past us. "Focus on posture," she reminds me.

At the field house, I change and leave the building first. Second team is just coming in, Blake in the lead. I feel his eyes on me. I glare back at him as he begins slowing. Coach Treat materializes beside me like a pale ghost. Blake pounds past us, but I hear him.

"Mine," he says as if it's a puff of hard breath.

· 9 ·
AIMEE

The whole day feels wrong, like people's emotions are all tangled into some sort of dark wires, yanking on each other, pulling against one another. At practice Coach notices my limp right away. When I'm in my shorts there's a pretty obvious bruise running all the way down my leg.

"You're not practicing, Avery," she says. "You're benched."

Even though it's pretty cold, I sit on the grass instead of the bench. It's that hard-core rebel in me, I guess. Hayley comes over right before drills and says, "Blake is out of control, Aim."

"I know."

"Look at your leg."

"Pretty, isn't it? Sort of a Barney the purple dinosaur look?"

"It's not funny, Aimee."

"I know. I know it isn't."

"Not everyone's on his side, you know? What he did was wrong. Even if you slept with that Alan guy, it would still be wrong."

"We haven't even kissed. We don't like each other that way!" The moment I say it, I realize that's a lie.

"Right." She lifts an eyebrow.

"I mean it," I mumble, and feel guilty for even thinking about Alan. Instead I start remembering all the sweet songs Blake made for me, all the times he'd get mad at other guys treating girls like possessions. How could he change so much? Maybe Courtney was right.

"HAYLEY! GET YOUR TUCHUS OVER HERE!" Coach yells way more harshly than she normally would.

Hayley rolls her eyes and runs off.

I watch. They're doing pressure passing drills and it basically sucks to be stuck here doing nothing. My hands cover my face. My body sits on the ground. I just exist.

Even though I try not to think about him because I've only just broken up with Blake . . . this whole thing with Alan? It's so weird. When we talk there's this funky connection thing going on and when he touches me, it's like the cliché of sparks and electricity. That's got to mean something, doesn't it? Something good in this world of bad? I can't believe Courtney mentioned the River Man. I've been trying for years not to think about him.

When I was around seven, I dreamed of this tiny airplane all broken in the woods with fire all around it in little bursts. In my dream, everything was the opposite of supersized; things were mini-sized, like toy sets. There was a man in a blue jumpsuit standing at the edge of the road. He looked lost. He lifted his hand to me, and I tried to take it.

That was the first dream I had that came true.

I tried to tell my mother about it during breakfast in the kitchen. She liked to hear about my dreams. If she could have had an automatic feed into my brain so that she could know everything I was thinking, she would have done it.

"There was a blue man," I said.

"Sweetie, don't talk with your mouth full." She smiled to make it not so much of a scold.

I chewed my English muffin and swallowed real fast. "And there was a little plane in the woods, but it was broken in half like Benji's toy plane that he dropped off his high chair, but it wasn't a toy. And there were lots of fire bushes all around." I got back to my muffin. My belly felt too liquid from so much apple juice.

My mom nodded. "Anything else?" I shook my head. "Well, that's an interesting dream," she said, which is what she always said. "I wonder what that means."

Later, she came out of the shower wrapped up in a white bathrobe. Her hair dripped onto the floor, making little drip noises, a sort of splat as the drops hit the ground. She smelled like her lilac soap. She crouched down, adjusted her robe, and then put both her hands on my shoulders and said, "Sometimes I see a man, too."

"Really?"

Her hands felt good on my shoulders, like they were holding me to the ground. She nodded. "On the river."

"On a boat?"

"No." Her lip quivered and steadied. "Just . . . just standing there."

She brushed some dirt off my shoulder and started to stand

up, but I didn't want her to go. I blurted, "What does the River Man do?"

She froze in place. "Calls me. He calls me. He wants my soul, and then once he gets it, he'll feed on it; he'll be so powerful, baby. He'll leave the river and walk into town and everything . . . everything will be gone."

Alan brings me home, and it's a ten-minute ride of awkwardness. We talk about Courtney. Neither of us mentions Blake. I thank him and scoot into the house as quickly as possible.

At dinner I want to tell Dad about Alan and Courtney, but I can't because Benji's yammering away about Cheetos and baseball and Gramps dating some woman named Doris, which is where he is now, and how disgusting girls are. I try not to be annoyed at Benji because I know he's just psyched that Dad's actually having dinner with us and not working late, but it's hard.

"How do they run with those . . . those things on their chest?" Benji moves his hands and totally inappropriately shows what he's talking about.

"Benji!" Dad acts horrified, but his eyes are laughing.

"You call them breasts, Benji," I say really slowly. I poke my fork in his direction. He scoops up some spaghetti.

"Well, they're disgusting," he announces, then shoves way too much spaghetti into his mouth. It dangles out.

"You're disgusting," I say. He shakes his head back and forth so the spaghetti flaps all around, flinging this way and that. "At least we don't have penises and scrota. That's what's really disgusting."

"Aimee!" Dad scolds.

102

"What? Like 'penis' is a bad word?"

"I was more worried about scrota," he says, and takes a sip of his wine. His eyes sparkle like he's not really mad.

"It's the plural of scrotum," I explain in a teacher voice.

"I know what it is," he says.

Benji's just looking at us, figuring things out. It takes him a minute to compute. Finally, he asks, "Is that the health class word for balls?"

We all crack up. My father almost snarfs wine out his nose, but he eventually manages to nod.

Benji starts chanting, "Scrota. Scrota. Scrota." We giggle for a good minute, but Benji's in fourth-grader overdrive and he can't stop it, he just keeps going. "Scrota. Scrota. Scrota."

My father has had it. "Benjamin. That's enough." Benji keeps chanting and Dad has to use his authority-figure voice. "Benjamin. I said no more."

He stops. He sulks. He stabs his spaghetti and twirls it around like a madman before saying, "Why not? It's not a bad word. It's not like the f-word or something."

"Any word is a bad word when chanted incessantly at the table," Dad says. He looks to me for help. I can't really give him any.

"It's a pretty weird word," I say.

Benji pushes his plate away, sad faced, feeling betrayed or something. "Can I be excused?"

My father and I look at each other like one of us should be the parental figure but neither actually wants to be. I scrape my fork around the plate. My dad sips his wine. Footsteps whisper across the floor upstairs.

Benji's back straightens up and his voice perks out, "What's that?"

My father holds his glass in midair. My fork stops by some clumped spaghetti. Dad puts the glass down slowly while Benji stands up. "It sounds like footsteps."

He races out of the dining room, smashing past the bookcase. A tea candle drops off and spins across the floor. Dad barrels after him. "Benji!"

His chair bumps up the Oriental rug, but I don't fix it. I just get up, too, rushing up the stairs into the hall. Benji's hopping in place, looking around. Dread fills my throat.

"I heard footsteps!" he bubbles out. "There's nobody up here. You guys heard it too, right? You heard the footsteps? And it smells. It smells like vanilla!"

I cross my arms over my chest and turn the hall light on. I force my throat to swallow.

"Did you hear it, Dad?" Benji keeps going, eyes big. My dad nods. "I think we're haunted!" Benji paces back and forth down the hall. He stomps to make footstep sounds. "It sounds like someone walking, like a woman."

I whisper out all my hope. "Like Mom?"

"Your mother is not haunting our house." Dad says it like an edict, like a judgment. "Aimee, why do you fill his head with this nonsense? What's wrong with you?"

I gasp, can't even think of what to say because I'm so shocked that my dad is talking this way to me. He never acts so mean.

Benji's eyes go big. "Then what was the noise?"

Dad waves his hand in the air. His eyes look to the left like he'll find the answer there. "The house settling."

Benji rolls his eyes. "Yeah. Right. Gramps thinks Mom is haunting us, too. Did you know that?"

He stomps off to his room and slams the door.

"Benjamin Avery! We do not slam doors in this house!" Dad yells after him, but his voice is defeated. He turns and goes back downstairs to the kitchen. I trail after him and we return to our places at the table.

"Dad—" I think about those footsteps, Courtney, Alan, and my dreams, and change direction. "Do you know anything about the man in the river?"

He stands up, giraffe-leg strides across the wide wood floor planks to the kitchen counter, and grabs a bottle of Glenfiddich. Scotch. He's switched to scotch, which means he's stressed. "What?"

I push my piece of garlic bread around my plate in a great big circle. "Mom saw him before she died."

"This is not a discussion that I'm going to have with you, Aimee."

"Why not?"

He pours his scotch into one of his special glasses that rounds out like a pregnant woman and has a pattern etched into the glass. His hands are steady, like mine. He could be a surgeon slicing into people with hands like that. He could paint.

"Because."

"Because why?"

He swirls his glass. "Because I can't." He takes a sip. His Adam's apple moves down and up with the swallow and release. Something inside me burns hot and hard, the way I know scotch burns hot and hard when you swallow it. Some sort of vital organ falls into itself, lost, lost, fire, burning into itself.

"Please, Dad . . ."

His voice comes out flat and dull. "Your mother lost a baby. She was very early on in her pregnancy and it . . . well, it pushed her over the edge, Aimee. She became obsessed with protecting you and Benji from some delusion she had. She'd stay up all night and say she heard footsteps, like you, only they were heavy, and there were scratching mice noises. She said she smelled dead things, not vanilla."

"I don't say that," I blurt out.

"No. But you are hearing footsteps."

"So is everyone!"

"The house was settling." He rubs his hands across his closed eyes. "She twisted things so they were frightening. She was crying out for attention just like you."

"Dad! It wasn't even me. It was Benji!" I push my chair away from the table. This day could not get worse. Courtney is sick. Blake and I broke up. According to my dreams, someone is in danger and I have no idea how to help. I had an awkward ride with Alan, and now this? This? He's comparing me to my mother. My voice is wood-plank hard because I am *not* crazy and I am *not* the only one who heard footsteps and it's unfair.

"Fine, then. You clean up. I made dinner." My feet take me away from the table.

"Aimee . . ."

"Dad?" The word comes out before I can stop it.

He swirls the amber liquid in his glass again. He is so tall and strong looking. Why is he acting so weak? "Don't make Benji think your mother is here."

"It was Gramps."

106

"I will talk to him, too."

"We aren't going to be Mom, Dad. We aren't her. You aren't going to lose us, too."

"Don't go there, Aimee."

My hands turn into fists but I nod. I will let him believe what he wants to believe, what he needs to believe. Even though my heart is heavy fire burning, I cross those wood planks of our kitchen floor and lift myself up on my toes. I kiss his cheek. I will pretend I do not need a dad to save me. I will pretend to be normal. He is weak. He can't help it. He is more like Blake than Alan. I think the whole world is more like Blake than Alan.

"I love you, you know," I whisper, because I do. I do love him, no matter what.

"You, too," he says, and that's when I notice the knife on the stove.

It's the big serrated-edge knife I used to slice the garlic bread. I point my finger at it, but my hand is not like my hand. It shakes.

He turns to see what's got my attention. His free hand wraps around my waist. He pulls me close. His words are more a curse than a prayer. "Holy God."

The knife, the foot-long bread knife, is standing up on its tip, perfectly balanced and slowly spinning around.

ALAN

I slow the truck to a crawl as I approach Aunt Lisa's house—home. Aimee caught it during the car ride, called me on it, so now I'm calling it home. Aunt Lisa's Chevy Tahoe is in the driveway. Lots of lights are on. I stare hard at Courtney's window, wondering if I'll see the shape of a man behind her pink curtains. Her light is on, but I can't see any shadow-men.

Pulling into the driveway behind the Tahoe, I turn off my truck. I can't help but look up at Courtney's window again. There is a shape. A dark form stands there, looking down at me. But the curtain is parted a little and I can see that the shape is female. Aunt Lisa. The front door opens and there's Mom, waiting for me, so I get out and go up to her.

"Alan, are you okay?" she asks, coming out on the porch.

"Yeah, I'm fine. How's Courtney? Is she okay?"

"She will be. A few stitches and a mild concussion. What happened?"

I study Mom for a minute, wondering why she's asking me about it. "What did she say happened?"

"She doesn't remember," Mom says. "Someone at the school told Lisa you carried her to the nurse."

"Yeah, I did." I pause and look around, stalling, wondering what to say, and finally just tell her what happened.

When I'm done, she steps forward and hugs me. "No more skipping classes, Alan Whitedeer Parson. Okay?" I nod. Mom sighs. "She's upstairs. We have to keep her awake until midnight, the doctor said."

"Let's go see her."

Courtney and Aunt Lisa are sitting on the bed. "Hi, Alan," Courtney says.

"Hey. You okay?" I ask.

"I have a headache. Thanks for carrying me to the nurse." She smiles at me. I guess she's done being mad about me barging into her room the other day.

"No problem," I tell her. "Aimee's pretty worried about you."

"I should call her," Courtney says.

"Later," Aunt Lisa tells her. "You can call her later."

"Hey, listen, the truck cost quite a bit less than I expected," I say. "I have money left over. How about if I take us all out for supper? No lobster, though. That's just gross."

Aunt Lisa puts up a mild protest, but I wave it away. Finally she turns to Courtney and asks, "Are you up for it?"

"Sure," Courtney answers. "I want onion rings."

I send Aunt Lisa and Mom downstairs, promising we'll be right after them. I turn back to Courtney. "You really okay?" I ask.

"Yes," she says. I study her face. There's no sarcasm. No meanness. She looks like a normal girl. Well, a normal girl with a stitched-up gash on her forehead and some bad acne, but at least the sores aren't raw and leaking like they were earlier.

Carl's Cone Corner is kind of an old-fashioned place. Like something you see in movies from the 1950s. They have a big jukebox in the dining room and the waitresses—two of whom I recognize from school—bring the food on roller skates and wear pink uniforms with short skirts. The food is really good, and no dead lobster eyes stare up at me while I eat.

Conversation about the framed pictures of celebrities on the wall dies down after a bit and there's a long pause. Courtney is sitting across from me, next to her mom.

"Do you go to church?" I blurt out. Nice. I meant to be subtle about it. I'm not real good at subtle.

Courtney actually seems to shrink away from the question. It's her mom who answers. "No, we haven't been in . . . I don't know. A long time. Why?"

"Alan?" Mom warns beside me. She holds a french fry just outside her mouth and the two syllables of my name start low and end higher, threatening.

"I was just asking," I say. "Do most people go to church up here?"

"Quite a few do." Aunt Lisa looks suspiciously at Mom. "Do you guys go?"

"No," Mom says, nudging me with her elbow so I'll be quiet. Aunt Lisa sees it.

"If Alan wants to go to church, we can find him one. What kind of church are you interested in?" she asks me.

"He's not," Mom says. "Not like you think. Alan follows the Indian gods." She puts air quotes around "Indian gods."

Courtney sits quietly, staring at her food.

"One god," I correct her. "Manifested in several forms. But that's not why I'm asking."

"Why are you asking?" Aunt Lisa asks. She's stirring her drink with her straw, uncomfortable. I know I have to kill this subject.

"I was just wondering."

"No, you have a reason." Aunt Lisa won't let it go. She is like her sister in a lot of ways, I guess.

"I was just thinking of the noises we've been hearing. You know, the scratching?" I poke a fry into my mouth like what I said is no big deal.

"The mice?" she asks.

"Yeah. Sort of. I mean, what if it isn't mice?"

"What do you think it is?" Her fingers are still pinching the top of her straw, but now she's not stirring. She's looking me in the face.

Mom wipes ketchup from her lips and slaps her napkin onto the table near my hand.

"I'm not sure," I say. And I'm not.

We get home around eight. There are no shapes silhouetted against the light of Courtney's bedroom. I almost start to wonder if I imagined it before. Aunt Lisa kills the engine and I start to open my back door.

"Just a minute," Mom says. I stop, my hand on the door handle, looking at her while she looks at Aunt Lisa. "We might as well tell them now."

Aunt Lisa twists around to look at me and Courtney in the backseat. "The mill is adding a shift," she says. "They asked for volunteers to work half the new shift until they hire new people. We agreed to do it."

"It'll be a lot of overtime," Mom adds. "Extra money."

"Okay," I say.

"We won't be home until nine tomorrow night and for a while," Aunt Lisa says.

"You won't be home?" Courtney squeaks.

Aunt Lisa runs her hands through her hair and her fingers get stuck in a tangle. She pulls at it distractedly. "Maybe I shouldn't do this. Not now."

She looks to Mom, who looks back at me. I know what she wants. We've never had much money. It took all Mom's savings to move us up here.

"It'll be okay," I say. "Me and Court can handle it. I've got the truck in case we need to go anywhere. We'll be fine."

"Court, you think so?" Aunt Lisa asks.

Courtney shrugs. It's a motion so small it would be easy to miss it. "I guess," she says. "I know we need the money."

"You sure?"

"Yeah," she says, but her voice lacks conviction.

"I'll take care of her," I promise, and pat her knee. Aimee would say that's condescending. I smile because I've already learned that about her. But at the moment, it seems appropriate, and Courtney doesn't object. Nothing else is said, and after a minute we all get out of the Tahoe and go to the porch, where Aunt Lisa unlocks the door.

The smell of decay rolls out at us like a fist when the front door swings open. We all back away gagging, except Courtney, who stands completely motionless in the doorway. I cover my mouth with one hand and throw the other arm around her shoulders and pull her away.

"What is that?" Aunt Lisa asks between coughs.

"Maybe your mice died." It's mean of me to say it, at least to say it as sarcastically as I do, but it just pops out that way.

Aunt Lisa nods with her whole upper body. "That's probably it. I put out some traps and poison this morning. I bet we got one."

"A dozen, based on the smell," Mom corrects.

I bet we never find a single dead mouse.

"I'll start opening windows." Aunt Lisa keeps her mouth covered and runs inside like a kid running toward the end of the high diving board. Mom goes after her.

"I don't want to go back in there," Courtney whispers. "He's there."

"Who is it, Court? Tell me."

She turns her pale face up to me and I see a deep sadness in her eyes, like she's just completely hollow behind her eyes.

"Not Daddy," she says.

I shake my head. "No," I agree. "Who is it? Do you know?"

"Not Daddy."

113

I hug her shoulders against me. "No, it's not your dad. But we'll be okay," I promise. "I've got some stuff in my room that'll help."

The house gets pretty cold with all the windows open. The smell goes away really fast, though. Too fast. It isn't natural. Aunt Lisa checks traps and cabinets where she left poison, but doesn't find any dead mice.

"They must have eaten the poison and died in the walls or something," she says. Mom agrees with her. I keep quiet, but stay close to Courtney.

"The smell's gone," Aunt Lisa observes. We start closing windows.

"Come on, Court, let's go upstairs and close those windows." I motion her toward the stairs. She follows meekly as I go room to room, closing windows. We do my room last. "Stay in here for a while, okay?"

She nods and sits on the bed. I go to a stack of cardboard boxes and start rummaging through them. One of the first things I find is an old University of Oklahoma cap I've had for years. The crimson has faded to near pink and the white OU stitching is frayed. And it stinks of old sweat.

"Here ya go," I say, stepping over and dropping it onto Courtney's head. "A little souvenir from my home state." I go back to my boxes, but from the corner of my eyes I see her take the cap off, look it over, sniff it and wrinkle her nose, but then she puts it back on her head, pushing her hair behind her ears once the cap is in place.

In the third box down I find my old nylon-and-leather

backpack from junior high. I take it out and open the main pouch. It smells like a garden despite the fact I have everything wrapped in plastic bags. I take out a few and toss them on the bed beside Courtney.

"Is that pot?" she asks.

"No. I wouldn't bring that into your house." I look at the bag she's studying. It holds a thick braid of dried grass looped around itself a couple of times. "It's sweetgrass. You burn it, but don't smoke it."

"An Indian thing?"

"Yeah."

The scratching begins beneath us. I swear I can feel my skin rippling over my skeleton when it starts. Courtney sits up very straight, a terrified look on her face. I can't help but feel sorry for her.

"It'll be okay," I say. "Give me just a minute here."

In the bottom of the backpack I find Baggies of incense cones and a little brass burner. I find the bag I labeled SAGE in big black letters and put a cone in the burner, then put the burner on my dresser. There are four or five plastic lighters in a side pocket of the backpack. I take one out and light the sage cone. The smoke drifts lazily from the brass. The smell is kind of like turkey dressing and pot.

"That smells . . . good," Courtney says. She hasn't really relaxed.

I nod and put all the unused stuff back into the backpack, keeping the sage cones on top. "It's sage," I tell her. "It's used to . . . to purify places."

The scratching gets louder, faster under the floorboards.

"Courtney? Alan? Are you two okay?" Aunt Lisa calls from downstairs.

"We're fine," I yell back. "We're in my room."

"Stomp on the floor and see if those damn mice will stop."

I stomp a few times. The scratching does not stop.

"I'll have to call an exterminator," I hear Aunt Lisa say. "That'll take care of a lot of that overtime."

"Courtney," I say, going to her and taking her by the shoulders, making her look me in the face. "Courtney, listen to me. If something is bothering you, harassing you, something evil, like a spirit, would you want it to go away?"

The scratching gets worse, like it's going to burst through the floorboards and come after us. Courtney trembles in my grip. Her eyes try to stray away from me, toward the floor. I shake her a little and she looks back at me, but I'm not sure she's seeing me.

"Do you want it to go away?" I ask.

She nods.

"Say it," I tell her. "Tell it to go away. Say it and mean it."

"G-g-go . . . away," she whispers.

"Louder!"

"Go away!" she screams. "GO AWAY GO AWAY GO AWAY GO AWAY!"

"Keep saying it," I tell her, hoping it's the right thing to do. I carefully lift the brass burner off the dresser and walk around the room with it, fanning the smoke and aroma around the room.

"Go away go away go away go away. Leave me alone," Courtney says, and now she's almost sobbing.

Beneath us, the scratching stops suddenly. It's replaced by a long, drawn-out groaning sound, like someone bending wood and holding it just before the breaking point. I can hear Mom and Aunt Lisa pounding up the stairs. They'll be here in a second. Mom will freak out on me.

"Onawa, help me," I whisper. "Great Spirit, help me."

The groaning stops as if cut off at the head.

"Go away go away go away . . . ," Courtney is still chanting.

I get to her just as Mom and Aunt Lisa appear in the doorway. I put my hand on Courtney's shoulder, and she stops. She looks up at me, her eyes still wide, but less scared than they were a minute ago.

"What was that?" Aunt Lisa demands. "Was Courtney screaming?"

"What's that smell?" Mom asks.

"The noise?" I ask, turning to face the women. "I don't know. The smell is incense. I thought it'd help get rid of the other smell. Is that okay?" I ask Aunt Lisa. Her face is all scrunched up with worry.

"It wasn't you?" She looks at the little brass pot smoking in my hand. "That's just incense?"

"Yeah. Sage," I say.

"Just be careful with the matches." Her voice is distant, troubled. She doesn't believe that I don't know what was making the noise. Would she believe me if I tried to explain it? I don't know, but I'm not ready to tell everything and have it rejected yet.

"We're okay," I say. "If you two have to work late, maybe you should go on to bed. I'll keep Court up until midnight. That's when she can go to sleep, right?"

117

Aunt Lisa nods, then says, "Yes. Midnight. You sure?"

"Yeah. Go on. Whatever the noise was has stopped. No more mice, either."

"You're a good boy, Alan," Aunt Lisa says, and now her voice is a little more relaxed. "Your mama raised you right."

"I guess," I say, and offer a weak grin. "I think me and Court are going to hang out in here for a while. Maybe unpack some of my stuff."

Mom says, "Don't stay up past midnight. You both have school tomorrow."

"We won't," I say. They leave, and I turn back to Courtney. "You okay?"

"No."

"You will be."

She shudders. "I don't think so. He'll come back."

Courtney makes me start another incense cone before she falls asleep. When she does, she's sitting propped up against the headboard of my bed, my stained and stinky University of Oklahoma cap still on her head. She looks more peaceful than I've seen her since we arrived in Maine.

"What have you done, cousin?" I whisper as I pull her into a more reclined position and put a blanket over her. "Did you invite this thing?" I look at the sudden acne on her face. Thanks to the magical informational powers of Google and Wikipedia, I now know that there are four stages to possession. The first is invitation. Obviously, something has been invited. At least, it's obvious to everyone who isn't over thirty and working in a paper mill.

The second stage is infestation and usually involves poltergeist activity. I glance at my dresser, where the broken picture frame lies. Third is obsession, and there's usually some kind of bodily change at that stage. Like sores. The last stage . . . full possession.

That's the Christian version. The Navajo call the whole thing Ghost Sickness.

Call it whatever you want, I think Courtney has it.

· 11 ·
AIMEE

I push away from my dad, cross to the stove in two strides, and grab the knife by the handle. Storming to the dishwasher, I shove the knife into the utensil rack, then slam the door shut.

We don't speak. Dad motions for me to sit down, but I don't because I'm way too freaked out. His face looks horrified. "Aimee!"

For a second I can't breathe. I'm too shocked. "What?"

"How did you do that?"

"You think *I* made the knife twirl?" The dishwasher stays shut. I check; even in my anger, I check.

His face blanks out. "That's the only logical explanation."

"Dad!" Every inch of my skin hardens up with hurt. He thinks I did that? He thinks I'm so crazy, such a liar, that I'd make a knife spin? I somehow manage not to swear at him, not to give him the finger, and instead stomp upstairs to my room.

"Honey, I'm sorry, but if it wasn't you—it—it—I can't—"

He's calling after me, but I don't go back. I can only be the peacemaker so much, you know?

Later, I get a text on my phone. It's from Blake: I AM SO SORRY. PLEASE DON'T THROW US AWAY.

I don't know how to respond to that, so I spend most of the night painting. I know this isn't normal. Paint thinner wafts through the entire house with its clean, sharp smell, but nobody wakes up. Nobody comes to my room to see if I'm okay. I would like to pretend this doesn't bother me, but it does. I would look out the window at the river, but I'm afraid of what I might see. That's why I don't sleep. I'm afraid of what I'll dream. But at 3:10, I give in. I close my eyes and lean back against my bed, sitting up, like that will keep the dreams away.

It doesn't.

I am below water. There's a canoe on the surface, and someone swimming. The water freezes against my skin. A seal floats by, sad eyes warning me, as I try to break toward the surface, and then . . . hands clutch my legs, pulling me down, down. My lungs are about to burst. My limbs are slow moving, stretching, twisting. Then I see who it is holding me: a man with eyes of water and a mouth that smiles, smiles, smiles . . .

You are mine . . .

I must be so wiped out from the nightmare that I actually sleep like I'm dead the rest of the night. No dreams. No fears. In the morning I go down to breakfast. I do not go kayaking. I can't trust the river, not today.

We all sit at the table, all four of us. If we put a dress on

Gramps we'd almost look like a perfect family. We've all got cereal and orange juice. It's strange.

"Dad doesn't think the house is haunted," Benji announces.

We all look at him. We all look at Gramps, whose spoon dangles from his fingers. "Your father doesn't believe in ghosts." He ducks the spoon into the milk.

Benji leans up in his seat, arching forward, eyebrows down and ready for a fight. "How can he not believe it? There were footsteps upstairs and *nobody was there!*"

"I didn't witness it," Dad says with his mouth full. He never talks with his mouth full.

Nobody says anything. Last night he said he can't believe in these things. I think it would hurt him too much, make him feel like he couldn't protect us like he couldn't protect Mom, and that makes me hurt for him so I try to break the silence. "Well, how's the Cheeto auction going?"

"We're at $850," Gramps announces. His eyes are proud. Benji whoops and Dad chokes on his orange juice.

"You're kidding," I say. "$850?"

Gramps raises his right hand. "Scout's honor."

"When were you going to tell me?" Benji demands. He pours extra sugar on his cereal. Dad reaches out and takes the sugar away.

"When you stopped being so cranky," Gramps says. He slurps more cereal, his eyes twinkling. He loves the running I'm-cranky-no-you're-cranky joke he and Benji have going.

Benji's mouth drops open and he points at his chest. "Me? I'm not the cranky one!"

"You two and your crankies," Dad says, and somehow the way he says it makes the conversation stop.

I try to think of something to say. I can't. I glance at my dad and wonder if he's thinking about the spinning knife, too.

"No river today, Aimee?" Gramps asks. "Kayaking's good for you. Good exercise, calms the mind."

"Nah." I shudder. "Not today."

"You need to sleep better. You're going to wear yourself out," he announces. "I found her wandering around last night. Had to tuck her into bed."

Dad's hand leaves his juice glass and clutches his coffee mug instead. "Really?"

My head feels like it's twisting around. "I don't remember that."

"Of course you don't," Gramps says into the awkwardness. "You were asleep."

Great. More ammunition for my father's "Aimee is crazy" theory. Dad changes the topic again. "The ER has been incredibly busy lately. The number of assaults is way up . . ."

I stop paying attention when he starts talking about the capital campaign for a new emergency room. Benji mouths, "Blah, blah, blah . . . ," which makes me giggle.

Dad's still there when Alan's truck pulls in.

"That him? Courtney's cousin?" he asks, shrugging on his suit coat and staring out the window.

"Yeah." I tug at his elbow. "Come away from the window, Dad."

"That's not much of a truck," he complains.

"It's fine."

"He's getting out. Blake never gets out."

"He's getting out?" I run to the window and look. He is.

123

He's actually getting out of the truck and striding toward the door. Oh, wow—he's so tall and he's almost smiling. My heart does some weird fluttery thing but I do not become completely ridiculous and put my hand over it or anything. "Guys don't get out of the car when they pick you up for school."

"They do if they want to get all kissy-faced," Benji pipes up. He's peeking out the window, too. "Man, he's huge. You'd have to stand on a chair to make out with him."

"Benji!"

"She's turning red," Benji gloats. "Girls only turn red when they like a boy, right? It's like all the hotness goes right to their cheeks. Gramps told me that."

My dad turns and looks at me. His eyes widen. "He's got a lot of hair there."

"It's nice."

"He'll never get a job with hair like that."

"Dad, shut up. Stop being such a suit." I grab my bag and rush to the door. I yank it open before Alan can ring the bell. His arm's upraised and his finger is ready to push. Everything inside of me sort of sighs out just seeing him. I touch the bulge the medicine bag makes on his chest. I can't help myself.

"Hi," I manage, blushing harder. I can't believe I just touched him like that.

He smiles. "Hi."

Benji materializes behind me. "Dad. They've said 'hi.' They've taken the first step, but like most teenagers, they're failing to make any other words. They are dumbstruck by love. Dumbstruck! Dumbstruck!"

I whirl around and my backpack slams into the door frame. "Benji! Stop! You sound like Gramps!"

He grins devilishly.

I turn back to Alan, trying to apologize. "That's my little brother."

"I figured that by the whole height thing and the teasing and the fact that you're both in the same house in the morning. It was either that or you just rent kids to seem more wholesome. I go for wholesome."

"Funny. BYE!" I yell and shut the door behind me. We walk down the porch together. My hip bumps into his leg.

He opens the door of the truck for me.

"How's Courtney?" I ask before he closes the door.

"Better . . ." He looks back at my house. "She's better right now, at least. I think. Her mom is taking her to school. She insisted." We get in the truck. It already smells like him, deodorant and earth and good. "I'm glad you're okay."

"You thought I wasn't okay?"

"I worried about you all night," he admits, and puts the truck in reverse so he can get us out of the driveway. The truck kind of moans. "I couldn't get you on your cell."

"My battery died. I forgot to charge it. Sorry."

For a second neither of us says anything. I try to ignore the heebie-jeebie feeling creeping up on me. On the ride in he tells me what he's learned from looking up possession last night. I tell him about my knife experience and how my dad thinks I'm somehow behind all the stuff that's happening in our house.

"But you think it's your mother?" he asks as he parks the truck.

We sit there for a moment. I must look scared or like I need comfort or something because he grabs my hand and says, "It's okay, Red."

Swallowing hard, I nod. "I don't want to be crazy."

"You aren't." He smiles, and I look away from his mouth to where our fingers touch as he says, "If you are, then so am I."

"That's not very convincing," I try to tease.

He laughs and says, "We should get going."

Just like that he lets go of my hand and we hop out of the truck. He doesn't lock his truck like Blake always locks his car. Not that I'm comparing them. Oh my gosh, we held hands. It was only for a second. Maybe Oklahoma people always hold hands. It doesn't mean anything. It can't mean anything. Blake would kill him if it meant anything.

During my free period I head to the library instead of the art room. I flip open my laptop and connect. The sweet librarian lady, Mrs. Hessler, smiles at me. She leans over the table, but she's careful not to look at my screen. She tries so hard to give us privacy.

"Let me know if you need any help, Aimee," she says. Her frog earrings dangle and sway against the bottom curls of her dark brown cropped haircut.

"Thanks," I say, and smile.

"You have such a beautiful smile." She straightens up. "Just like your mom."

She nods as if satisfied with her statement and turns away. I google "hex counter" and get all this crap about decimal counters.

"Great," I mutter. Meanwhile, I check out the Cheeto bids on eBay. The picture Gramps took makes it really look like

Marilyn Monroe. It's kind of freaky. I click back to the search engine and type: "protect from evil."

Bingo. The first site is some sort of healing medieval chapel based in the United Kingdom. It says that people vulnerable to psychic attacks are already nasty and already busy manipulating other people. But it also says there's a whole other category of people who are vulnerable, and those are people who have healer personalities. They are the kind of people who are ultra caring and compassionate and kind of absorb all the emotions of the people around them.

"We have workshops!" it says. "Sign up now."

"England is a little far," I mutter, and scroll down the page to where there's a special section about techniques to prevent psychic attacks. One of them is creating a protective field of energy, like a white light.

"*Ha!*" It's like what I do when I try to heal people.

Two freshman kids look up from their computer with amused expressions.

Mrs. Hessler gently calls over, "You okay, Aimee?"

"Yep. Great, thanks." I lower my voice to the appropriate library volume level. "Sorry I was loud."

Mrs. Hessler's smile is heart-singing. "It's good to be happy in the library."

I give her a cheese-ball thumbs-up, then read through the page really quickly, before googling "protective herbs." I am going to do everything I can to protect the people I love. That's that, River Man. Aimee Avery is on your ass. People think I'm all peace and love all the time, and I am, but part of that is wanting to keep people safe—safe from arguing, from meanness, from evil river men . . . The problem is that except for occasionally healing Benji's baby cuts and scrapes, I haven't actually practiced healing people. It always felt too much like my mom, too much like crazy . . .

There's still time, so I look up "Alan Parson." There are 2,190,000 results, and most of them have to do with the Alan Parsons Project, which I guess is some ancient rock band. So I narrow the search to "Alan Parson Oklahoma football."

There is article after article. The first thing I pull up is a newspaper account from *The Oklahoman* newspaper's online section. The headline reads: FOOTBALL PRODIGY PARSON LIFTS TEAM TO WIN. There are even pictures of him running on the field, ball clutched to his chest, his thigh muscles straining against his uniform.

He clutched me to his chest.

I close my laptop. I am being ridiculous. Okay. Big breaths.

I almost groan out loud. This is happening way too fast and everything is way too heated.

"Aimee? You okay?" Mrs. Hessler asks again.

I nod.

"I heard Courtney passed out yesterday. How is she doing?"

"I don't know," I answer honestly. "She's supposed to be in school today. I haven't seen her, though, but even before today she wasn't always acting . . ."

"Like herself?"

"Yeah." I pack up my stuff. "Exactly."

The bell rings. The freshmen leap out of their chairs, gathering up their stuff. I do the same.

Mrs. Hessler taps me on the shoulder right before I get to

the door. "Aimee?" I stop and turn around, wondering if I've broken some library rule. "When Courtney passed out, did she do anything funny?"

"Her eyes rolled into her head." I shiver. I hate remembering it.

"Oh . . . oh . . ." Mrs. Hessler looks strangely uncomfortable. "Did she have . . . Was there a lot of acne suddenly?"

I pull my computer tightly to my chest. "Yeah. There was. Why?"

She fiddles with her fingers nervously. "No reason. I was just wondering. That's all. Do you need a slip? Are you going to be late?"

"No." I can't quite figure it all out. "No. I'll be fine. Thanks, Mrs. Hessler."

"Wait a minute, Aimee." She goes to the counter and writes out a slip anyway, then she pulls out a pink file folder and walks back to me. "Take this. Read it. Okay?" I hesitate, but she pushes it into my hands and says, "Please. It's information I've collected. It's . . . well, you read it and make your own conclusions."

I take the folder, totally confused. "Thanks."

She raises her hand and waves as I hustle away. I turn back and look. She's still standing at the door, watching, a very sad expression on her face.

I open the folder in math because I can't wait. The first page is tiny articles from some old-fashioned newspaper. There aren't even any bylines on them. Mrs. Hessler has circled one with a red felt pen. It's from 1876.

DEATH IN RIVER—Last evening's entertainment in East Goffs Town, by the "Goffs Harbor" club, was attended by many, and the program was carried out favorably. The essay by Mrs. Joshua Petengale was received with great favor and exemplified much labor in composition.

However, post the performance, Mr. Emulus Black, though suffering from a cold and fever, insisted that he could indeed make it back to his home on the Union River without assistance. This assertion seems to have been mistaken. Early this morning portions of Mr. Black's body were found upon the river banks by Mrs. William Goodale. The means of his demise are not currently apparent and may not be suitable for the finer sex's reading.

Shuddering, I look up. Mr. Block is droning on. The next piece is also a microfiche, but seems to be an editorial.

TOWN CURSED?—With the recent death of Mr. Emulus Black, the old heathen rumor of East Goffs Town's curse has resurfaced. For those unfamiliar, it is said our town's esteemed founders angered Indian woodland spirits by building this fair community without making sacrifices to trees and river. It is the opinion of this newspaper that belief in such legends is morally dangerous and criminal.

I want to go get Alan. Instead, I flip to the next page. It's another microfiche article circled in red.

> MYSTERIOUSLY INJURED—Doctor M. S. Hutton of 24 Maple Avenue came staggering into the First Congregational Church Sunday morning in an overcome condition, about a quarter of an hour into the service. He was unable to converse much, but it is said that he kept uttering the phrase, "Man in the river." After a cursory examination, it became apparent that the respected citizen had been sorely injured with blows to the head and bore thick scratches around his wrists and ankles. Preparations to carry him to the closest doctor, his colleague, one Dr. Llewellyn Allen in Blue Hill, were unsuccessful because he rapidly died from his injuries or from the shock which had befallen him. A group of men from the church attempted to spot any men injured in the river but could not. No one else from the town is missing. What happened to the good doctor is as yet a mystery as far as we can ascertain at this time.

There are three more articles from the same week talking about two women going missing. They were last seen by the river. One woman's body was found dismembered on the shore. There is a bit of a panic in the town. People are not allowed to go to the river by themselves. The newspaper runs a picture of the woman: she is small-faced and large-eyed and beautiful.

She reminds me of my mother.

The next page is dated 1938. In the headlines, there are more mysterious deaths in the river. I flip through some more. It's the same stories every couple of decades. People die. They are found dismembered.

I put my hand on my forehead, like that's going to keep my thoughts under control. I turn a page. It's a newspaper story about my mother. It doesn't say her name.

> A Goffstown woman died in the Union River
> Sunday morning. Coast Guard units, local police
> and the harbor master responded to the scene.
> Foul play is not suspected.

I put my head on my desk.

I swallow hard. I will not cry. The desk is cold against my forehead. It smells like lemon cleaner, and if I close my eyes it is dark—dark and nothing, which is what I want to be right now. Nothing.

"Miss Avery?" It's Mr. Block, with his comb-over hair and big red cheeks. "Miss Avery? Are you with us?"

People laugh.

I lift up my head, blinking against the light. "Not really."

People laugh more, like I'm making a brilliant joke, but I'm not.

Mr. Block lets himself smile for a second, then hitches up his green cords and scratches at his bald spot. He leans back so his butt is resting on the edge of the desk and knocks off a pencil. Emily scoops it up off the floor and gives it back to him.

"Thank you, Miss Portman," he says, then turns his attention to me. "Miss Avery, how about you tell us about the fundamental theorem of calculus."

Ugh.

It is all I can do not to bash my head back down against the desk. It's so heavy. My voice is heavy. But I push myself out of the bleak and say, "It's that integration and differentiation are contrary operations."

"Contrary?"

I blink. "Inverse. I meant inverse."

He shakes his head. "I like contrary. That's good. That's really good."

He smiles again, and I know he's throwing out a lifeline to me, but it's like I just can't reach out and take it. He lifts himself away from his desk as though movement is the easiest thing in the world and scoots over to the blackboard to write it out:

$$F_{ba} F(x)dx = F(b) - F(a)$$

He turns and smiles at us. "There it is folks, the secret of the universe."

If only it were that easy.

Right before she died, my mother's feet were always moving. She'd sit down, and her feet would tap, tap, tap on the floor like they were revolting against the stillness of sitting, like they were meant to move and move and move.

One time we were having lunch, even though it was only

133

about 9:30 in the morning. Benji was in this car-seat thing that could be taken in and out of the car and she put it on top of the table, next to a stack of library books we'd just gotten that morning. He slept there, rocking gently, his toy teddy blankie draped over him. I was having lunch—Annie's macaroni and cheese, the all-natural kind, and some apple juice. My mom sat down. She stood up. She sat down. Her foot went *tap-tap-tap* against the floor.

"It's hard to sit still," she said. "Aimee, it's just so hard sometimes for Mommy to sit still. There's time to sit still when you're dead." She gave this funny laugh, short and hard. Her laugh stuck in my throat, made it hard to swallow my Annie's macaroni and cheese. "Or maybe I should say there's time to lie still when you're dead, time to lie still when you're dead, I mean. Oh, what do I mean? I have no clue. No idea. No clue. People's jaws are so interesting, aren't they, Aimee? You could almost imagine their skeletons when you look at their jaws."

I looked at her jaw; it was pointed, thin. The skin stretched over it. She had boo-boos on it, small sores.

"You're going to be quite the artist and you should draw people's jaws first, I think, because that's how you know the structure of the face. Oh, that sounds like I'm talking about a house, doesn't it? The structure of a face. The structure of a house. The structure of a heart." She stood up. She stared at me. Her face was sleek and nothing. "I'm going to go outside and cut down some trees. I do not like those trees leaning near the house. It's not safe. My family has to be safe. That's my responsibility."

She rushed toward the door. It was March. She didn't have a coat on. She didn't have boots on. Snow covered everything.

"When I'm gone, you watch after Benji," she said. "You keep him safe."

And then she was gone for good.

I dreamed the night before that happened. I dreamed about her at the river, walking to the edge with a big machine in her hand. I dreamed that there was a man standing in the river, his face a skeleton. He was ready for her. I think he might be ready for us, too.

· 12 ·
ALAN

I have first lunch, and when I get to the cafeteria Aimee is already there with Hayley, waiting for me at the end of the lunch line so we can go through together. Her hair stands out like a fire in a world of fog. I want to walk up to her and bury a hand in her hair, ruffle it up a little before running my hand down her back.

I look at the line, then glance around the cafeteria. Looks like they're pushing chicken fingers and mac and cheese today.

Her little oval of a face becomes almost as red as her hair. She shakes her head as Hayley whispers something to her. I try to think of something to say and brilliantly come up with, "How's the Cheeto?"

"Bidding was up to $850 this morning."

I stop moving forward with the line. "Are you kidding me? For a Cheeto?"

"A Cheeto with boobs."

"I wonder if I can find John Wayne in one of these chicken fingers," I muse. I survey the crowd. Blake's at his regular table, glaring at us. Great. I wonder if just talking to Aimee is a punishable offense.

Aimee doesn't notice him. She laughs, then says, "I'll look for Buddha's face in my macaroni."

"We'll retire from high school and live off our freaky food fortune," I say.

Hayley smiles. "That would be brilliant."

Aimee starts to say something else, then stops, looking at something behind me. I turn around and see Courtney approaching the back of the line. She looks sick. Her face is swollen and covered in zits. A lot of them are leaking, and people are pointing and backing away from her. Her expression is weird. She looks angry, but amused. Her eyes are too bright, like she has a fever.

"Get away from me," she growls at the general population. Yes, growls. Courtney's head whips around and she singles out a tall boy in a Boston Red Sox jersey. The boy's face goes pale. Courtney looks around again and picks out a brunette girl in a Goffstown High School Student Council T-shirt. She staggers toward her and the girl backs away, panicked.

I push out of line and start back toward her. Aimee is right behind me. Courtney turns her head to look at us, and her lips, which I can now see are dry and cracked, split in a wicked grin.

I stop. This is not the girl who fell asleep in my OU cap last night.

Her eyes focus on Aimee.

"Court?" Aimee whispers. "You okay?"

Her mouth opens but no words come out.

"Come on, Courtney, let's go," I say, reaching out to her. "I'll take you home. You look like you don't feel good."

Next thing I know I'm flying over the blue railing that separates the lunch line from the rest of the cafeteria. I land on a table, sliding across it and into the laps of two people sitting there. Their food is smashed into my clothes. The cafeteria is deadly silent.

"Court?" Aimee asks. "Court, can you hear me?"

Then, just like yesterday, my cousin folds up like a rag doll and starts to fall. But Aimee is there, and this time she catches Courtney. She can't hold her up, but she slows her fall so that Courtney doesn't crash to the floor again. Everson and several other teachers are running to them while I struggle to get off the knees of the guy and girl at the table. Blake is laughing behind his hand as he strides up the aisle. I finally manage to stand up. Chicken strips and sticky macaroni fall off my right side and back.

"Sorry," I say, then hurry back to Aimee and Courtney. Blake is already there. He has his arm around Red's shoulders like she belongs to him.

"Don't pick her up!" Everson yells. "Get back! Everyone just get back. Go eat your lunch." He jerks a radio off his belt and gives orders. "We need an ambulance in the caf, right now. We have a girl down."

Blake is pulling Aimee away from Courtney and saying something to her, but I can't hear it. I can only stare at Courtney and remember how she was last night. I try to push my way through to her.

"She's my cousin," I insist. Everson and the others hold me back. Everson is solid, like a wall. What was he at Colorado? A linebacker? Defensive end? He doesn't move.

"Settle down, Alan," he says.

"Is she okay? Is she breathing?" I demand.

"She's breathing." He puts his hands on my chest to stop me. "Help is coming."

I have this urge to lash out, to try to knock the vice principal out of my way. It comes and goes quickly. You just don't hit teachers and principals. Especially not principals built like brick walls. "She's got a concussion," I explain.

"I know," he answers. "She needs a doctor. We've got the ambulance coming. She'll get help." He looks me over. "Go to the office and tell Ms. Murillo I sent you to get a clean shirt, then go see if you can clean the cheese off your jeans in the bathroom."

I look past him to Courtney lying on the floor, out cold, not moving, an empty husk of a person.

"She'll be okay," Everson promises.

"Come on, Alan, I'll go with you." Aimee is there, taking my hand in hers, pulling at me. Blake is standing in the background, staring. Everson looks at her and nods.

I follow Aimee to the office and she tells the secretary I'm there for a clean shirt. The secretary goes to a cabinet and pulls out a blue GHS shirt and hands to it me. I mumble a thank-you, then Aimee pulls me out of the office and toward the nearest restroom.

"Go change and clean up," she says. "I have something to show you after."

★   ★   ★

I come out of the restroom with my black Motorhead T-shirt wadded up in one hand. My hip is damp from scrubbing the sticky cheese off the denim. Aimee is still there, waiting on me. I wonder if she's made up with Blake. I wonder if she'd tell me if she has.

"They just took Court out on the stretcher," she says. "She was awake. I got to hold her hand and tell her we love her. She was acting groggy but not—you know . . ."

I have to look away. A lump jumps up in my throat and my eyes water just a little. I didn't even really know my cousin a week ago, but after last night we've become family. I nod, then turn back to Aimee and figure to hell with Blake. I grab her and crush her against me and kiss the top of her head. I didn't know *her* last week, either, and now she is my only anchor in a world that is getting more screwed up by the minute.

"We have to fight this thing," I say into Aimee's beautiful red hair that smells like sunshine and flowers and sanity.

"I know," she says, and her voice is muffled against the new blue fabric of my chest. I realize how tightly I'm holding her and ease off a little, but don't let go. There's still the threat of watery eyes and I'm not ready for her to see that.

"What can we do?" she asks.

"I don't know." But I think I do. The question is, can I do it? Am I strong enough? For the briefest second I wish my father were here to tell me, to witness, but I tackle the wish away.

Considering the circumstances, I figure Mom will understand. We go back to the office and I tell Ms. Murillo, "I'm going to the hospital with my cousin."

"Me, too," Aimee announces. "He's my ride today."

Ms. Murillo has a perky voice and a short, sassy haircut. She's obviously heard all the excuses kids can think up. "I can't let you leave unless someone checks you out."

"I'm sorry, ma'am, but I'm going," I answer. "I don't want to be rude, but really, I'm not asking. I just thought I should let someone know."

"Let me call your mom and see if it's okay with her," she suggests, reaching for the phone on her desk.

"I can't—"

"Alan, it's better this way," Aimee says. "I'm sure your mom will be okay with it, and it'll keep you out of trouble."

"What's the number?" Ms. Murillo asks.

I start writing my name under the names of other students who were checked out by parents. There's a line for the adult to sign. I leave it blank as she finishes calling my mom.

"Aimee, let me call your dad," Ms. Murillo says. A few minutes later we're in my truck and Aimee is telling me how to get to the hospital.

AIMEE

"This is it?" Alan says.

"Yeah." I rub a hand across my eyes, trying to see it the way he would, trying not to think about how nice Blake was in the cafeteria, how he comforted me when Court went crazy. It was like he snapped back into nice Blake again. I hate that. Life would be so much easier if people were like buildings—if they didn't ping-pong back and forth between nice and mean, angry and loving.

Maine Memorial Hospital is solid and steady. It's not a huge hospital by anybody's standards. It's brick, and kind of squat and sprawling because it's always a big ordeal to raise money in the capital campaigns to add stuff like a new maternity wing or an ER. It doesn't have any double-decker parking garages or fancy things like that.

"I know it's not big, but it's a good hospital, I swear. They'll take care of Courtney here. I mean, they'll do the best they can and everything, but—"

He interrupts. "It's not something a stethoscope and a blood test can fix."

"Right." I nod and point to a section of parking lot. "You can park there. That's Dr. Mason's Mini Cooper and that's Doris Bailey's sedan. Doris is my dad's administrative assistant. She's worked at the hospital for fifty years. She's sixty-eight. She's never had another job. She makes really good pie. I'm babbling. Oh . . . I'm sorry I'm babbling. I'm just so worried about Courtney."

He unhooks his seat belt after he parks and pulls me into him for another hug. I kind of wonder if Oklahoma people are big on hugs or if it's just him. *Does it mean something?* He says, "I know. Me, too."

It is our second hug ever. The good smell of him drifts into my nose, although it's mixed a little bit with cafeteria cheese.

His breath brushes my hair. My hair is happy. "I know."

I pull away and just say it. "I'm so worried about Court, but I'm scared of going in there. I'm scared of what might happen. I mean, I'm scared of her—not her, but . . . what's inside of her, you know?"

His hand reaches down to my cheek. "Me, too."

"Really?"

He nods just the slightest of nods.

I try to gather up my strength. "Blake still likes me."

His arms stiffen around me. "Do you like him?"

I let myself think about it for a second, just to make really sure, but then I say, "No."

We wait there for a second. A cop car pulls under the emergency room platform. Sgt. Farrar unfolds his giant body from the car and steps into the building. He looks busy and worried, stressed. Someone said the cops have been super busy lately. I can't remember who it was, though.

"Do you want to tell me what you're thinking about?" Alan asks.

I shake my head like a little girl but I tell him anyway. "I was always afraid of being a freak again." I tell him about the séance. His eyes tell me he understands. Believes. "I was always afraid of people thinking that I was crazy like my mom. But it's not me. It's Courtney. I mean . . . she's become what I was always afraid of becoming . . . And Blake? He's not that kind of crazy, but he's not nice right now. He's mean and he's threatened me and you and . . . We can't like each other, Alan. It's not . . ."

I don't have a word to put in there. It's not . . . Safe? Right? Time?

His eyes are so deep and brown and solid. They are nothing like the river. "You can't help who you like." He takes a deep breath. "You ready?"

They don't let us see her. We go talk to Doris, but she tells us they're running MRIs and CT scans on Courtney's head, checking for tumors; we aren't allowed in during all that. Courtney's mom doesn't want Alan to have to see it, or Courtney, right now. She thinks it's too disturbing. Alan shakes a little with worry, but it isn't until we're back in his truck that he completely loses it.

"I should be in there." He pounds his back into the seat. It shudders from the force. "I can help. They aren't going to find any freaking tumors."

"I know." I try patting his arm. It doesn't seem to work.

144

"I can't believe they're trying to protect *me*. I should be the one protecting them!"

I take a deep breath. "Alan, it's not like love and protection are one-way streets."

He does a double take. I raise my hand before he can object and soldier on.

"No. Seriously. Listen. You love them. You want to protect them. That's good. But you also have to respect the fact that they love you and want to protect you."

"But they can't—not from this."

His anger fills the air, hot and dangerous. He punches his steering wheel. It makes the whole truck shake. Two Goffstown police cars pull up and an ambulance follows them in. It must be an assault victim or something. Rob, this nurse with 1970s rocker hair, all big and curly, gives us a thumbs-up and yells, "What's happening?"

I wave back and do the whole polite smile thing.

Once he's gone Alan looks sheepishly at me. "Did I scare you?"

"A little."

His hand swallows mine up. Then he reaches for me and folds me into him. "I would never hurt you, Red."

"I know," I mumble, but I never thought that Blake would hurt me, or Court, and they both did. I say more clearly, "I would never hurt you either."

We pull apart a little bit and he studies my face. "I believe you."

"Good." I laugh and try to lighten the mood. "Why don't we go to my house? I'll show you the river."

He agrees, but I can tell it's hard for him to drive away from the hospital.

"She's with doctors. She'll be okay. They'll do their best to take care of her, and your aunt and your mom, too," I promise. "And we'll go back. As soon as your mom calls. C'mon. You know you hate it in there. It'll be good for you to be outside, for us to be outside. You'll have your cell. It'll be okay."

He shudders a little, like the decision is that hard, but then he pulls out of the parking lot and we go.

"This is amazing," he says as we climb up to the tree house. He touches the plywood where Benji and I have drawn things. He finds the knight with the long dark hair right away. He smiles. "Is that me?"

I nod, but I'm embarrassed. I turn away and step farther onto the little porch. I point toward the river. "Those are our kayaks down there. I used to kayak every morning, but now . . . you know . . . the river is kind of freaking me out." I stop.

He turns me back around. "Aimee . . ."

My hands seem no longer under my control, and they move up to his face. It's a bit of a reach. He sighs when I touch him. I sigh, too.

He takes one of my hands and kisses each knuckle. "You're nervous."

"I babble when I'm nervous," I say too fast and too jokey, but I have to be jokey because the way I feel is too intense, too real. It's like he's some super-strong magnet and all I want to do is press against him.

"It's not babbling, but it's nice, and you only do it when

you're nervous." His breath brushes against my hand with every word. He straightens up a little. I move with him. "Do I make you nervous?"

"Yes. No. A little. Not because I'm afraid of you, but because . . . it's . . . oh . . ." I lose my words because he's kissing my knuckles again. "I still have paint on my hand."

He flips it over and kisses right where there's a bit of dried sky blue. "I like it. I like everything about you."

I swear my knees are about to buckle. I grab for him.

He laughs softly. I can't believe he did that. I can't believe I feel like this. It's so different from Blake, so much bigger. I force myself to sound teasing, like my feelings aren't in some big swirly jumble. "What? Like you've never made a girl weak-kneed before?"

"I'm weak-kneed, too," he says.

"Really?"

"Swear."

"Let's go inside. I have to show you something. I was going to show you at lunch but it all went crazy," I explain. "I even thought we could talk to Court about it, too, because, you know . . . she was getting better."

We go back inside the tree house. Alan can't really sit up straight unless he's in the absolute center, so he half lies across the floor, propped up on an elbow. I hand him the folder.

"Mrs. Hessler gave it to me. She's our librarian. She was friends with my mom. She asked if Court had any sores. I think she knows something." I start to leave.

He reaches out and touches my ankle. It's a light touch. "Where you going?"

"I was going to let you read. I didn't want to bother you."

His hand strokes my foot and calf lightly and I swear it sends these good shivers all through me. It's ridiculous. Blake never made me feel this way; never made me feel as if the whole world had gone static-electric and power-charged.

Alan rumbles out, "What did Doris say when you apologized for asking about Courtney? 'You're never a bother.' She's right."

He grabs on to my ankle and tugs gently. I laugh and flop down next to him. He rearranges himself so that he can sit up better. I curl against his side and close my eyes, listening for danger, listening for any signs of badness, of evil. What stinks about it is that I don't have any idea what I'm listening for. Does evil have a sound?

Alan wraps his arm around the front of my shoulder. His voice is husky-deep and smooth-slow and melt-worthy. "Is that comfortable?"

"Yep." It's all I can manage. "Read it, okay? Do you mind?"

He kisses the top of my head. "Of course not."

I settle in for the duration and try to keep my mind off of Courtney and how worried I am. I try to keep my mind off Alan, too, and how good he smells, because, let's face it: now is not the time, right? At least not in my little brother's tree house, anyway.

She feels so right nestled up against me. The smell of her perfume, shampoo, and girliness is very distracting as I open the folder and try to concentrate on what's inside. My arm is around her, my forearm against her chest, my hand on her shoulder. I've never been this comfortable with a girl before. I can't believe it's only been a couple of days. We're so comfortable that for just a minute I start to let myself think that all this is okay, that we can just be a couple. I can't think about that now, though. I mean, Aimee just broke up with a guy, and Courtney's dad just died, and . . . there's just too much happening.

Instead, I focus on the open folder in front of me. It looks like printouts of old newspaper articles. I read the first one, then the next few. One is much newer, and I feel Aimee kind of flinch a little when I uncover it. I read it quickly.

"Your mom?" I ask. She nods but doesn't say anything. I

look through a few more pages, all relating various deaths that have something to do with the river. Finally, I close the folder and kiss the top of her head again. "You okay?"

"Mm-hmm." She snuggles her shoulders up tighter against me and all I want is to kiss her, but it's too soon, way too soon.

Instead, I clear my throat and say, "This is the river right here? Where your kayaks are?"

"Yep."

"I was there the other day, before I saw the shape in Courtney's room. It seemed so peaceful."

"Usually it is. It's tidal but it feeds off some lakes up in the country. The ocean's not far that way. That's where Courtney's dad died."

We're quiet for a minute, both of us thinking, I guess. She turns her head to look at me and suddenly our lips are millimeters apart.

She inches back, but only by a fraction, and says, "The whole town thinks that my mom killed herself, that she was really crazy. People teased me about it when I was little. They said that I was crazy, too."

I want to kiss her so badly, to just once feel her lips against my lips.

"You're not crazy, Red." My voice surprises me. It's about eight octaves deeper than normal. Her face is so close. Her eyes mist up. She blinks hard like she's trying to hold back tears.

"We shouldn't do this," she says. "I mean, I want to do this, but we—it's—I want . . ."

I swallow so hard and so slowly that it's like my Adam's

apple gets stuck halfway down my throat. Her eyes turn into some sort of plea.

"I know we shouldn't do this," she says again.

She sucks in her lips a little bit and totally changes the topic. She tends to do this, I've noticed. Her brain jumps around. "Do you think the River Man is him, that first guy, Emulus Black?"

"No." I say it without hesitation, which surprises her and me. "Some places attract evil. Some things in nature have evil souls, just like people. Maybe this is an evil river spirit."

"Like a nymph, but a man?" Her breath is warm and sweet-smelling and I want to keep breathing it into my body as soon as it comes out of hers.

"Yeah, I guess."

"So, this thing has maybe been here forever?"

"Maybe. Maybe somebody called it from somewhere else and bound it to the river. Maybe it just found the river, found people here, and stayed."

"It seems like it's affecting everyone. People are cranky, fighting. It's like some sort of virus of evil, you know?" She shakes her head and sighs. "What can *we* do?"

"That's the question, isn't it?" I say. "That'd be easiest. Just turn it all over to someone else, someone who knows what he's doing."

"What's the other option?" Aimee asks. Her eyes, so close, are huge and green, like a meadow filled with sunshine. "Can we make it leave Courtney alone? Can we make it go away completely, so it won't ever hurt anyone else?"

"I don't know." I explain to her about the stages of possession.

"The acne?" she asks.

I nod. "It's the obsession stage, and it seems to be getting stronger. Yesterday, I think she was totally possessed for a little while when she threw the door open. Then she passed out. Maybe the spirit was exhausted. It spent all its energy possessing her before she had submitted to that stage, really. That's why she was able to be so normal the rest of the day. The thing wasn't strong enough to harass her anymore."

"And now? What happened today? Is she completely possessed?"

"I don't think so. She's normal sometimes. Once the possession is complete, she won't be herself at all. Ever."

"Will . . . will he kill her then?"

"I don't know. He might just use her to spread his evil for a long time. Or maybe not . . . ," I say. We talk for a second about how it seems to be affecting other people, too, sort of bringing out their worst traits somehow, making them meaner. It's not as full-on as it is with Courtney, but people are being arrested for domestic violence, people are getting in fights at school. Good people, Aimee says. People who have never been in trouble before. She thinks this might even be why her brother and grandfather are having such intense moments of crankiness lately, why her dad's not been coming home as much, why Blake freaked out.

"What can we do?" she asks, nestling in against me.

"You remember I told you I was scared?"

"Yes." She sounds so serious.

"I've been thinking that maybe there's a reason I'm here. You know, maybe it's more than Mom wanting to move in with her sister. Maybe the Great Spirit sent me here to fight this thing."

"That's deep, Alan."

"Yeah. Maybe it's all bull. Maybe I'm being, I don't know, arrogant, thinking I can fight this thing."

"Can you?"

"I really don't know. I've never done anything like this. It's not like all members of Native American nations are mysterious, magical shamans . . ."

I tell her my whole story. I tell her what I've always known and how much I really don't understand. "I'm just a half-breed bastard who can't even get a tribal ID card. The little bit I know about Ghost Sickness, the ghost dance, medicine, and all that is from the Internet and books, and no self-respecting one of us would ever publish the really important stuff."

"Your guide, though," Aimee says. "She called you Spirit Warrior."

"Yeah, but wouldn't I need training?"

"Maybe it's a calling," she says. "You know, something that's innate in your nature and just comes forward when you need it."

"That sounds too easy."

"What exactly does it mean, 'spirit warrior'? Is it like an exorcist?"

"I think it's more," I answer. "Like a shaman. You know, everything from making charms to doing exorcisms. But . . . I don't know. Who am I to do any of that?"

"If you were going to try to do something, what would it be?"

I can't help but smile at her psychological tactic. "If I tell you what I would try if I really was a shaman, then you'll just tell me I should try it."

"Caught me, didn't you?" she asks, smiling back at me.

"Yeah. Nice one, Miss Avery. Going Dr. Phil on me."

"So, what *would* you do? If, of course, you were going to try something?"

I think about it. "A few things, I guess. When I burned the sage incense last night, the scratching stopped and she went to sleep. I think we should do a smudging in Aunt Lisa's house."

"Smudging?"

"It's—" I stop and pull back a little to see all of her face. She looks serious, but I feel self-conscious. "You're okay with this? I mean, it might seem kind of hokey if you don't believe in it."

"Alan, I've seen my best friend turn into some kind of monster. She threw you—yes, threw you, a great big football player who saved a lot of games for his team in Oklahoma, according to your hometown newspaper—she threw you across the cafeteria today. That was not Courtney Tucker. Yes, I believe."

"Okay. So we're on the same page here," I say. It still takes all of my strength to keep from kissing her. She wriggles around until she's lying on the tree house floor, her face beneath mine.

"Yes," she says coyly. "Same page. What is smudging?"

"You take a bundle of dried sage, light it on fire, and you walk through the house with it and fan the smoke around with feathers. I think they have to be owl feathers. And you pray to

154

the Great Spirit, asking him to bless the house and drive away any evil spirits."

"Is that it? Will that work?"

"I don't know." I hang my head a little. "I keep saying that, huh? I don't know. I really don't. But I think smudging will not be enough. At best, it might buy us some time, give us a few days for something else. Something more extreme."

"What?"

"Exorcism."

"Really?"

"Yeah."

She looks up at me in a very serious way, and I wish I could give her some deep philosophical words promising that I can do it and that everyone will be okay afterward, that life will go on like it should. Instead, I can only smile at her like a guy trying to hide the fact that he's just torn a major ligament.

"How do you do that?" she asks.

I can't bring myself to say "I don't know" again. I clear my throat. "I'll have to do some more research. There may be certain prayers that have to be used. I think I have to fast and do a sweat lodge first so that I can be purified."

She grins up at me. "So you'll be pure, like new snow? Are you pure, Alan Parson?"

God, she's beautiful.

"What's that?" she asks.

We both lie there completely still for a minute. Far away there's a noise like a truck barreling up the street. But it's no truck. We both know it. Her hand trembles. My heart hiccups in my chest. Still, we sit up to face it. Looking out the A-frame of the tree house, we can see a cloud of old leaves and dirt moving toward us up the street ahead of a strong and completely unnaturally focused wind.

"We should get down," I urge. Loose hair lashes across my cheek.

"Not on the ladder."

I lean over the edge. No, we can't get caught clinging to the side of the tree. I turn around and lunge for Aimee, grabbing hold of her and covering her as best I can with my body as a wave of leaves and trash crashes into one end of the tree house. She screams beneath me. The wind is so strong I'm afraid it will get under us and throw us out of the tree house.

"Onawa!" I yell into the wind. "Great Spirit, protect us."

The wind finds a voice. It roars around us, swirling in the tight confines of the tree house so that the wood groans and stretches. Some boards are splintering around the edges. The tree rocks madly, like a frenzied fan at a Slayer concert. Inside my head, the voice of the wind is screaming at me, challenging me.

The tree house echoes with demonic laughter. It fades as the wind rushes out the opposite end from the one it entered and flies off down the slope toward the river. Sticks and pebbles litter the floor. Dry autumn leaves and a ragged bit of newspaper flutter and collapse around us like dying birds.

Under me, Aimee is sobbing. I push myself off her, but pull her close against me. She clings to me, crying. I want to cry, too. That was damn scary.

My cell phone rings. I take my arms from around Aimee and fish it out of my jeans pocket. It's Mom's ringtone.

"This is my mom," I say. "She'll tell us that Courtney is better. She's resting."

Aimee nods. "I know. We were wrong. It's like he recharges from her now, gets all his energy out of her and then uses it up doing crazy stuff, and then sucks it all out of her again."

Not a good thought. I hit the button to accept the call.

"Alan, where are you?" Mom asks.

"I'm at Aimee's."

"Who?"

"Aimee. Courtney's friend."

"Are you okay?"

"I'm fine, Mom." Almost shaken out of a tree house by an evil spirit, but otherwise fine. "How's Courtney?"

"She's resting. Finally." Mom sounds very tired.

I look at Aimee. She heard and nods at me.

"She settled down all of a sudden, didn't she?" I ask.

"Ye-es. How did you know?"

"You won't get mad?" She doesn't say anything. "Mom, I don't think Courtney has a tumor, or any kind of disease. I think it's something else. I think there's a ghost or something bothering—"

"Alan, please. Please. Just don't. I've let you read what you want, let you pretend you're some Native American, even let you wear that disgusting bag around your neck, but you can't . . . This isn't about you, Alan."

Aimee looks very, very sorry and I know she heard every word.

"Okay." It's all I can say.

"I swear, Alan," Mom goes on. "You think, what? She's possessed? Like in the movies?"

"I guess not." I swallow down the anger bubbling up my throat.

"Don't you dare mention that to Lisa. You understand me?"

"Yeah. I understand."

"If you're okay, I'm going to stay here for a while," Mom says. "Lisa is still frantic and almost exhausted. The doctors are talking about giving her a sedative, too. That's what they did with Courtney. They pumped the poor girl full of tranquilizers. It took a long time for them to work, though."

"Was she cussing at everyone?"

"Alan," she warns.

"Just asking."

"This isn't a game."

"I know, Mom. I know it isn't a game."

"I don't know when they'll let Courtney go home. If they keep her overnight, and I can only imagine they will, Lisa wants to stay here. You might need to come get me."

"I will. Bye."

I put the phone back in my pocket.

"Sorry," Aimee offers. I wave it away like it's nothing, but she knows. She grabs my hand and holds it tight in both of her little hands. Touching her doesn't make me feel like I'm getting shocked anymore, or like I'm seeing visions; instead it's just warmth, a healing kind of warmth. I remember what she told me about dreams that evening we first talked on the phone.

"You see things, don't you? Things that have happened or that will happen in the future?"

"Sometimes." There's fear in her voice. That doesn't comfort me.

"What do you see for Courtney? How about me? Us?"

She shakes her head. "I can't. I see bad things, but nothing . . . nothing solid. Just threats. So far."

Her eyes look toward the river. She shudders and says, "Let's go inside."

"What if we ate it and replaced it with another Cheeto? Do you think they'd notice?" We have homework spread out on the kitchen table, but we've barely looked at it. Who can do homework in the presence of such an expensive Cheeto?

Aimee laughs at me and takes the plastic bag out of my hand as if she were afraid I might actually do it. "I think they have every bump on this Cheeto memorized."

She looks at the Cheeto, then puts it back on top of her refrigerator. I can't believe I was just holding a Cheeto that is already worth more than I paid for my truck.

"You can eat dinner with us," she says.

"Would your dad mind?"

"Of course not."

I shrug like I'm totally cool and not at all nervous about meeting her dad. Then I remember something else. "How did you know about those newspaper articles about me saving games?" I ask.

"I might have googled you."

"That sounds dirty."

"It would really go a long way toward impressing my dad if you helped me with dinner," she says. "And stayed to eat it with us."

"I don't know. If I had a hot daughter like you and I came

159

home from work and found some guy playing house and cooking dinner with her, I'd probably shoot him."

"I am not hot."

I can't help but laugh at her.

"Gramps will be home first. Today's his day to visit friends at the senior center. Then Benji. Dad's always late, but he's been better the last couple of days."

"Great."

"What?"

"It's like two practice runs before your dad gets here. If your grandpa doesn't throw me out and I survive the wicked glare of your little brother, then I get to face off against your suspicious father."

"What would he be suspicious of?"

"My intentions toward his daughter."

"And what are your intentions?" She smiles a teasing smile and again I want to lunge across the table and kiss her.

"You're the psychic on this exorcism team," I say. "I suspect you know my intentions."

· 15 ·
AIMEE

Gramps tromps through the door and doesn't even pause when he sees Alan at the table doing homework with his giant long limbs sprawling everywhere. He just puts his hat on the coat hook, takes his shoes off, and slides on his bright yellow Crocs, which are hideously ugly. Then he Croc-walks over to me, kisses the top of my head, and says, "Well, who do we have here?"

Alan stands up, hitting the table with his thigh. Papers jiggle. He reaches out his hand. "Alan Parson, sir."

I half want to laugh but the other half of me is so proud that he's polite.

Gramps takes his hand and shakes it. "Good to meet you. I'd ask if you were tutoring Aimee, but I know she doesn't need a tutor. Is she tutoring you?"

"No, sir . . . I . . ." Alan looks to me for help.

"We're just hanging out," I say.

Gramps nods. "What happened to the other one?"

"He turned out to be a racist," I finally admit.

Gramps digests that pretty quickly and nods at Alan. "And you're the race he was *ist* against, huh? You Native American?"

Alan's fingers twitch a little. "Part. Navajo."

"Good. Good. This place is too damn white anyway." Gramps heads toward the fridge.

Alan's smiling this ridiculously large smile and just watching him. It's pretty obvious he likes Gramps.

"He's Court's cousin. He and his mom just moved here from Oklahoma," I explain, then feel like a total jerk. "I'm sorry. I'm talking about you in the third person."

Alan just smiles even bigger and shrugs.

"Aimee tell you about our Cheeto? Looks just like Marilyn Monroe." Gramps whirls around. "You do know who Marilyn Monroe is?"

"I know." Alan sits back down at the table. He stretches out his legs beneath it. His calves are on either side of my legs. "I think it's amazing what people will pay for it."

"I'll tell you what's amazing." Gramps makes us wait for it, pouring some water. "What's amazing is that we even had a bag of Cheetos in this house in the first place, with Little Miss Health Nut here." He gestures to me.

Alan clears his throat. "She can't be that bad if you're having hamburgers for dinner."

"You staying?" Gramps asks.

Nodding, Alan looks to me for verification. "If that's okay."

"It's okay." Gramps asks me, "You tell him what we're having?"

"Burgers," I say innocently.

"Not *ham*burgers. *Veggie* burgers. You ever have veggie burgers?"

"Uh . . . no. I'm from Oklahoma. If it doesn't bleed, we don't eat it."

"Exactly." Gramps claps him on the back. "Man after my own heart. Your brother home yet?"

It takes me a second to realize that he's talking to me again. "Benji? No . . . I think the Vachons are dropping him off."

Gramps snorts. "He'll put you through the wringer. Don't let him bully you. He's all of four foot eight, but he's one intimidating little son of a gun."

"I won't," Alan says.

The door flies open and there's Benji. He stands there gaping and then points at Alan. "It's him!"

Nobody says anything.

Benj rushes over to Alan. "You are freaking huge. Your hair is like eight feet long. Do you have split ends? Aimee's always whining about her split ends."

"Benj," Gramps interrupts. "Why don't you go change into some clean clothes?"

"What? And leave the lovebirds alone?" Benji singsongs.

"Yes." Gramps smiles and pushes him toward the living room and the stairs. "Exactly. Notice the lovebirds doing their homework. Maybe you should do the same."

At that moment I don't think I've ever loved anyone more than I love Gramps.

We eat. Alan even swallows the veggie burger. Dad works

late, doesn't show up, and then it's time for Alan to go. I walk him to the truck.

"I don't want you to leave," I say.

He touches the side of my face with his fingers and the whole world spins out of control in this crazy-good way. I think he's going to kiss me, but he doesn't. His fingers drop and I almost think I imagined it. He says, "I know."

"You'll be safe, right?" I pull in a big breath. "Nothing will happen, right?"

"Nothing will happen." He folds me into a hug, but it isn't long because it's so obvious that Benji's watching from the window. "You call if you need me."

"You, too." I hate pulling away. I hate how it's suddenly so cold without him. "Tell me if you hear anything about Courtney. Deal?"

"Deal."

He drives away, and suddenly the night seems a whole lot darker and a whole lot more sinister. A twig snaps in the woods. Wind blows a leaf across my foot. I hurry inside, but honestly, I don't know if it's any safer in there.

Dad comes home, making apologies and explaining that Courtney seems a little bit calmer, although they're keeping her sedated overnight at least. I warm him up some food, go upstairs, and paint for a while. I can't focus, though, so I do the horrible obsessed girlfriend thing and google Alan again. I pull up picture after picture of him on the football team making play after play.

I know nothing about football. I really know nothing about

Alan. What if he's playing me? What if Courtney has a brain tumor? What if those dust storms were just dust storms? A cold wind blows through my window. I shiver and leap over my bed to shut it. Something is on my windowsill. It's a rock. There's a word painted in yellow on it: MOM.

My right hand drifts down. My finger touches the rock. It's cold and gray, round, and about half the size of my palm. My finger moves toward the word, the bright stain of it against the stone.

The paint is still wet.

"Dad!" I scream-shriek it. I stare at the tip of my finger. A dot of yellow stains it. "DAD!"

He thunders up the stairs, but Benji gets there first. He stands at my door, pajama-boy with crazy-wild hair. "Aimee?" He rubs at his sleepy eyes.

My dad bullets past him, leaps on my bed, pulls me into his arms. "Honey? What is it?" He rocks me into him, rocks us back and forth like a lullaby movement can make it all better. I stare into the gray T-shirt he always wears to bed.

"Aimee?" Gramps's voice finds me. "You have a nightmare?"

I pull away from Dad, making big eyes so Gramps knows I'm lying. "Yeah."

He looks at Benji, nods at me, puts his hand on Benji's shoulder, and says, "Off to bed, kiddo. Nothing to see here."

"I get nightmares all the time," Benji mumbles. "I don't wake up the whole house."

"Benji!" Gramps warns.

My dad pulls me in to him again. He's warm from being asleep under the covers. "I am so worried about you, kiddo."

His voice is a broken rocking horse trying to rest, trying to find something solid for balance.

I lean away from him. "I went to shut my window and I found that on the sill."

I point to the rock.

"A rock? You screamed about a rock?"

"I didn't put it there."

"Maybe Benji?"

"Look at it, Dad. It's got paint on it. It says . . ."

He leans his long trunk across my comforter and peers at it. "Did you paint that on, Aimee?"

I yank my knees to my chest. "Dad! No."

"She didn't do this," Gramps says. I'm not sure when he came back in the room. He crosses his arms in front of his chest. "You know that."

"Dad! Did you or did you not see a knife spinning on our stove the other day? I am not the kind of genius who can do stuff like that. And did we or did we not all hear freaking footsteps upstairs? They sounded like Mom! You know they did!" I push myself far, far away from them, against my bed. "I know you think I'm crazy like her, but I'm not!"

Even I can hear that it's like I'm trying to convince myself.

Silence.

My dad whispers, "Your mother was not crazy."

"Son—" Gramps starts.

"She wasn't!" Dad lunges off the bed, lumbering toward him like some sort of angry grizzly bear. "Don't start with that, Dad."

"That's not the point," I interrupt. "The point is that

166

there is a freaking rock on my windowsill and I did not put it there."

My dad's shoulders loosen. He straightens back up. Gramps eyes him, and then walks past him without a care in the world and comes close to me. "Where is it?"

I point.

He grabs it by the edges, careful not to smear the paint. I look from one to the other. Two guys with sleep-tired faces and fight-ready bodies, identical chins, and balding heads. Lean and strong, but so tired.

Dad says, "Tell us about Courtney, Aimee. Her mom hinted that you thought something was going on, but she wasn't buying any of it."

"Are you going to believe me?" I ask him.

"I'll try," he says.

I pull the pink folder out of my backpack. "You can start with this. Mrs. Hessler gave it to me."

"Mrs. Hessler?" Dad's eyes get big. "Really?"

"If you read that, it'll help." I choose my words carefully, trying to make like I'm calm. "I think that something from the river is trying to possess Courtney. I think there's something really bad happening here."

Eventually they both go into their bedrooms. I hear my father check every door, every closet, every window until he's sure the house is secure.

It's too hard to try to sleep. My ears are on hyper-alert mode, listening for ghost footsteps. I get up and paint. I've barely begun when Alan texts me. YOU OKAY?

YEP. YOU? I text back. CALL ME?

I am so glad to hear his voice. We whisper into the phone about Courtney, the rock, the River Man, and what happened in the tree house, which is somehow easier to do on the phone than in person.

"He's just trying to scare us," I say, staring at the two sets of eyes in my painting. They are the same shape, but not the same inside. They are the same form, but not the same intent.

As I paint, Alan tells me the stuff he's learned about exorcisms. He's done most of his research on the Internet and he has one book that had a paragraph about it. He insists that if he's going to try to exorcise Courtney he has to do it alone, that it's part of the tradition and process. That freaks me out.

"I wish you didn't have to do this on your own."

"I can do it."

I fumble with a paintbrush. I try to wipe the paint off with some thinner, but it's ocher and it's stubborn. "I know." I drop the brush head-down into the bottle to let it soak.

Alan says, "What if he tries to hurt you when I'm not there?"

I turn away from my painting and go back to my laptop, where the images of Alan are still on the screen. He's the one I'm worried about. "He won't hurt me. He can't."

"How do you know?"

"I just know."

"Red . . ."

"Look, it's not like he has a gun. What has he done? Possessed Courtney. Thrown something at you. Made a huge dirt storm thing. Maybe he leaves a rock in my room, but maybe that's something else, like Benji playing games or me sleep-walking or some other ghost. Give me a break. Either way, it's lame."

I shut the laptop. I flop over onto my bed and hug my giant tiger. It's a Princeton tiger. Gramps went to Princeton. The night is dark outside my window. You can't see Benji's tree house or the river or anything that could be lurking, but you know it might be there. I pull down the shade and touch the sill where the rock was. No matter how brave I can make myself, sometimes thinking about the darkness and the river and the night, thinking about my mom standing out there that one time . . . it makes me not quite so brave.

"I wish you were here," I say.

"I wish I *was* there."

I think for a second. "Come over."

"What?"

"Come over. We can protect each other. You could climb up the tree. I could sneak you in."

"Your dad will go ballistic."

I don't answer.

"What if your grandfather catches me? He'll kill me."

I don't answer.

"Aimee?"

I wait. I wait. I think, *Please be brave for me, Alan.* I wait. I close my eyes but that's too dark, so I open them again and stare across the room at the painting I'm working on. I need to add more layers to it. I need to add more depth, but I can tell, now, at least, what it's supposed to be.

Two women.

169

The same.

But not the same.

You can tell this by looking in their eyes.

I say, "I'm scared."

I grab the paw of a teddy bear. He's old. He's seen a lot of stuff, this teddy. He's seen me.

Alan's voice is husky. "You are?"

I think about what Courtney said. I think about what I might have inherited. I think about the man from the river who haunts us. I feel so alone, and all I want is someone to wrap his arms around me. Okay, not just someone.

My voice is tiny. "I'm really scared and there's . . . there's more I should tell you . . ."

"Okay. I'm coming over."

My phone beeps to let me know I have a text message.

I'M HERE.

I am so glad the phone is working tonight. One minute later he's outside my window. I pop off the screen. He wedges himself through.

"Tell me Blake never did this," he whispers.

"Blake never did this."

Alan hugs me to him, kisses the top of my head. I try to mold myself into him, like we're two pieces of sculpting clay meant to return back together.

"Aim . . ." My fingers stretch out across his back. He pushes away a little so that he can see my face. "Aim . . . you want to tell me what's going on?"

I pull away from him. Even though it's hard, I pull away,

and go sit on my bed. He comes across the room, trying not to make noise as he steps. He sits next to me, holds my hand. The bed sinks down with his weight, but it's good.

He points to the painting. "That you and your mom?"

I nod. I try to breathe.

"Aim?"

He makes my name a question and I know I have to answer. I know he deserves an answer after driving here in the middle of the night. I try to give him one. "I'm afraid of him, but that's not what I'm most afraid of."

"What are you afraid of then?"

I point to the painting.

He pulls in his breath. His fingers tighten around my fingers. "That you're like your mother?"

The word comes out all by itself.

The word comes out even though I don't want it to.

The word comes out and it is "Yes."

"Aimee." He soothes quiet words into my hair, rocks me back and forth, back and forth like a baby while I cry. "Aimee, it's going to be okay. You're okay. You're okay."

"I know." I hiccup. "I know."

I wipe at my face with my hands. I try to breathe normally, but what is normal? I try to breathe. Gramps's snores hammer through the walls. Once in a while, a mouse scampers over the roof, scratching, searching for food to eat, places to hide.

"Courtney thinks I'm crazy or something. She implied it in Advanced English the other day."

"That wasn't her, that was him. You know that. It's just him working at your fears."

"I don't want to be crazy," I say. My dad implied it, too.

"You aren't crazy." Alan's lips tighten together. Then he opens them again. "'Crazy' is a stupid word."

"I know. Actually, 'stupid' is a stupid word."

"You're okay, Aim."

I make my fingers relax, trying to understand. I glance at the painting across the room; me and my mom. It's too much. I hide my face in his shirt. He smells toothpaste-clean.

"I don't think I'm crazy," I say.

"Okay."

I push away from him. He is not mad. His eyes hold my eyes. "Whatever happens, we will deal with it, Red."

The story everyone knows is that my mother killed herself. She had an ax. She walked into a river. She had a mental illness called bipolar disorder. Sometimes she was regular. Sometimes she wasn't. But that might not be the truth, not the whole of it, at least. But either way—either way, one thing is sure.

"She left me," I say. "My mother left me."

"I know," Alan says. "But she didn't have a choice. You have a choice, Aimee. You can choose. We can manage this."

I half laugh. "'Manage this.' You sound like a lawyer."

He wiggles his eyebrows. He is trying so hard. "I know."

I swallow. I swallow five times at least. He just tucks me against him. He presses his lips against my hair, and it's like he's pressing promises there. "Thank you."

"For what?"

"For finally trusting me."

"Alan, that is so sappy."

He shrugs. He pulls me back into him. "It's true."

I play punch him, but my heart's not really in it. "Are you going to freak out about all this?"

He sniffs in. "Not till tomorrow, probably, when I'm home and you don't need me. Cool?"

I snuggle in closer. "Cool."

"I'll stay until you fall asleep," he whispers. "Then I'm going to sneak out."

We flatten ourselves down against the mattress. He puts one arm beneath my shoulder, curls into my side, and pulls his other arm across my lower rib cage, holding on.

"It'll be okay." He is sleepy voiced.

"Are you sure?"

I dream all night. I dream of an upturned kayak, hands ripping me apart, water, Alan crumpled on a floor. I dream and dream and dream, and the River Man's voice echoes through it all, telling me that we will all be his.

In the morning it's Alan's gasp that wakes me up. Sunlight fills the room.

"Crap!" he mutters. "Crap. Crap. Crap."

I sit up straight, trying to figure everything out. He's throwing open the window, about to slide outside, but something across the room catches his eye.

"Aim . . ." His voice is a warning sign.

I don't want to look. But I look and my heart stops, really. It stops. Then starts again, hard, painful, pounding. He grabs my arm and pulls me into him, but I've already seen.

Someone—something?—has thrown paint all over the picture of my mother and me. The red of it oozes across our faces, dripping like horror-movie blood. But worse than that is the message printed in scratchy style over the whole thing.

HE SHOULD NOT BE HERE.

"I really, really wish I could believe Benji snuck in here and did that," I say as I hold Aimee pressed hard against my chest. She shakes her head.

"He wouldn't."

"No." This seems way too much for an ornery little brother. At the same time, as weird as it is, it seems kind of tame for the thing that attacked us in the tree house. "Aimee, is it possible that was done by somebody else?"

"Gramps? No, he wouldn't—"

"Not Gramps. I was thinking . . . well, maybe your mom?"

She raises her head, her big green eyes wide, but doesn't say anything.

"If it was our friend from the river, don't you think he would have done something . . . I don't know, more physical? Like in the tree house? This is messed up, no doubt, but maybe it's your mom's spirit telling you something."

"I've been thinking the same thing," she says. "But I don't see why she'd say you aren't supposed to be here. Plus, red paint looks like blood. I wish she'd used blue or something."

"Well, you did leave the red tube open. I saw that when I came in." She just stares at me, and it's so obvious that she's trying really hard not to freak out, so I try to ease the tension. "Maybe she knows that I have to get out of here before I get you in trouble. My mom'll have a cow, too, if she wakes up first and I'm not home. I saw a doughnut shop. I'll take some doughnuts home, eat, and come back to get you."

"School?" Her perfect little nose wrinkles up and I almost laugh out loud.

"I think we need to carry on as close to a normal routine as we can so the parental units aren't hovering over us. They probably won't like what we're going to try to do. We need to be normal, get Courtney home, and then we can fight this thing." I go to the window.

"Okay." She's still looking up at me. "Maybe she means him—the River Man thing isn't supposed to be here."

"You should put that painting away so no one sees it," I say, then move as lightly as I can over the short stretch of roof to the edge and jump to the ground below. I stay low and run from the yard, hoping none of Aimee's menfolk look out their windows at that particular moment.

I drive to the little doughnut store and buy a dozen assorted doughnuts, then race home. Mom and Aunt Lisa are both up when I get there, but it looks like they haven't been up long. "Alan, where have you been?" Mom asks. "I thought you were still in bed."

"Couldn't sleep. I got up early and went out. Thought I'd take care of breakfast today." I put the doughnuts on the table. Aunt Lisa's face is pale, with dark circles under her watery eyes. "Any news?"

"She was awake this morning," Aunt Lisa says. "She talked to me a little, and she seemed like the old Courtney. She asked about you."

"She did?"

"Yes." Aunt Lisa hesitates, like she isn't sure she should say anything more.

"What did she say?"

Aunt Lisa looks to Mom, then back at me. "She asked me to tell you to be strong. To do what needs to be done."

That stands up the hairs on my arms. "She said that?"

"Alan, what's going on?" Mom asks. "What did she mean? What are you doing?"

I think about it. I tried to tell her already, and she wanted no part of it. Would she believe me now, with Courtney's cryptic message? Probably not. I shrug and shake my head. "I don't know what she means. She probably had some kind of dream."

"That's what the nurse said," Aunt Lisa tells me.

"Are you going to work today?" I ask. Both women nod.

"Lisa, you shouldn't," Mom says. "You should take a nap. Go to the hospital."

"They told me there's nothing I can do there," she says. "We need the money. If—if something is seriously wrong . . . well, I might need my sick leave then."

"Aunt Lisa, she's going to be okay," I promise.

She nods, then comes around the table and hugs me.

"Thank you, Alan. Thank you." Her voice is husky and thick in my ear. "What would I do without you and your mom here?"

"Move to Oklahoma and watch me play football, probably," I say, trying desperately to lighten the mood while I hug her back.

I grab a couple of doughnuts and a bottle of OJ from the fridge and run out the front door, pretending I don't hear Aunt Lisa telling Mom what a great kid I am.

Aimee's dad meets me at the front door of the house. He's not a big man. I mean, he's tall, but average build. I suppose the intimidation factor comes from just knowing he's Aimee's dad. He opens the door and waves me in.

"Come on in, Alan," he says. "I'm sorry I didn't get to see you last night. I heard you choked down one of Aimee's veggie burgers, though. It must be love."

"Uhh." Okay, I wasn't ready for that, and he has a good laugh over my dumbfounded look before holding out a hand. I shake it, and it's probably the weakest handshake I've ever given. He laughs at me again.

"I was only kidding," he says. "I'll tell you, though, Aimee really seems taken with you. I appreciate you coming up to the house to pick her up and being here to meet the family last night."

"I, umm, was glad to do it," I manage to stammer out. "She's a great girl."

He nods, then his face gets serious. "She's having a bit of a rough spot right now. Bad dreams and stuff. I don't know what she's told you about her mother. We lost her a while back, and it's been pretty hard on Aimee."

"She told me," I say.

He looks at me in a weird way, like he's surprised Aimee would have already mentioned that. "She told you, huh?"

"Yes, sir. We've, well, we've talked a lot."

"I see. Well, okay then." He pauses, and his forehead wrinkles up. He's wearing a white dress shirt and dark slacks. I suppose he'll have a tie and suit coat on pretty soon. "Alan, will you promise me something?"

"Sure."

"Be . . . be good to Aimee, okay?"

"Yes, sir, I will. I mean, I would never do anything to hurt her."

"It's just that, you're new here, and I don't know you," he says. "It isn't personal. I trust Aimee's judgment, and, like I said, she's really taken to you, so I have to trust you're a good kid. You seem like a good kid. Just, please understand, she's still my little girl."

"I know," I say. "I promise, nothing will hurt her while I'm with her." He gives me a really strange look then, and I realize how dumb that was. Not at all what I meant to say. He just wants me to promise to stay out of her pants. "I just mean, you don't have to worry about me, Mr. Avery. Aimee is safe with me."

"That's what I wanted to hear," he says, and offers his hand again. This time I grip it hard, like a man is supposed to, and pump it quickly a couple of times.

"What did you two just agree on?" Aimee asks from the

179

stairs. "Dad, did you just sell me for a goat and a couple of chickens?"

"You're worth much more than that, honey," he says, releasing my hand and turning to face her.

"I had to throw in a whole cow," I say. "Gramps wanted it for the steak."

Her dad gives a short bark of laughter that he covers up real fast with a hand while winking at me. Aimee just sticks out her tongue.

"Your colon will thank me for that veggie burger, you know," she says. "And for all the ones to come."

"You two better get to school," her dad says.

"Sir, can you tell me anything about my cousin? Aunt Lisa said she was awake and talking this morning."

"Sorry, Alan, there's not much I can say. Regulations and all." His face tells me he really is sorry he can't give me any news. "I promise we'll do everything we can to help her, though."

By now Aimee is off the stairs and standing beside me, her backpack strap held loosely in one hand. I scoop the pack off the floor and throw it over my shoulder.

"I can carry my own backpack," she protests.

"I know," I say. "But that veggie burger gave me so much energy that my colon said I have to carry your backpack to say thank you."

Her dad laughs again and says, "I think he's going to keep you on your toes, Aim."

She gooses me in the side and I can't help but flinch. "I think I can handle him," she says. "Now let's go, Alan. I heard

180

Benji brushing his teeth. Or sharpening them to get whatever Dad left of you."

"It was nice to meet you, Mr. Avery," I say, then open the door for Aimee. She doesn't seem to consider that an affront to her feminist side, but her dad notices and smiles at me. I give him one more wave, then follow Aimee to my truck.

I want to put an arm around her shoulders as we back out of the driveway, but instead I ask if she's okay.

"I am now," she says.

"Well, Aunt Lisa told me Courtney was talking this morning."

"She was?"

I tell her what my aunt reported.

"Do what needs to be done?" she asks.

"Yeah. That was freaky."

"Do you think she knows what's going on?"

"Probably. I don't know. Maybe. I think she knows there's some kind of spirit taking possession of her sometimes. Has it told her to stay away from me? Does she know that it believes I'm some kind of threat? I don't know. From what she said, I think so. I think she senses something."

"It might try to hurt you?"

We pull into the school's parking lot and I start looking for an empty space. "You mean it might try to throw me across the school cafeteria or something?"

"Or something worse."

"I'm more worried about you." I ease the truck into a slot between a Camaro and a Saab. I kill the engine and we sit quietly for a minute.

"I'm not going to be able to concentrate on school today," she says.

"Me, neither. But we're running a little late, so we better do the best we can." I open my door to get out. We're almost to the front door when I hear a voice behind us.

"It's the slut and her Injun chief who skipped practice yesterday."

Aimee and I stop in our tracks. We both know who it is.

"Ignore him," Aimee says in a whispery hiss. "He's not himself. I'm positive. He would never say that, not normally."

"Aimee, it's going to come to fists eventually," I say. I start to turn around, but her grip on my arm becomes frantic. It turns out that I don't have to go to them; Blake and two of his friends come around in front of us.

"What's the matter, Parson? Your slutty white squaw already got you whipped?" he asks. His friends laugh. I recognize one of the guys from my algebra class. The other one might be in German with me; he's a bigger guy with broad shoulders and a square jaw. The algebra guy is like Blake, tall and lean.

"Shut up, Blake," Aimee says. "I can't believe you've turned into such a jerk. What happened to you?"

The air vibrates with something hard and evil.

"Aimee, you just sick of white guys or something?" the algebra guy asks. Blake grins real slow, and I visualize my fist busting those lips wide open. There would be so much blood.

"You're being an idiot, Chris," Aimee says. She whispers to me. "He's normally nice. Really. They aren't acting right."

"You not speak English today, Tonto?" Blake asks.

"Don't do it, Alan," Aimee warns, obviously sensing the tension in my body.

"Not here," I promise. It's the best I can offer. Getting suspended from school wouldn't bother me. It's happened before. But I can't do that to Mom. Not so soon here in a new place. Not with Courtney in the hospital.

"He speakum English!" Square-jaw exclaims.

"Does Lauren know you're acting like a dumb-ass, Noah?" Aimee asks him. "Or are you just worried she might decide she likes Alan better than you, too? Jealous?"

"I don't have to be jealous of anybody, especially some stupid Indian," Noah says with an edge in his voice that tells us he's lying.

"Come on, Alan." Aimee pulls on my arm. I glare at Blake, ignoring his henchmen, and take a reluctant step behind Aimee. Back in OKC the girls I knew would have demanded I fight in this situation. All this is more than a little confusing and frustrating. I know I could take Blake, probably without breaking a sweat.

Aimee thinks she can push right between them and on toward the school. They move to let her pass, but the three of them close around me and I'm convinced we are going to get physical right here and now, until another voice stops everyone.

"You young men better not show up in the office needing a tardy slip," Mr. Everson announces. At some point he's come out of the school and is just ten yards from us. I see Blake's face flush up to his hairline. He steps away from us.

"We won't," Blake says. His friends look like sheep caught on a highway.

Aimee is still pulling at me, so I follow her. We pass the vice principal, who turns and falls into step with us. He opens the door and follows us in.

The first bell rings and neither of us have our books for first hour. "Go to class," she says, pushing me away. "I'll see you in bio. But that was not normal. They're not usually like that."

Focusing on algebra is impossible. Thinking about Blake's friend sitting three rows over and two desks ahead of me is useless. Keeping an eye on the teacher and my book open to the problems I'm supposed to be working on, I begin writing a note to Aimee, since the algebra teacher is tough on cells.

> *We need some things. We need real sage and sweetgrass. And rocks. We can't use river rocks. Not because they're from his river, but because river rocks get air pockets in them and can explode when they get hot. Where can we get some granite rocks? And the other stuff? And we need a place where I can build a sweat lodge and keep a fire going. Like a campsite or something. Any ideas?*

I fold the paper and slide it under the front cover of my biology book, which is under my open algebra book. Then I try again to focus on the math problems. I still don't see the point of this, but Aimee can't date a loser who can't pass his algebra class.

Back in Oklahoma, my sophomore English teacher made us read a short story called "The Bride Comes to Yellow Sky," all about how a sheriff in the Old West brings his wife to town and then won't fight the local bad guy.

"Man is a barbarian at heart," Mr. Walker had said. "Women bring a civilizing influence. When a woman enters the picture, men behave differently. Even Scratchy Wilson recognizes that."

I hadn't at the time. It was just a dumb story. But now . . . I look at the back of Chris's head and think about how I would have fought him and Blake and the other guy, Noah, if Aimee hadn't stopped me.

Finally, the bell rings and we're free to get out of this class to shuffle off to the next one. I get there before Aimee. She smiles at me when she comes through the door, and I pass her my note as she walks by to sit behind me. I hear her unfold the note, then scribble something with her pen. She hands the paper back to me.

Craft Barn probably has the sage and sweetgrass. It'll be dried. People use it to make potpourri and stuff. They might have granite rocks, too. If they don't, Bergerman's Lumber sells rocks for people to use as lawn decorations, so they might.

The bell hasn't rung yet, so I risk turning around before Mr. Swanson comes in. "Sounds good," I say. "I also need a tarp, or something like that. Something that will hold in the heat. Heavy canvas."

"You're living in a place where shipping used to be

everything," Aimee says. "I think we can get some canvas like they use in sails. Will that work?"

"Front and center, Alan," Mr. Swanson calls. "We'd all like to spend the hour gazing at Miss Avery, but we wouldn't learn much about photosynthesis that way."

"I bet he's learning a lot of biology from her," some girl across the room says in a joking tone that gets most of the class to laugh. I don't laugh, and I know Aimee isn't laughing. I'm sure she's blushing.

"Blake's going to kill him," some guy mutters, and then Mr. Swanson gets the class back under his control and begins a discussion about water treatment plants pumping waste water back into rivers.

"The moral of the story," he says as the bell rings to end our time together, "is to live as close to the head of the river as you can."

I take Aimee's hand as she gets squished among all the students trying to squeeze out the door. "See you at lunch," she says before we have to go our separate ways.

Square-jawed Noah doesn't say anything to me in our German class. I half expected him to create some kind of problem, but he's acting calm and normal and kind of looks embarrassed. I guess him, Blake, and Chris must share one set of balls, and it takes all three of them to say anything. Or else Aimee's right and something really is affecting people—and it's powerful. Really powerful. Anyway, there are no fights, and we all recite the lines Fräulein Gray feeds us until class is over.

No one in the cafeteria asks me directly about what

happened yesterday, but I see them looking at me and whispering about how my little girl cousin threw me over the railing and onto a table. Then Aimee grabs me by the arm and we join the chow line.

At the lunch counter, she takes a salad and I hold out my tray for a glob of mashed potatoes and some chicken fried steak fingers with a side of corn. "Maybe I should get an extra helping for Gramps," I tease.

"I'll have you eating healthy eventually," Aimee promises. "It's just a matter of time."

I think again about the bride going to Yellow Sky and civilizing all the men. I sigh and admit, "Probably so. Seems like I'll do about anything for you."

She only laughs and leads me to an empty table. We sit down and people flow around us. A few wave at Aimee, but nobody makes a move to sit with us. Aimee's friend Hayley is sitting at a nearby table crowded with people I vaguely recognize from various classes. Are they giving us space? Because they think we're a couple? Of course not. Because of Courtney. Something's wrong with her, centralized in her, and they know it. And we're too close to her. It's like the thing that has infected her has tainted us, too.

"Why do we need Court out of the hospital to do this?" Aimee asks. "I mean, why can't we just go to the river and do . . . whatever it is you need to do?"

"The evil spirit has to be focused somehow," I explain. "Confined. For whatever reason, it picked Courtney. Since she's the focal point, we have to have her before we can get rid of this thing."

"I wonder why it picked her?" she asks as she stabs at a tomato in her salad. She adds, "This time," before eating the tomato.

"I don't know. I think it has something to do with her not accepting that her dad is dead." I push my tray away. "I can't eat. I have to fast. I should have remembered. School just makes me feel like a dog that has to do this when one bell rings and do that when the next one sounds."

"So you're just not going to eat anything?"

"No. Nothing but water. I have to be ready."

"You think it'll be soon?"

"Yeah, I think so. We should get that stuff today. Can you come home with me after school? I want to check Courtney's room while nobody else is home."

"Searching for clues?"

"Yep." I watch her eat a few bites. Her jaw is very sexy when she chews.

"What?" she asks when she sees me watching her.

"Nothing." I smile at her. "I think I'll go to the bathroom and see if I can text Aunt Lisa."

I leave her there and go to the restroom around the corner from the cafeteria.

Sitting on the toilet of a closed stall with my pants up, I text Aunt Lisa. ANY NEWS?

After a few minutes I get a response. SHE SEEMS FINE STILL WAITING FOR SOME TESTS STAY AT SCHOOL!

I write back, WILL DO. I stand up and pocket my phone, then open the stall door.

The fist that hits me in the face isn't well aimed, but it's enough of a surprise that I stagger backward and trip over the toilet. I fall against the wall, and before I can catch myself three of them are in the stall with me, punching at my face and body. I see Blake's face, so twisted with rage that he barely looks like himself. I can't get my balance, can't stand up under the attack. All I can do is cover my face, but I've already taken several hits and it feels like at least one of them is wearing a class ring.

Somewhere far away I hear the call: "Fight!"

The fists keep coming as people pour into the restroom, yelling and jostling to get a better view of the action.

Finally I'm able to kind of roll forward and stand up, though it offers my right side to several kidney shots. Fortunately, the confined space keeps them from getting in any really good punches. I shove at the first body I find, then drive a fist into Blake's face. His nose crumples and blood bursts out of his nostrils, but it's like he doesn't even feel it.

He laughs at me, but it isn't his laugh. It's the River Man's laugh. I've heard echoes of it before in the wind.

Then Mr. Burnham is behind Blake, his arm around Blake's throat as he drags him out of the stall. Everson is behind him and grabs Chris and Noah by their jacket collars to pull them out.

"Come on," Everson says. "You all can have some time off to get over this." He turns them toward the bathroom door, ordering the spectators back to lunch, then looks at me. "Come on, Alan. You, too."

Arguing would sound weak. Mom won't understand. Even Aimee might not understand. I wipe some blood off my face,

189

feeling the sting of a cut, then follow Everson and Burnham out of the bathroom.

Aimee's there, her green eyes wide and concerned.

"Sorry," I say as I pass her. I offer her a smile, but it doesn't erase the worry on her face.

· 17 ·
AIMEE

Boys are stupid. That's all there is to it. Boys are just stupid. Even if the River Man is making people meaner than normal, they had this in them somehow, somewhere, this need to punch.

When Alan comes out of the bathroom with blood all over his face and the Blake posse with him, I swear I am ready to kill him. But he is *so* bloody. He's hurt. I start forward, but Mr. Everson gives me this look that tells me I'm not supposed to interfere.

"Aimee." There's a hand on my arm. Hayley's hand.

"What?"

"Are you okay?" Hayley's trying to shield me from the crowd.

"Disperse! Disperse, people!" Mr. Swanson and some other teachers are trying to settle us down.

"Yeah," I say, staring into her big brown eyes. "I'm okay."

She steadies me. "You're swaying."

"What?"

"You're swaying. Your hands are shaking." She steers me away from the cafeteria and down the wheelchair ramp toward the off-limits elevator. "You need to sit down, away from the idiots."

We park ourselves on the floor by the elevator. It's a nook, really; the only door is to the resource room and it's shut. The floor is cold on my legs. I lean my head against the wall. It's cold, too.

"I never knew Blake was such a racist," I babble. "And he's fighting, which is not like him, and . . . oh . . . They hit each other. I can't believe Alan hit him back."

"I think it was three on one," Hayley says, all hard and mean-sounding. And for a second she gets this crazy, blood-thirsty look on her face, but it fades away and her voice goes back to singsong sweet. "He had to."

"Three on one!" I cringe, thinking about the blood. "He's hurt. He's hurt and he's probably going to get suspended, and I can't do this . . . I can't do this alone. I can't . . ."

"Aimee. Do what?"

"Be here. Exist. Go to class. It's all messed up. Courtney. Blake. Alan. Everything." I lean forward and Hayley rubs my back. Her hand makes little circles. It's comforting. It's like something a mom would do. I sniff. "You are so nice."

She smiles at me complimenting her, just like Courtney would. If Courtney were here, she'd be the one comforting me right now. Hayley says, "Thanks. So are you."

"I don't feel nice right now."

"I swear nobody's being nice lately. It's like the whole town is having steroid rage."

For a second I want to tell her everything, about Courtney

192

and the rock and the painting and the tree house craziness. I want to tell her about my mom and Alan and possession, and how sometimes it's so hard being the only girl in a house full of men. Suddenly something sharp and painful stabs at the side of my head. My hand goes up to my temple. I can always make Benji's bumps and pains go away; I wish I could do it to myself.

"Aimee?"

Hayley's voice seems so far away. I try to focus on her.

"Aimee?" She says my name again. "Are you okay?"

"Yeah." I stand up. My head's still throbbing. "Yeah. I just figured out something I have to do."

Her face is a mess of worry. "You're white. You're still shaking."

"I'm good. I'm good, Hayley." I lean in, kiss her cheek. She smells like one of those Victoria's Secret garden scents. "Thank you for being such an awesome friend."

Mrs. Hessler meets me before I even get close to the restroom, which is an essential step in my plan. Her eyes are skittish, nervous. She touches my arm briefly and says, "I heard that Courtney's in the hospital and that Blake attacked her cousin."

I nod and wait. She's holding me back from what I have to do.

She pulls a book out of her bag. There's a bookmark stuck in it, and she opens to that page. "Read this."

I look around. "In the middle of the hall?"

"Please, Aimee."

She sort of hustles me over toward the wall. Leaning

193

against it, I start to read. It's an article written by Roslyn Strong that talks about dragon imagery in North America.

"Skip ahead to the story," Mrs. Hessler urges.

I do. The story is about a Wabanaki hero named Glooskap killing a dragon in Maine, or what would later be called Maine, right around here. The dragon dies.

"What are you trying to tell me, Mrs. Hessler?" I ask, handing her back the book.

"What if the dragon died in our river? What if Glooskap bound a European demon or dragon to our river after taking it out of a possessed settler? The Wabanaki knew of the continuing dangers, but the settlers, being arrogant, stayed, even though they were warned that the evil from the river ebbs and flows like the tide, affecting the entire town while the demon tries to take over a body."

"Like it's doing with Courtney," I whisper.

"And like it did with your mother. She was my best friend, you know, just like Courtney's yours." *She was?* How did I not remember that? Cloudy memories come back to me of Mrs. Hessler bringing over Christmas cookies, and she and my mother going out to dinner all dressed up. Mrs. Hessler wipes at her eyes, which have filled up with tears, and I pat her arm as she continues, "I found another story that says the demon is destined to remain here until it finds a vessel or is sent back to the darkness by a lion from the west."

Could that be Alan? "But why?" I ask.

"Why what?"

"What's this—demon—trying to accomplish? What makes him evil in the first place?" I watch people scurry to class.

"Native American legends rarely give a reason for their monsters acting the way they do. It's our culture, our modern culture actually, that tries to understand them." She clears her throat. "And my best guess is that a total possession of Courtney would allow him to transport himself out of the river, and he would be free to roam wherever he wants again, like he did before Glooskap bound him to the water."

A sadness grows inside me. "He tried to do this to my mom, too, and nobody saved her."

"She died trying to save all of us, Aimee. When she went to the river with that ax and drowned, she was trying to fight the demon, the River Man—or at least prevent him from fully possessing her."

"That was brave," I manage to say, even though my insides are clenching up with sorrow. I miss my mom. I miss her so much. Someone coughs down the hall.

"Yes, it was." Mrs. Hessler coughs, too, a tiny bark.

"Why didn't he move on then? Why not just go after another victim to possess?" I ask.

She shrugs. "I don't know. Maybe he only has enough power to focus on one at a time. It seems like his evil comes in spurts, separated by at least a decade."

I push away from the wall, give Mrs. Hessler back her book, and hug her in the process. She smells like vanilla, just like my mom. "Thank you."

I say that and then take off into the bathroom, back to my original mission, armed, finally, with a tiny bit of knowledge.

★ ★ ★

I pretend that I've thrown up. I'm pale enough that I look sick. I convince Ms. Murillo that Dad and Gramps are both unreachable this morning. It works. I am free to leave school. I triple lie and say I have a car outside, and I'll drive myself home.

If you cut through the woods it doesn't take long to get to the hospital. The cross-country trail in back of the school takes you half the distance, and then if you go across a blueberry barren you can hook into the Starbald Road and walk the rest of the way. So that's what I do. The trees are almost naked of leaves. Their branches are eerie, like bare, reaching fingers, gnarled and hungry. They remind me of the man in the river reaching, grabbing, pulling down. I stop for a second and listen. The wind rattles the trees.

Hauling out my cell, I debate whether to text Alan. I decide to.

HOPE U R OKAY.

I press SEND and pocket the cell, listening again. Everything scares me today. I know Alan's probably still getting chewed out in Everson's office. I know he probably won't even see the text. I also know that I didn't tell him what I'm doing. And I know he'll be mad.

Sometimes, though, you have to do it alone.

I race ahead a few yards and then think about it again. Court might have her cell. I text her: OK IF I COME SEE YOU NOW?

I walk forward and hope for a reply. My cell beeps, telling me I have a message. I open it and read: YES!!!! COME QUICK.

That's all it takes. I run.

The woods surround me for a mile. The path is full of

tread marks and rocks. Roots stick out from trees, but I've seen them all before. We run here for soccer about twice a week. Our coach calls them conditioning runs, and I've never been so happy about them as I am right now, because with every footstep the sky gets darker above me and the woods groan a little more with the wind, but hey, I'm conditioned, despite the bruises on my leg.

I bullet ahead. One foot. Another foot. Over and over again.

Just when I enter the rolling, treeless barrens, an eagle screeches above me. I look up and trip over a rock, but don't fall. I can't figure out what the eagle is trying to tell me, but I figure it's some kind of warning. He battles the wind with his massive wings, struggling to remain in the updrafts. He's trying to stay near me but can't quite do it.

The wind pushes against me, suddenly hard and deliberate. Some hair escapes my ponytail, thrashing into my face. A blueberry bush rips away from the dirt and crosses the tiny, narrow dirt trail in front of me. I avoid it, but just barely. Another one rips up and almost chases me down the trail. Dirt and twigs whisk around me, making it hard to see.

Suddenly this doesn't seem like such a good idea.

"Man!" For some reason, I don't swear. Swearing seems like it would give everything bad even more power.

I'm halfway between the high school and the hospital, almost to the road, when a rock hits me square in the spine, right below my backpack. I tumble forward. My backpack slops into my body. Pain ricochets through me. Another rock hits my calf. I scramble up as fast as I can, lurching onward.

I am almost to the road, but there's even less cover on the

road than there is here. Turning back into the woods seems crazy, though.

"You won't stop me!" I yell.

There's no noise, nothing except for the sound of the wind—but I can feel him laughing at me. Every single bone feels it. Every single neuron trembles with it. Fear builds up inside my stomach and tries to slow me down, dragging like the flu, getting dumped, failing a test, and having the ugliest zit on your nose all combined into one dense lump.

Courtney is more important than that.

I scramble forward. A bush sideswipes me. I fall, roll sideways, and hit the dirt road. My hands, scraped and bloody, push me up off the dirt. I sprint. There's a rumble in the distance, deep and loud. It reminds me of the tree house attack.

I stop and quickly search for shelter. There is none, just rolling blueberry barrens and the naked road. My heart staggers in my chest. My feet stagger on the road.

The debris storm is on the barrens. It's a mini-tornado of bushes, rocks, and branches from the forest. I think there's even a squirrel caught up in it, the poor thing. A wooden NO TRESPASSING sign swirls around. I run harder. There's no way I'm going to make it. It's three times as fast as I am. My bruised leg aches, but I run hard.

My breath comes out in sharp pants as I sprint forward. I glance behind me. That's when I realize that what I've been dealing with isn't even the real storm—that's about a hundred feet back. The sign swirls to the front. The screeching noise hurts my ears. It's fifty feet away now. There are nails in the sign. Thirty feet. I turn. I stand. I face it. Fifteen feet. I dive forward, wrapping my hands over my head. I curl into a ball, my back-pack sticking up.

It hits.

A nail rips into my pack, tearing a hole in the side. My whole body jerks. Dirt smashes into me. Something hard hits my arm. I can't open my eyes to see what it is. The sound of the storm roars through me. My whole body trembles. I scream. I know I scream. Dirt goes into my mouth. I clamp it closed. I start praying . . . I start praying to God and begging for my mother, for Alan, for anyone. Something barrels into my side. I roll and I'm face up now, on top of my backpack. Pebbles and rocks pelt me.

"God!" I scream it. "God help me! Mom! Mommy!"

Something scratches my face. I close my mouth again, trying to keep the dirt out. I manage to get on my side again, underneath most of the force of the wind and debris. The prayer my mom taught me when I was little soars through my head.

> O God, who made the heav'n and earth,
> From dreams this night protect me.
> Destroy each succubus at birth,
> No incubus infect me.

It doesn't seem appropriate, but I don't care. I turn back over so my face is to the ground.

No incubus infect me. No incubus infect me. No incubus infect me.

While I'm chanting this, my heart is screaming one name with every double beat it takes: *Al-an. Al-an. Al-an.*

There's some kind of noise, loud and bleating.

Through shielded eyes, I see movement that's not the wind. I can just make out a dump truck stopped beside me, right in the storm. I scramble toward it. The tires are massive and smell like horse poop, but I don't care. I yank myself up to the cab. Some paper flies out of my backpack and joins the whirl of wind. The door opens. A man shouts, "Hurry! Hurry!" He pulls me inside. While I'm sprawled on the seat he reaches right over me and yanks the door shut. The truck shudders from the smack of the wind. It reeks of Polo cologne and chew and right now I think those are the best smells in the entire universe.

The guy's voice shakes. "Holy crap, what is this?"

I sit up and stare out the windshield. Bushes and trees are flying by. Branches are smacking into us. Rocks are pelting the side of the truck. "Drive!" I shout.

He hesitates for just a second, then shifts into gear. I pull off my pack and inspect the damage. It's not too bad. My hands shake so badly that I can't fix my hair. I don't know why I try.

"What is this? A tornado?" the driver asks.

"I don't think so. We don't get tornados in Maine, do we?"

"I don't know . . ." He starts stuttering and loses whatever he was going to say. He's in his early twenties, with a short blond crew cut and a lot of stubble. His eyes are wide and scared. Both hands clutch the wheel. He's sweating and peeking over at me.

Something big and hard slams into the side of the truck. It shakes. We keep going.

He swears under his breath. "You okay? You're a mess. Holy . . . Holy . . ."

The truck swerves a bit from the force of the wind.

"We're almost through it," I say. I point ahead. "It's lighter up there."

"Hold on. I'm going to floor it." He does. We rush forward. We break through the swirling debris. He doesn't slow down. "I think I should take you to the hospital."

"Great. Good."

He swallows hard. I realize I'm clutching my pack. The sunlight seems so bright. It's crazy to be able to see clearly again. I touch my face. I'm bleeding. My leg aches. My back kills. I'm a total mess. I start, instinctively I guess, to work on my ponytail again. We're almost at the hospital.

"I don't know how you survived that," he says almost reverently.

"I stayed low." We bump off the dirt road and onto the pavement. "Wait." I suddenly think of it. "How did you see me? Why did you stop right there?"

We're in sight of the hospital. He pulls into the emergency room turnaround.

"No, seriously, why did you stop?" I ask. I touch his arm. He's still shaking. "You saved me."

"Do you think that storm's still out there?" he asks.

"I don't know."

He rolls the truck to a standstill and sets the brake. "You'll think I'm crazy."

"Please. I won't. I promise. What just happened *was* completely crazy."

He closes his eyes for a second, like he's remembering. "There was a woman standing there. She was glowing gold, almost." He glances over, to see if I think he's crazy,

201

I guess. I motion for him to go on. A muscle by his eyes twitches. "And I just knew that I had to stop, you know? I knew that someone needed help."

"Me." I swallow hard. "I needed help."

He nods. "So I stopped and I yelled. You didn't answer. I honked the horn. I couldn't go out there. I hope you don't—don't think I'm a coward, but I didn't know how I could—stuff was flying all around." He wipes at his face with his hands. "I'm not making sense."

"You are." I touch his arm quickly. "Thank you."

He turns his head to look at me. "You're a mess. Let me help you in."

"No," I try to object. "I'm okay, really."

He's already out of the truck and opens the door. He reaches for my hand.

"Thanks." I hop down. Everything aches and throbs. My mouth tastes like dirt. "I'm okay."

"You're not steady. I'll bring you inside," he says.

"No. I can do it," I insist. "Thank you, though. Thank you for finding me."

He nods vigorously and hands me my backpack, holding it so things don't fall out of the rip. "Glad I could help. You better go inside."

I hobble into the emergency room entrance, but don't go to Intake. Instead, I turn left and go up the corridor toward the elevator. There's only one hall for kids, on the top floor. I stagger into the elevator, which is happily empty, and press the CLOSE DOOR button, then the number 3.

I'm scared, but not horrible scared. I think Alan is right. I think every time the River Man does something big like this he gets tired. I think all magic (good or evil) depletes your energy, so he's weaker right now. So now is the perfect time for me to try to heal Courtney. He quickly recharges, though; my theory on that is he feeds on fear, on Courtney, on pain.

The elevator grinds to the third floor and stops. The doors open and Mary Harmon, a tall, red-haired nurse, is walking down the corridor in front of me. I slide out of the elevator and to the side just as she turns around to see who's coming. I'm hidden from view, which is what I want, because I know that if anyone sees me like this there'll be a lot of questions, and they *will* shove me back into the ER and call my dad. That can happen later. Right now I need to get to Court. I need to get there while the River Man is still weak.

The elevator doors slide closed. Mary's footsteps flip-flop away down the hall. I count to five and slip out behind her. She turns the corner in the hallway and I hurry, looking at the charts outside the doors, reading names, searching.

Finally, halfway down the hall—TUCKER, COURTNEY.

I slip through the doorway, grab the metal handle, and shut the door behind me.

Courtney is sitting up in the bed. She's not restrained, which is a super-good sign. She turns her head when the door shuts. "Aim?"

I smile at her. It's hard to do. Her face is still a mess. Her eyes are weak and tired, cloudy even. She looks so tiny beneath the thin white hospital blanket. "Courtney?"

Her eyebrows lift up a little bit. There's an IV line attached to her, but it looks pretty mild. I hope it's just fluids to keep her hydrated. She lifts up the hand without the IV line, but doesn't get it up very far.

I go to the bed. "How you doing, honey?"

She squints a little. "You called me 'honey.'"

I shrug. "I know. It's weird."

"My cousin must be wearing off on you." She forms the words slowly, like it's an effort.

"Probably." I drop my backpack on the floor. It makes a hard clanking noise. Court startles and then focuses on me.

"What happened to you?" she asks.

"A little mishap."

"Mishap?"

I take her free hand in mine. It's cold and still has sores. Mine's not much better: all cut up and dirty. We are not two glamour queens at the prom right now. For a second I wonder what Blake would say; then I ask, "How are you?"

"Amazing," she says, and softly laughs.

Tears peek out of the corners of her eyes and start to roll down her cheeks. I use my free hand to wipe them away.

"Alan and I are working on something, okay?" I tell her. "We won't let this keep happening to you, Courtney, I swear it."

"Very melodramatic, Aim."

"I mean it."

"I know you do." She closes her eyes, like it's all too much.

"Where's your mom?"

"Working."

I make sure nobody's lurking and whisper, "Do you know

how sometimes when you or Benji get scratched up, how I focus really hard and try to make you feel better?"

Her eyes open. "Yeah. Your dad said it was just the power of suggestion."

"I love my dad, but sometimes, he's a putz. It's like he's so afraid of what happened with my mom that he denies anything that even hints at the supernatural," I say. "Can I try it?"

She closes her eyes again, weak.

I panic for a second. "Court?"

Her hand tightens around mine. "Yeah. You can try."

The light above her bed flickers. In the dark, for just a second, I think I see the shape of a man. The light steadies out. There's nothing there. I loosen my grip on her hand and take some deep breaths.

"Does Alan know you're doing this?" she asks.

"Yeah," I lie. "He's just stuck at school."

"You're not?"

"Got an excuse." This time I close *my* eyes, spreading my fingers out just a little bit, and put one hand on top of Courtney's freezing forehead. I put the other over my own heart. I breathe in; I breathe out. The centers of my palms start to tingle in perfect circles. Power twirls there, I know it does. It's not freak power—it's my power. Mine. My fingers separate a little. I imagine white light, good white healing light enveloping Courtney.

"Heal, sweetie," I whisper. "Heal. Be safe."

The whiteness flows over her. I can feel it leave me, leave my hands, stretch out over her. She makes a funny chirping noise. I open my eyes. Her skin is clean. The sores are gone. Her eyes flutter open, meeting mine and widening in shock or fear. Her mouth moves to make a word, but I can't hear it.

Something inside my head stabs against my brain. The last thing I see is Courtney slowly, weakly reaching toward me, and then my knees buckle. I am gone, just gone.

· 18 ·
ALAN

"Alan, you go to the nurse while I deal with these three," Mr. Everson says as we near the front of the school. He looks to Mr. Burnham and says, "Pat, will you get a towel for Blake here?"

I go on to the nurse's station. She isn't there, so Ms. Murillo comes in and helps me find some hydrogen peroxide, cotton balls, and Band-Aids. There are a few cuts and some bruises already forming on my face, but it isn't as bad as I'd expected.

"You boys and your bumps and bruises." Ms. Murillo puts a butterfly bandage on the worst of my cuts, a shallow gash under my left eye, probably made by a ring.

"I'll be okay," I say. "I guess I better go see how long I'm kicked out of school."

She smiles at me in kind of a sad way as I leave her. Mr. Burnham stands guard over Blake and his cronies where they sit in plastic chairs against the wall outside Everson's office. Blake holds a towel over his face. I can see bloodstains on the white cloth. I guess the one shot I got was a good one.

"Come in here, Alan," Everson calls. I go into his office with all the Colorado Buffalo memorabilia. "Close the door and sit down." I do. "Tell me what happened."

I was in a stall. Should I say I was taking a crap? I decide to be honest. "I went to the bathroom to text my aunt and ask if my cousin was any better," I tell him. "Courtney is in the hospital because of what happened yesterday, you know."

"I know," he says. His eyes are intense, like he's going to pin me against the back of the chair if I lie to him. "Go on."

"I went to the bathroom so I wouldn't get caught with my phone out. I went in the stall, texted my aunt, and she texted back, so I was leaving. I didn't hear anybody come in. I opened the door and somebody hit me in the face. Then they were in there with me, just basically trying to beat the sh—I mean, beat the crap out of me."

"Looking at Blake's nose, I'd say they weren't the only ones punching."

"They had me against the wall," I argue. "I was off balance. I couldn't even stand up because I tripped over the toilet when they came in hitting me. I threw one punch and I guess I got lucky. Then Mr. Burnham was there and broke it up."

Everson glares at me for a long moment, and I just know he's going to call me a liar, say nothing like this ever happened until I came to the school, that I'm just a bad person, all kinds of stuff that means this is my fault. Instead, he says, "I'm inclined to believe you, Alan. Those three told me you started the fight, that they were already in the restroom when you came in, but

Mr. Burnham saw you go in first. He says they watched you and went in after you and that someone yelled there was a fight right after that."

I nod. I'm not sure what to say. "Thanks."

"It doesn't get you off the hook," Everson says. "We have a zero-tolerance policy on fighting. You threw a punch. That makes it a fight."

"I understand."

"It's an automatic three-day suspension."

I can't say anything. I can only think about how disappointed Mom's going to be. Not to mention Aimee. Her face when I came out of the bathroom . . . shock, disappointment, maybe anger.

"You're living with your mother and aunt, right?" Everson asks.

I nod. "Yes, sir."

"How about your dad?"

I look up and find the determination to return his stare.

"I've never met him." Just saying this makes my stomach hollow out even more.

"Your mom's going to be upset about this?"

"Oh yeah. She will. I promised I wouldn't fight. But I had to. They had me cornered in that stall."

"Well, let's call her. What's the number?"

The conversation is painful, and after a minute they agree I'm suspended for three days and can drive myself home.

"I think we're done here, Miss Parson." Everson punches a button on his phone and Mom is gone. "You've got a good mother there," he says.

"Yeah. I know," I say.

He scrawls on some papers and hands them to me. "Bring these to me when you come back." I take the papers and stand to leave. "Alan, try to stay away from Blake. I've known him since he was a freshman. He's not a bad kid. All this is kind of a surprise to me. Maybe he just needs some time to get used to the idea of having someone faster than him, and getting over Aimee. Don't go looking for trouble, okay?"

"I won't," I say. There's already enough trouble to go around without having to hunt down some stringy cross-country runner to fight. Everson nods and I leave his office. Burnham and the other three guys are gone.

I halfway expect Blake to jump me on the way to my truck, but there's no one to be seen. Off to the south, though, the sky is dark, like there's a storm moving in.

In my truck I check the messages on my phone. There are two. The first is from Aimee: HOPE U R OKAY. I write back, I'M OK. SUSPENDED. PICK YOU UP AFTER SCHOOL.

The second message is from Mom. GO STRAIT HOME. Mom isn't the world's best speller, especially in texts.

It's early. Mom won't be home until late, and there are things I need to buy. I head for home to get some cash out of the metal box I keep in a drawer of my dresser. With a couple hundred dollars in my pocket, I drive to the Craft Barn on the outskirts of town.

"Yes, we have sweetgrass and sage," the middle-aged woman tells me. The store isn't huge, but I'd been walking around it for at least fifteen minutes without finding anything but baskets and candles. She leads me around a few corners to a little back room that's got some dried plants. "Here's the sweetgrass. Now, we don't have a lot of it because it's native and so easy to find growing wild. You're new around here, aren't you?"

"Yes, ma'am," I answer.

"Thought so. Lots of people have this growing right in their backyards and they just mow it down like a common weed. Can you believe it?"

"Some people just don't appreciate nature," I say.

"The sage," she says, beaming with approval as she moves up the aisle a little and waves toward a section filled with dried sage, "is another story. We have lots of it. People love it in their potpourri, and it's harder to come by in the woods."

"Thanks," I say. "Is there any chance you sell granite rocks? The kind you'd put in a lawn display? Not huge, just about this big?" Using my hands I make a circle that's somewhere between the size of a softball and a bowling ball.

"No, nothing like that," she says. "You'll probably have to try Bergerman's for that. Do you know where that is?"

I shake my head, so she gives me directions. I thank her and she leaves me.

I grab a dozen bundles of both sweetgrass and sage, then find a roll of heavy brown twine and head for the checkout. Purchases made, I follow my directions and find Bergerman's Lumber, which isn't half the size of a Lowe's or Home Depot, but is surprisingly well stocked. A guy in an orange vest takes me outside and shows me pallets of granite in various sizes and shapes. I put seven stones in a cart. Each stone is about the size of a football, and they make the cart really heavy.

Back inside the store I find the tarps and pick out a heavy

canvas one. Aimee suggested sailcloth, but I don't know where to get that without her, so this will have to do. I also pick up a small tree saw and a good hunting knife. I'm in the checkout line when my phone vibrates in my pocket. I don't check the text message until I get all my purchases into the bed of my truck.

CAN U COME 2 HOSPITAL? It's Aimee. Why is she out of school? I write back: B THERE SOON.

Something's up. I jump into the truck and take off as fast as I dare. No way I'm going to follow my suspension and disobeying Mom's order to go "strait" home with a speeding ticket.

From the hospital parking lot I text Aimee: WHERE R U? She immediately responds by calling me.

"Alan, are you here?" she asks.

"I'm in the parking lot."

"Come to the top floor. Room 312."

I come face-to-face with a wide-hipped, severe-looking nurse as soon as I step out of the elevator. "Can I help you?" she demands.

"I'm looking for 312."

"Just down the hall." She watches me as I make my way past the nurse's station, like maybe I'm going to steal a pen or peek at a computer screen or something. As I walk, I reach up and run my fingers through my hair, like I'm combing it out. That always gets to the older, conservative types who don't like long-haired guys. Behind me, I hear the nurse grunt and stomp off in the other direction.

That's when Aimee steps out of a room ahead of me and waves me closer. She does not look right. I only get a quick glance before she ducks back in. I pick up the pace and push through the door and into the room.

"Alan!" She lunges at me as soon as I'm in, throwing her arms around me and hanging on like she's drowning. I hug her back, then grimace.

"You smell like dirt, Red. What's going on?"

She looks up at me and I see the pain, fear, and exhaustion in her face. And the dirt under her eyes, the scratches on her cheeks and forehead. A tear leaks out of the corner of her left eye and leaves a trail through a coat of grime as it runs down her cheek.

"What?" I ask. I hold her at arm's length and look her over. Her clothes are filthy, with small tears and bits of sticks and grass and leaves stuck to her. "Aimee, what happened?"

"He attacked me," she says, then she breaks down for real, pushing her way back into my arms. While I rub her back and stroke her hair she tells me about the attack and her rescue by a dump-truck driver. "He saw a golden woman in the road who made him stop."

"What?" This is all too much. I don't know what to think. "What do you mean?"

For the first time I take note of Courtney, sitting up in a bed across the room. She's trying to act like she's not watching us, but she so is.

"What do you mean, Aimee? A golden woman?"

"It was my *mom*. She made the driver stop. At least, that's what I think. I didn't see her. He did, which means all of this is real. We aren't delusional."

"We already knew that." I hug her and rub her back some

213

more and think about it. "Sounds like we have some help, then."

"Mmm-hmm," she breathes against my chest.

Courtney has waited long enough. "Hello? I'm the one in the hospital. Is anyone going to pay attention to me?"

I laugh and hug Aimee tighter, bending to whisper in her ear. "You okay?"

"Been better," she says.

We walk toward Courtney. Aimee is just sort of hanging on my side and I know it's more than her being glad to see me. I gently push her so that she has to sit on the bed, even though she's dirty. I look around, then pull up the room's only chair and sit facing them.

"Your face," I say to Courtney. "It's cleared up."

"Aimee did it," she says, smiling at her friend. I look to Aimee for an explanation and she nods.

"Yeah. I can do that."

"Do what?"

"Heal things." She shrugs it off like it's no big deal.

"She does it all the time," Courtney says. "She did what the doctors here couldn't do." She gives Aimee a worried look, then adds, "Not that they didn't try. I know they did, but they're not made of awesome like you are, Aim."

"They're just not equipped to cure you, Court," I say. It's time to just blurt it out. She has to be on board with it or this thing won't work.

"Tell me," Courtney says.

"You have what the Navajo call Ghost Sickness," I tell her. "It's, well . . . it's like demonic possession. An evil spirit—"

214

"You mean like in the horror movies?" Courtney interrupts.

"Yeah, like that. All the stages are there. Except the last one, and I—we—think it's happening."

"What is it?" she asks.

"Total possession. He—this thing—has taken possession of you already, but he isn't strong enough to stay yet. He takes you for a while, then gets weak, or distracted or whatever, and leaves. That's when you collapse."

Aimee says, "That's just what I was thinking."

Courtney is nodding, but her face shows her fear. "What if he gets stronger?"

"He'll take over your body and won't leave," I say. "Not until . . ."

"I'm dead," she whispers. She pulls her knees up and presses her forehead against them. Aimee, sweet Aimee, leans into her and hugs Courtney as best she can.

"It's going to be okay," Aimee promises. "Alan knows how to fight it. We'll make it leave you alone."

"I just wanted my dad back," Courtney says without lifting her head. Her voice is muffled against the blankets covering her legs. "He said he could bring Dad back to me."

"Who is he, Court?" I ask. "Did he tell you his name?"

"River Man," she whispers, as if saying it will bring him, and maybe it will. Aimee and I both look out the window, then at each other. I shake my head.

"Is that the only name he told you?" I ask.

Courtney moves her head against her knees, indicating "yes."

"Alan and I—we will get rid of him," Aimee promises

215

again, but she's looking at me. I try to smile at her, to reassure her, but I know it's a weak smile at best.

"We'll take care of it. But it's going to take all three of us." I put my hand on the back of her head and add, "You have to want to get rid of this spirit, Court. Do you want that? It means that you have to give up trying to get your dad back, give up for real."

She raises her head and we can see that her face is streaked with tears. I can't help but be amazed at how healthy and clear her skin looks. Aimee really did that? "Yes," she says. "I want it to go away. I want to be normal again."

I get out of my chair and go to the bathroom to get a cool, wet washcloth. Aimee sits still and lets me dab at the cuts and wipe away the dirt on her face. The cold water seems to do her some good.

"What do we do next?" she asks.

"Build the sweat lodge," I say, then look at Courtney. "Have they said anything about when you're going home?" She shakes her head, so I look to Aimee, who shakes her head, too. "What are they gonna do when they see her face all healed up?"

"I'm not sure," Aimee says. "My dad will suspect I was up here."

"Will he let her go home?"

"It's up to her doctor."

We plan. It's obvious that the River Man is getting stronger, more active. I explain about the sweat lodge and Aimee tells us about all the new information Mrs. Hessler gave her.

"This is bigger than us, isn't it?" Courtney asks.

"That doesn't mean we can't beat it," Aimee says, grabbing

Courtney's hand and squeezing it. "It doesn't mean we won't win."

Getting out of the hospital is much easier than expected. The hallway outside Courtney's room is deserted, and Aimee seems to know just when to round a corner and scuttle toward an elevator or door. We make it to the parking lot without anyone recognizing her, which amazes me, considering the first time we were there.

Aimee is visibly worried as we cross the open area from the hospital to my truck. Her eyes keep darting around as if expecting the tornado to come after us again, but I assure her that the River Man's probably weakened after the big dirt storm. Nothing happens, and we're soon safely in the cab of my old Ford. I wish she'd snuggle up close to me and I could throw my arm around her once the engine's started, like a normal guy would with a normal girl.

"You're really okay?" she asks.

"I'm fine. I'm more worried about you."

"I'm okay. I want to help with the sweat lodge."

I smile.

"What?" she demands.

"The best way to do the sweat lodge is to go in it naked."

"Completely?"

"Yep." I wait, and she doesn't say anything. "You still in?"

"Um . . . We'll see. Maybe I'll just stand guard outside."

I laugh and drop the truck into drive.

"You want me to show you the place in the woods now?" Aimee asks. "The one for the sweat lodge?"

"Not today. I don't want to irritate Mom any more than I have. Everson was actually pretty cool. He told her he believed I was just defending myself. Maybe she won't be too mad."

"I hope not. Maybe it would distract her if I came over?"

"That might work," I agree. "She asked about meeting you. How about if you come over after dinner to help with my homework?"

"You're not going to invite me for dinner?"

"Fasting," I remind her. "Plus, Mom and Aunt Lisa are working late, so it's not like we'll be having a real family dinner, especially while Courtney is in the hospital. About seven thirty? If Mom doesn't ground me, I'll come get you."

"Deal."

"In the meantime, promise me you'll get some sleep."

"Rest? In the middle of the day, with Benji coming home in less than an hour?" She laughs. "For you, I promise."

· 19 ·
AIMEE

Nobody is home yet, which is such a good thing. I clean up as best I can, but I'm still scratched and bruised. I flop on the bed to rest because I'm pretty darned drained from healing Courtney, but I can't get my mind to calm down. I need a cover story, and I can't even think of one. How do you tell your grandfather and little brother that you were attacked by a demonic dust storm? They'd think I was insane.

Even though I'm freaked about everything, I feel lighter, steadier, because Courtney's face is clean of sores and Alan's got a plan, and I—me—Aimee Avery—used my freaky healing hands to help someone.

The place I do the best figuring is in the kayak on the river. I smile. It's perfect. I'll figure out how to stop him by going on his territory. He's weak now, and the river isn't just *his* territory—it's mine, too. I want it back.

Plus, it has the added bonus of Gramps and Benji not

seeing my scratched-up self right away. I pull on a bra, T-shirt, and fleece. I grab a cotton knit hat, which does not make me look too hot, but it does keep my ears warm.

What I can't figure out is the link between Courtney, my mom, and the guy in the river. I can understand that there's this history of death here. I can understand and even believe that some sort of evil is killing people, but I don't understand the logic of it. What makes it happen when it happens?

I double-check my PFD. All the buckles are good. The river is smooth and calm, and for a second I don't push with my paddles, just letting the tide take me where it wants to. A crow flies across the bow. Its wings break the air. It lands on a branch and watches me.

"What do you think?" I ask. "Why us?"

He squawks out an answer, but I don't understand it. Of course I don't. Instead, I put my paddle in the water and pull myself out of the current, choosing my own course. I decide to move up the river, toward town.

When I first hear the yelling, I think he's a seal.

My eyes don't work right in the afternoon sun. Light hits the water at an angle that makes everything shadowed. That's my excuse. That's why I think he's a seal. But the thing is, seals don't talk.

Still, I just stare for a second, no longer paddling, and my messed-up head thinks, *Seal*.

The guy's head pokes up from the river water just long enough for him to spit and scream at me, "My buddy! I lost my buddy!"

He dives back under again.

For a second (that's all, I swear), I wish I hadn't gone upriver. For a second, I wish I'd paddled out to the bay. Then I remember my dream: the overturned canoe, being below the water, breath gone. My stomach drops into the bottom of the kayak.

I blow my emergency whistle and paddle my kayak faster, looking up and down the river for other boats. Nothing. No, delete that—there is something, an upside-down blue canoe, spinning in an eddy. I stare at it and swallow, paddling even harder. The water where the boy dove under is choppy from his splashing. He's barely submerged at all.

His head pops up again, wet and oozy from the tidal water. He slams his hands against the top of the water. He looks at me. I'm maybe twenty feet away. It's early October, in Maine. The river water is colder than an icy shower.

"Don't dive!" I yell. I don't know why I expect him to listen.

He splashes his arms frantically. He's lost it. The guy has completely lost it. "My buddy! We gotta get him!" He dives again, a shallow dive, a nothing dive.

I put everything I have into pushing my kayak across the water, fast, digging the paddles into the cold. Water splashes me, tastes like salt. An eagle watches from a tree on the point. I wish he could come down and help.

The boy struggles just below the water's surface to the right of my kayak, swimming without reason, twisting his torso, slowly. He surfaces again and stares at me with wild eyes. His lips are blue. I recognize him. Noah Chandler, one of the guys who pummeled Alan.

"I lost him." He spits water. He flails around.

221

My heart leaps into my chest. Someone else is in the water. Like my dream. My fault. I didn't warn anyone. I was too busy worrying about Alan and Courtney to worry about my dreams.

I look around, trying to push the panic back into my stomach where it belongs. "What happened?"

"My buddy!" He starts to dive again, but I let go of my paddle and catch him by the shirt. I'm a pretty strong girl, but I won't be able to hold Noah for too long, even though he is weak from fear and being in the water. Adrenaline has run out and left him. He's in the river, and it's not just the cold that might get him. Old-fashioned newspaper headlines flash in front of my eyes, details of deaths, men with scratches around their wrists, bodies dismembered.

"You've got to get out of the water!" I tell him, barely hanging on. "Now. You have to get to shore."

I point my paddle toward the river grass and mud flats, a good fifty feet away.

He grabs the kayak near the bow, rocking it. I lean the other way to keep from going over. "Grab with both arms. I'll take you in, then look for your friend."

He doesn't move, but his eyes fill with hate. He stares at me. I am turning frantic now, too. I have to find the other boy. The eagle spreads its wings, swoops above us, and then down the river. Seconds pass. Time wasted when the person underneath the water might be dying. Noah doesn't say anything, but his arms wrap around my bow and I paddle in to shore.

He crawls onto the land. He doesn't shiver. He is past shivering. His jeans and shirt are wet and drag him down. I pull off my life jacket and my fleece and give the fleece to him.

"You need to stay warm," I say. I yank the emergency blanket out of the wet bag my dad stores in the kayak. I throw it over him.

He doesn't look up. He puts his head in his hands, hiding, and his voice comes out in a croak, "My buddy . . ."

"I'm going to call for help." I do it as fast as I can. I have to get back on the water and look for the other guy. I call 911 on my ugly little cell phone and tell them where we are, then smash back into my life jacket, zipping it up, thanking God for my dad always insisting on being prepared, bringing a cell phone, bringing a whistle. I look at the boy. He *was* Noah Chandler: my age, hanging out with Blake, beating up Alan, and being a certified tool, but now I can only think of him as a boy. He is sobbing, sobbing. The sky above us is cloudless and beautiful.

"I've got to go back out there. I gotta get my buddy," he mumbles, shaking his head, trying to stand up, but unable to make it. His lips shake.

I put my hand on his chest to make him stay put, and the wetness of it chills my hand. Then I hop into the kayak. "I'll go. You stay here. Help is coming."

I have to use the paddle to push off the muck. I turn the kayak back into the river and I look and look, but the water is not clear. It's muddy and I can't see far. Eel grass covers some of the river bottom. Old lumber from logging and shipbuilding obscures other parts.

I blow my whistle. That will help them find us, although nobody really uses the river in October. Still, I called 911. The Coast Guard will come with divers. The harbormaster will come down the river from Ellsworth. They will all come to rescue the boy, but I know, just like his friend knows: he is already gone. The river took him. The river took my mother. No, not the river, the man from the river, the man of the river, him.

"Help!" I yell.

Yelling is no good.

I blow the whistle again—long, short, long. I don't know if this is the SOS signal, but it's the best I can do. The eagle returns, landing in a tall tree on the opposite shore. The wind picks up. I blow my whistle again. My hands are wet and cold, almost numb, but I keep paddling, searching beneath the surface. On the shore, Noah Chandler rocks back and forth. Out in the water, a seal nudges his head up and looks at me. I look at him. His eyes are big and brown and sad. He looks at me. I look at him. There is no point in searching, he tells me. There is no point at all. We both look away.

I crisscross the area over and over again, whistling loud and shrill spurts for rescuers to hear. The eagle watches. Noah shudders on the shore, and I keep making kayak passes, back and forth, back and forth, until the harbormaster comes, and then I do it with him. He drives so slow, his fishing boat barely makes a wake. Every so often he looks at me, and I look at him. Just like the seal. He shakes his head.

Nothing.

I call my dad. I want to tell him where I am. I get Doris. He is in a meeting, but she'll tell him. I call home. Could Gramps or Benji answer the damn phone? My heart plummets, my muscles shake, and I'm not sure if it's because of the cold, or because I'm tired, or because I'm scared. I leave a message.

"Hey, Gramps. Um. It's me. I'm out on the river. There's been an accident. I found a boy in the water. The other one's still missing . . . I'm going to be late for dinner . . . But, um, don't worry, the police are—"

BEEeeeppp.

The answering machine cuts me off. Our answering machine does not like long messages. Neither does my dad.

The Goffstown police arrive. They had to get a fireman to launch his private boat so that they could get down the river. They ask me questions. Well, just one of them, the tall one from Florida, Sgt. Farrar.

"Now, sweetheart," he says, leaning over the side of the boat while I float next to it, holding on to the gunnels so the tide doesn't take me away. "I'm gonna have to ask ya more questions later, but can you tell me real quick what's happened?"

And I tell him.

"Do you know either of these boys?"

I shake my head, which is kind of lying. "I don't even know who the other boy is. I didn't ask his name."

But I *do* know who he is. He's Chris Paquette, the other guy who beat on Alan with Blake. It has to be.

"Ever met the other one? Noah? See him at school? At the skate park?"

The skate park? I reposition my fingers; they are stiff and blue, like dead things. I look up at the officer, and when I do I see past him to the never-ending sky.

"Yeah. I mean I know Noah. He's friends with my ex-boyfriend. He's on cross-country." My voice shakes.

Noah's still huddled there on the shore, alone. No one is taking care of him, and he looks so cold. I had the dream because I was supposed to protect him. I was supposed to protect both of them. I did a horrible job; a horrible, horrible job.

My dad comes at the same time as the Coast Guard. Our red tandem kayak plows around a curve in the river. I've never seen him paddle so fast. His paddles smash through the water, each stroke pulling him closer to me.

Normally, he paddles slowly, stops, watches for eagles, for seals, tries to understand the currents. I tease him that he's not getting much of a workout, and he always says something corny like, "Not all workouts are for the body. Some are for the soul."

It is so good to see him. He zips his kayak right next to mine and leans over, grabbing at my arm and whispering, "Oh, honey . . ."

The Coast Guard takes over. They make a grid pattern using sonar equipment. Then they start diving. That frees up the police department to talk to Noah. He looks skinny and pale, rocking back and forth on the shore between the big men in their yellow firefighting coats. They load him into the boat and take off for the town pier.

The shore seems empty, just tree after tree standing tall and crooked, bearing witness while my dad and I decide to search downriver, away from the Coast Guard.

"Maybe he's on the shore somewhere," I say, even though I know better. "Maybe he's just exhausted and on the shore."

My dad nods. He gives me sad eyes. We both know that I'm making things up, just believing what I want to believe and not what my gut rumbles at me. We glide, letting the river take us. "We'll follow the current the way it would have taken him," Dad says, pushing his baseball cap over his head.

"Would that work?" I ask. "Is the current the same on the top of the river and the underneath part?"

He scrubs a hand across his face and rubs at his cheeks. "Usually."

The river takes us away. It takes us far, and quickly. The river is tidal. Its movements can be swift and deep.

Swallowing, I adjust my grip on the paddles and say, "I think things are really, really messed up."

One of his hands leaves his paddle and he leans over to grab the side of my kayak, hanging on to me so that neither of us floats away from the other. "Because?"

"People are dying on the river."

He repeats it. "People are dying on the river."

"It's—" I start to explain.

"I know what you're saying," he interrupts. "But I think you're leaping to conclusions here, Aimee."

"I know you don't want to believe it's true, but Dad, Mrs. Hessler showed me all these newspaper articles, and there've been all these weird deaths on this river over and over again. Maybe this whole place is cursed or something."

He lets go of my kayak and says, "I love you, Aimee. I just want what's best for you, but sometimes, it's so hard."

I nod. The current ripples the water, moving it one direction, then another.

Finally he says, "Do you still have those dreams?"

"Yeah." My voice is super quiet, so quiet he might not even hear it, but he knows what I've said.

"Did you dream this?"

227

"I don't know. I think so. It's why I don't want to sleep—that, and I can't . . . I can't sleep 'cause I'm so nerved up by everything that's happening—the footsteps, Courtney, the . . . everything. I just don't want to get as bad as Mom was, you know? I don't want . . ." Something inside me breaks again, but not totally. One sob makes its way out, and my dad hurries his kayak toward me, slamming it into the side of mine. He reaches out and grabs me, holding on hard. Tears wash his face.

"I won't lose you, too, Aimee." He squeezes out the words. "I won't let you go."

"You won't," I say, then I repeat it. "You won't."

We cling to each other, aching inside with fear and love and loss for my mom. But we still have each other. We are alive and breathing and we love each other, and that has to be enough.

After a moment, we break apart. I reach out and wipe the tears off his craggy face and we start searching again, and the kayak feels lighter, like I suddenly weigh less, like I can suddenly move through the water.

I think of the river as brown, but that's not totally true. The river changes color. Sometimes it's brown like its muddy bottom, sometimes it's blue like the sky. Sometimes it's both, brown beneath but blue on the surface, and that's the way it is when I start paddling, turning my kayak sideways, trying to keep it in place, a horrible sadness pressing down on my chest as I stare into the water.

"Daddy!" I yell, and he looks at me, stunned, maybe because I have stopped, or maybe because I am suddenly using a name I haven't used since Mom left us and "Daddy" didn't sound right anymore.

"Daddy!" I give a few quick paddles, trying to maintain position on top of the water when the currents try to pull me another way. "Chris—he's here."

He stares. He brings his kayak over to mine and peers into the water. He can't see anything. "How do you know?" The muscles in his shoulders tighten. "Do you see him?"

"No," I say, "but he's here."

He adjusts his hat, squinting his eyes at me. "How do you know, sweetie?"

What do I say? I close my eyes so I don't have to look at my dad's face. "I don't know. I can feel him."

"Feel him?"

"It sounds stupid. I know it sounds stupid, but can you just believe me for a second?"

He nods. He believes. He pulls out his cell phone and calls a number. He uses his hospital CEO voice. Whatever he says works. My dad gets the Coast Guard. I don't know how he makes them listen, but he's good at things like that. He can talk people into things, my dad. That's his gift.

"I love you," my dad says after he hangs up. "You know that, Aimee, right? You know that I love you and your grandfather loves you and Benji loves you."

I dip my paddle into the water. The current ripples around it, separating, then coming back together. I nod.

"We'll get through this, pumpkin," he says.

"That's what Alan said."

"He's right. We will."

I nod. The Coast Guard boat engine sounds closer. "I love you, too."

* ★ ★

229

The Coast Guard pulls the dead boy out of the water. It takes two divers. When they haul the boy up, my father and I watch from our kayaks. My dad holds us together, gripping my kayak's bow with his big hands.

When they bring the boy out, I start to shake. His arm is missing. So is his leg. My dad takes his arm off my kayak and grabs me by the shoulders. He pulls me to him in an awkward kayak hug, and somehow manages to not tip us both over.

Our life jackets bump together, which prevents good body contact. I can smell him though, an indescribable fatherly scent. For a moment, that's all I smell. I smell him more than the salt of the river, more than the crisp ache of death, more than the ripeness of mussels ready to be plucked from the mud. The eagle flies overhead and cries to us, a loud squawk.

The Coast Guard boat motors over and a guy says, "Young lady? Ms. Avery? Can you identify the body?"

My father keeps his arm around me, but I can feel the tension in his biceps, how they tighten. My father moves his neck and says, "Surely someone else can do this."

The Coast Guard man says, "It would make things easier. We don't know what shape the other boy is in. He hasn't even told us who this is. And it looks like there might be some dangerous marine life involved."

"Marine life? How?" my dad's voice powers out.

"There are long slash marks around his wrist," the man says. "Appendages are missing."

"We don't have sharks here," I say.

"Not only sharks can do this," Coast Guard Man agrees. His face shows how upset he is. His muscles are all so tense.

The skin below his eye twitches. All his rugged handsomeness has turned into fright.

I pull my head away from my father's T-shirt and open my eyes. I swallow air that tastes like gasoline from the boat, not like my river. Where has my river gone?

The Coast Guard man stares at me. I know him. He's married to the lady at Finn's, the nice waitress, the one everyone calls Cookie, who winks at everyone and gives you chocolate chip cookies when no one in charge is looking.

His mouth moves, but I don't really hear him because everything seems muffled somehow, like my ears are full of water. His mouth moves again. I think what he says is, "Aimee . . . please?"

His eyes are sad, too—another man with sad seal eyes. Water collects in them, but it hasn't moved past the borders and down the cheeks.

"Okay," I say.

The boy's name was Chris Paquette.

His shirt is gone. Maybe the river ripped it away and took it out to the ocean with the tide. His skin is pale, pale like all Maine boys' skin is until August, when the sun finally gets through to them. His lips are blue. The ends of his left-hand fingers are blue. Tiny hairs spread across the middle of his chest like eel grass. His blond hair is darkened by the water. A yellow thermal emergency blanket covers his bottom half. But it's the large gashes—five of them around the remaining wrist—that kill me. The gashes are so deep.

I swallow again and try to speak, but I don't have to.

"That's Chris Paquette," says a voice, and I realize it's my dad. "He's a junior at the high school. He lives on Pioneer Farm Way. His mother works for me at the hospital. She's a nurse. This will kill her. That boy was her world."

"It's a hard thing," Coast Guard Man says.

My dad straightens up because he's finished with this. "I'm taking my daughter home now."

Coast Guard Man nods. "The reporters might be calling. The police definitely will. Your daughter's a hero, Mr. Avery. We could've lost two boys today."

My father nods back, and for a second I imagine they are both bobblehead dolls on a car's dashboard, nodding, nodding, nodding away.

"She's a good girl," Dad says.

He does not say I'm a wimp, but it would be truer. *A good girl, but a little cowardly*, is what he should have said. *She has dreams, you know; sometimes they come true. People think she might be crazy like her mother.*

My dad and I paddle home together past the shores of the Union River, where there are still more trees than houses.

"Are you mad at Mom?" I ask.

"Sometimes," he says. We move across the water. "Mostly I just miss her."

"Me, too." I stop paddling for a second to get some hair out of my face. "Do you think you could hang out at home a little more? We kind of need you."

"I promise I will, Aimee, and I am sorry that work keeps me so busy . . . I . . . I love you all so much, and this . . . this

232

craziness that's going on . . . it reminds me of what happened just before your mother left us, and it scares me. I hate to say it, but it scares me, and denial and false blame isn't going to make it go away. I am sorry I did that to you," he says, his paddle slicing the water. I start to tell him it's okay, but he raises a hand to stop me and instead says, "The boys will be waiting for us."

We paddle some more; we're almost home, but I'm really slowing down. I'm so tired, and my head is so full, and my stomach feels like it's full of river water—murky, salty. Every time I take a breath I think of Chris Paquette's body. Every time I stop listening to my heartbeat, I hear Noah Chandler shouting, "My buddy! My buddy!"

"Do you think they were drunk?" I ask my dad.

"Maybe. Maybe drugs." He turns his kayak into a current that carries him faster than me. I follow. "It's such a calm river this afternoon. I don't see why they'd capsize."

We have a floating dock. When you walk on it, it sways with your weight. Sometimes when a big boat powers by, it makes a wake that bumps the dock all around. You have to try hard to stay balanced. It would be easy to wind up in the water; one misstep, that's all it takes. There are a lot of things swimming under the water, but that's not where I look right now. I look up, toward the eagle, toward the sky. I don't know why the eagle reminds me of my mother. Usually it's the seals that make me think of her.

My mother used to write little notes in my lunch box. She'd draw pictures of cats and dogs, cartoon mice and birds on scrap pieces of watercolor paper. She'd color them in with

233

watercolor pencils and write things like: *Have a happy Tuesday! I can't wait to pick you up from school and give my good girl a great big hug. XXXOOO Love, Mommy.*

I saved every single one of those notes in the first Harry Potter book. If you open the book, they flutter out of the pages like wishes falling all over the floor.

The first thing I do when we get back is head up to my bedroom. I find that Harry Potter book in my bookcase, tucked between *Buried* and *Looking for Alaska*. I open it up. All the lunch box notes are on the same type of paper, a lightweight watercolor paper. But there's one note in there that's on yellow lined paper, like from a legal pad. It's always been in there; I just never got it out before. I always thought it was some of her insane ramblings. I never understood what it meant. Now I think I might.

It flutters out. I unfold it.

Aimee, I am trying to stop him. It might not work. But I have to try, honey. I have to make him stop haunting us all. Your father can barely sleep anymore because of my dreams, and I know . . . I know you have them, too. Know I love you, that I'll always love you, no matter what. XOXOX to infinity and forever. Love, Mommy.

My lips fold up and in. I say out loud, like she's here sitting on the braided rug right next to me, "An ax was an incredibly stupid idea. You cannot kill a ghost thing with an ax. And he dismembers people. What were you thinking?"

I can almost hear her soft whispery voice say, "I don't know."

I shake it off, stand up, and look out my window. A Coast Guard cutter is chugging up the river, going slow but leaving a monster wake.

Benji bursts into my room. His eyes are wide. "Aimee, are

you okay? I heard you found a dead guy." He throws himself across the room and into my arms, toppling me back into the bookcase. "You better not do anything stupid."

"What are you talking about, Benji?"

He shrugs.

"Don't do anything stupid," I repeat. "Sometimes you sound just like Gramps."

I muck up his hair.

"Gramps is right sometimes," he says.

"True," I admit, tucking the yellow paper into the pocket of my fleece.

He puts his hands on his hips and eyes me like he's some eighty-seven-year-old man. "So, you aren't going to do something stupid, are you?"

"Why do you think that, Benji?"

He squints. "Because I'm brilliant, that's why."

· 20 ·

ALAN

The smell of sage fills my room. It's just the incense. I'm saving the bundles I bought at Craft Barn for the actual ceremony. Now I'm sitting cross-legged on a rug on my floor, a smoking incense burner on either side of me, and my face is painted with black and red Halloween makeup. I'm wearing only a pair of shorts and my medicine bag.

The rug, about four feet square, is an off-white color with a black medicine wheel on it. It is the wheel of life, outlined simply in black—a circle divided into quarters with thick lines indicating the four directions. I sit in the center, facing North. The North quarter of the wheel is white; East is yellow; West is black; South is red. I do not fully understand the wheel, but I know that each direction represents a different phase of life. Since my vision quest, I have begun facing North during meditation. This is the direction of adulthood.

On a shelf above my bed, a small stereo plays a Yeibichei

song. It's on repeat so the song will not stop. The chant, recorded in the 1930s, rises and falls, rises and falls, playing a repetitive, melodic sound.

I've painted my face with an arrow pointing up from my chin, around my nose, and between my eyes, its tip aimed toward the sky. It symbolizes my conscious thought rising up from my body. Small cougar tracks—not drawn very well—mark Onawa's path from my hairline down my left cheek and neck to my chest, ending over my heart.

I hope Onawa will come to me.

Rolled in a sock in the back of a dresser drawer is a plastic bag with a few dried pieces of peyote. I was tempted to use it, just a tiny piece under my tongue, but even a small piece can produce a psychoactive response for several hours. I'm already suspended from school. No way I can let Mom come home and find me "stoned" on my "Indian drugs." The incense, music, and symbols will be enough.

Hands folded in my lap, I close my eyes and try very hard to clear my mind. It isn't an easy thing to do. Aimee keeps creeping in. Her smile, her red hair, her emerald-green eyes. Then I think of the scratches on her perfect skin, the dirt caked under her eyes, and the horror she must have felt as the dust storm chased her.

I focus on my breathing. In . . . out . . . in . . . Thoughts dissolve and crumble away. The sound of the music and the smell of the burning sage become muted and vague. Out . . . in . . .

"Onawa." I whisper it into the darkness behind my eyelids.

In . . . Eyes in the darkness of my mind. Green eyes. Out . . . Aimee? No. Feline eyes. Feral, but not malicious.

In . . .

"Onawa."

She's there. Her golden face looks back at me, illuminated by the light coming from her green eyes. Around me I feel space closing in, pressing against me as Onawa looks at me impassively. There is a message in her eyes, but I can't read it, not with the very air squeezing me.

Then I get it. Danger. There is danger all around me.

The pressure lessens a little. Onawa's way of letting me know I'm right.

I continue to breathe. Out . . . in . . .

"What can I do?" I ask without words. It is just a thought I send outward, toward the eyes.

Onawa looks away from me at the same moment that I feel a gentle heat in my chest. I follow the cougar's gaze and see a vague line of people standing nearby. The line fades in the distance. I feel a kinship with these people I do not recognize. The warm feeling in my chest grows as I look at them. One by one, they turn to look at me, and I see that they all have my face.

"Are they . . . my ancestors?"

Onawa turns her attention back to me and the line of people retreats into the darkness.

"Aimee?" I ask.

A fire appears above Onawa's head. The fire is Aimee's hair, though. I know this. There is a woman tending the fire. The woman looks like Aimee.

"Her mom?"

Onawa doesn't answer.

"Who is the River Man?" I ask.

The fire and woman break apart and fade away. The air presses around me again, but now it is cold and smells like a stagnant river. There is a feeling, something that can only be evil—ancient, nameless evil. I feel panicked, suffocated, and suddenly afraid. Then the feeling is gone.

I tell myself to breathe.

In . . . out . . . in . . .

The smell of incense comes to me. There's a sound. Not music. Something else. Onawa's glowing green eyes dim. I grope for focus.

"Don't leave me."

Out . . . in . . .

"Alan Whitedeer Parson! Listen to me!"

Onawa's eyes blink once, twice, and are gone. There is only the smell of sage and the sound of silence. I open my eyes. The room is filled with electric light. My windows are squares of darkness behind my angry mother.

"What the hell are you doing?" she demands.

"Meditating. Did you turn off the music?"

"That chanting? Yes, I turned it off. What is all over your face and chest?"

"Paint."

"Wipe it off. There is a cop downstairs. He wants to talk to you." The anger flickers for a second. "What's going on, Alan?"

"A cop?"

"Put some clothes on and come downstairs." She has wood shavings in her hair and she smells like oil and sawdust. Her face is pale, and her eyes show more fear than anger now.

"Okay." She starts to walk away, around me and toward

the door. "Mom?" She turns back. "I don't know why the cop is here. I promise . . . Unless it's about my fight at school . . ."

She nods her head once and leaves the room, closing the door.

I get up, and the movement is anything but graceful. My knees are stiff and my legs want to cramp. I put my hands on the edge of my bed and stretch my legs behind me. My cell phone is on the bedspread. The red light is blinking; I have messages. I pick it up and check. Six messages, all from Aimee. I check the most recent one.

PLEASE CALL ASAP!!!

I have missed calls, too. From Aimee. Something *is* wrong.

Mom is downstairs with a police officer who wants to see me.

I pull on some sweatpants and a black Rob Zombie shirt. It isn't until I walk past the mirror on my dresser that I remember the facepaint. I step into the bathroom to scrub off the paint that can be seen on my face and neck, then go downstairs. Mom and the cop, a pot-bellied blond guy with a pair of chins and a buzz cut, sit at the dining room table. Aunt Lisa isn't around.

"There he is," Mom says. "I'm sorry he made you wait."

"That's okay," the cop says as he gets to his feet. He's a few inches shorter than me but outweighs me by at least a hundred pounds. He extends a meaty, sweaty hand, and I shake it as he says, "I'm Deputy McKinney, Alan. Can I ask you a few questions?"

"What about?" I ask.

"Sit down, Alan," Mom insists. The cop settles back into his chair, and I think of a turkey squatting on a nest. I sit across from Mom, facing the deputy.

240

"You were in a fight today at school, weren't you?" he asks.

"Yeah, I guess. It wasn't much of a fight. Three guys jumped me in a bathroom. I only got one hit in before the teachers broke it up."

"It looks like they worked you over pretty good."

"It looks worse than it feels," I tell him.

"You know the boys who did it?"

"Sort of. I mean, we've only been in Maine since Saturday. I know two of them from classes, and Blake is in cross-country with me. He's my girlfriend's ex."

"That's Blake Stanley?"

"Yeah."

"The other two boys? Do you know their names?"

"Chris and Noah, I think. I don't know their last names."

"Have you seen them since you left school today?"

"No."

"Are you sure?"

"Yeah."

"You were suspended for the fight?"

"If you know about the fight, you know I was."

"Alan," Mom warns. "Answer him."

"Yes, I was suspended. Three days." I look at Mom while I say it.

"What about the other boys?"

"I don't know. Everson said three days was the required suspension for fighting. I assume that's what they got."

"Did you come right home after you were suspended?"

I swallow and can't look at Mom. I focus on a small mole on McKinney's temple instead. "No. I went to Craft Barn and Bergerman's Lumber and to the hospital first."

Mom gives a frustrated sigh. "I told you to come straight home."

"I had things to do."

"Alan, can you prove your whereabouts between about one PM and four PM?" the deputy asks.

"Why?"

He ignores my question and repeats his own. "Can you prove you were at Craft Barn and the lumberyard and the hospital?"

"I don't know. I guess. I have receipts."

"I'd like to see them."

"They're upstairs. You want me to get them?"

"Please."

I try to act calm and uncaring and cool, but my heart pounds harder than my feet as I throw myself up the stairs and into my room. I grab my jeans off the floor and fish out the two receipts from a hip pocket, then go back downstairs. I hand them to the cop as I sit down and watch him study them.

"Sage, and what's this?" he asks. Sweetgrass shows up as "Sweetgss" on the receipt.

"Sweetgrass."

"The weed? Why'd you buy that?"

"An Indian thing," Mom says. "His father was an Indian and Alan tries to be."

"I am half Navajo," I say, and don't care that I sound defiant. "I burn the sage and sweetgrass like incense."

"I see," Deputy McKinney says, but it's obvious he doesn't. He looks at the lumber receipt. "Tarps and . . . granite?"

"Yes."

"What are those for?"

Damn. I do not want to go here. Mom will blow a gasket. Maybe not now, not in front of the cop, but later.

"More Indian stuff?" he asks.

"Yeah. For a sweat lodge."

"Sweat lodge?"

"It's like a sauna in a tent," I say.

"Oh." He looks at the two receipts for another minute, then puts them aside. "The receipts put you at the stores at about one thirty and a quarter after two this afternoon. You say you went to the hospital?"

"My cousin's there. She's a patient."

The deputy looks to Mom, who nods confirmation. "Courtney Tucker, my niece."

The cop nods. "She's okay?"

I wait for Mom to answer, wondering if they've gotten word about Courtney's recovery. "She seems much better, from what I heard just before you got here," she says.

"I'm glad to hear it," McKinney says. "Your cousin can confirm that you were there?" I nod. "Anyone else?"

"Aimee."

"Aimee Avery?"

"Yeah. I met her there. She was already in the room with Courtney."

"Anyone else? Did you talk to any nurses or doctors, maybe a receptionist?"

"Nope. Well, actually there was a nurse standing there when I got off the elevator. What's this all about?"

The deputy takes a deep breath and looks at his thick index finger as he draws circles on the white tablecloth. "We pulled

243

Chris Paquette out of the Union River late this afternoon. He's dead. Noah Chandler was there, too. He's in the hospital now. Hypothermia and shock. He can't talk to us yet."

I stare at the cop for a long time. His gaze is on his finger, but I know he's watching my reaction in his peripheral vision. This is crazy. "You think . . . what? I drowned Chris?"

"What time did you leave the hospital?"

"I don't know. A little after three."

"Where did you go then?"

"I took Aimee home, then came here. I've been upstairs in my room since then."

"What have you been doing up there?"

None of your damn business. I want to say it. I open my mouth to say it, but I can feel Mom thinking I better not say it. "Meditating," I say.

"What's that? Like praying?"

"Yeah. Like praying."

"Do you use drugs for that? LSD? Pot?"

Oh. My. God.

I shake my head. "No."

"Aimee found Noah in the river, looking for Chris," the cop says. "Then she found where Chris's body was trapped underwater."

"Oh no. Is she okay?" Now it's my turn to stare him down, to demand answers. "Is Aimee all right?"

"She's fine."

"I have to call her. She's supposed to come over tonight. She wants to meet my mom." I look from the deputy to Mom, then back. "She's okay? You saw her?"

"I saw her. She's fine." He hesitates, then asks, "Alan, I'll ask you one more time. Be honest with me. Did you see those three boys again after school?"

"No. Was Aimee— Wait. Three? You only mentioned the two at the river."

"We can't find Blake Stanley." His voice is dead and flat, not quite accusing, but not *not* accusing, either.

"You don't really think I did something to them, do you?" I can't believe it.

He shrugs and his face softens a little. "Not really," he admits. "Even before this." He waves at the receipts, making the folded bits of paper flutter. "But, considering the circumstances, I had to ask."

"Thank God," Mom says. Her shoulders sink inward as the tension falls off her. Did she really think I'd done something like that? Why? How could she even think it?

"I should go and leave you folks to your dinner plans," McKinney says. He fishes in an unbuttoned shirt pocket and pulls out a crisp white business card that he lays on the table by the receipts. "If you think of anything that might help, please call me. Chris's mom . . . she's not taking this well."

"No," Mom says. "What mother would? I'm so sorry for her."

I nod. I'm sorry, too. Another river death. Another newspaper story for the school librarian's collection. If we fail, me and Aimee, how many more will there be?

"A lot of people die in that river," I say. I say it more to myself, but the cop and Mom both stare at me.

"What did you say, son?" McKinney asks. I hate it when men who are not my father call me "son."

"The river. A lot of people have died in it. The librarian at school has a folder full of old newspaper clippings about it."

McKinney nods real slow, like I've revealed I know some deep, dark secret about his little town. Maybe I have. This *is* Maine. Maybe the whole damn state is like some creepy old Stephen King story. "I guess so," he says. "Well, I should go. We're still looking for Blake. Please call if you think of anything. I can show myself out."

He leaves us and I sit still, waiting for Mom to start griping about the suspension, about me not coming home after school. She doesn't, though.

"Did we bring all this bad luck with us from Oklahoma?" she asks.

"It was already here, Mom. I think it's been here for a long time."

She doesn't respond. She looks so sad. I reach across the table and take her hand.

"I'm sorry, Mom. About the fighting, and not coming home like you told me to."

She only nods.

"You talked to Aunt Lisa? Courtney is better?"

"Yes. Even her face has cleared up. All the tests are negative. They're going to send her home tomorrow, but she needs to stay home the rest of the week. Someone's supposed to stay and keep watch over her. Lisa was going to."

"I can do it," I say. "I mean, I'm going to be home, anyway."

"That might work. Are you hungry? Your friend is coming over?"

"I already ate." I don't like lying to Mom, but she frowns on the idea of fasting. "Aimee wanted to come over. I don't know now. She's been calling and texting, but I didn't know it."

"You had that chanting stuff up too loud."

"I guess. Can I go call her and see if she's okay and coming over?"

Mom nods, so I race back up the stairs.

Aimee answers on the second ring. "Alan! Where were you? Are you okay? Oh God, I was so worried. Chris Paquette—he's dead. I found him. I found him in the river."

"I know, Aim. I know. Are you okay?"

"You know?"

"A cop was just here. He thought I might have done it."

"Are you serious?" She sounds as shocked as I was.

"Yeah, but it's okay now. I think. He left. He said he was convinced I didn't do it, but . . . whatever. Are you okay?"

"I'm okay. Just freaked. I want to come over."

"I'll come get you."

"Okay. Umm. I'm not sure Dad will let me go. But can you come anyway?"

"Yeah. I'll be there in a few minutes. Mom doesn't seem as mad as I thought she'd be. And she wants to meet you. Ten minutes?"

"Okay."

"Aimee . . ."

"Yeah?"

"The cop who came to my house? He said Blake is missing."

I don't really ask Mom's permission. I just announce that I'm going to pick up Aimee as I head for the door. She doesn't protest—at least that I can hear before the door closes behind

247

me. I make it to Aimee's house in seven minutes and am getting out of my truck in her driveway when a white van with a satellite dish on top of it slams to a stop in front of the house. A woman with a microphone and a man with a video camera spill out the sliding side door and rush at me like rabid linebackers.

"Are you here to see Aimee Avery?" the woman screams at me as she crosses the lawn in ridiculous high heels and a beige skirt that's too tight to allow her to run as fast as she wants to. "Do you know about the boy pulled out of the river?"

I turn away from them and catch a glimpse of Benji looking through the curtain in the front window. Big man hands pull him back and the curtain falls into place.

The newswoman is beside me now, shoving the microphone under my nose like it's an ice-cream cone. Her cameraman stands behind her, pointing his lens at me. This is what I wanted a week ago. I wanted to be the football star, with the media surrounding me. Now I just want to swat the microphone away and break the camera.

"Were you a friend of Chris Paquette?" the woman asks, her voice shrill.

"Leave me alone," I say. "Leave Aimee alone. Go chase an ambulance." I turn around and make for the porch, but she follows.

"What can you tell me about Chris?"

The front door of the house opens a crack and Aimee's hand motions me forward. I sprint up the three stairs. The door opens and I slip inside. Aimee slams it behind me and throws herself against me, talking into my chest.

"Those people won't go away," she says. "They've been

parked up the street, just waiting for something to happen. I'm sorry. I should have warned you."

"It's okay," I tell her.

"He sure does have some long hair," Benji says.

"Benj," his dad says, but he's grinning. So am I.

"Can you come over?" I ask Aimee, then I look at her dad. "Is it okay if she comes to my house? My mom's there and wants to meet her."

"I don't know," he says. "Aimee's been through a lot today. I think some rest—"

"Dad? Please?" She lifts her head from my chest and looks at her father. "I'll be okay. I won't be gone long, and Alan will bring me home. Won't you?"

"Of course. Yeah."

"What about our paparazzi out there?" Gramps asks.

"Here." I press my keys into Aimee's hands. "You just go straight to the truck and get in and lock your door. I'll block them while you run."

"Alan," her dad warns, "don't do anything stupid. Don't break any cameras or push them down or anything."

"I won't." I peek out a corner of the window. The reporter and her lackey have retreated to the van. They're sitting in the front, talking. He's not holding his camera. "Okay," I tell Aimee. "We'll have a few seconds to get to the truck before they can get out of the van. You ready?"

She nods. "Bye, Daddy."

"Alan, be careful with her," he says, his voice almost a plea, like he's lost her.

"I'll guard her with my life, Mr. Avery. I swear it."

"Whoa. That's deep," Benji says.

"Let's go." I open the door and guide Aimee in front of me like she's a blocking tackle not moving fast enough to get out of my way. I maneuver her through the door with my hand, my eyes on the defenders scrambling to get out of the van with their equipment. "Come on, Aim, we gotta move."

Aimee jumps off the porch, sags for a moment as her bruised leg threatens to give, and then she's up and loping for the truck. I charge straight at the cameraman, wearing my game face. He stops and looks around his camera like what he was seeing in his viewfinder couldn't possibly be right. He starts backing away, almost tripping over his own feet. The newswoman drops her microphone to her hip and moves to the side.

Aimee makes it into the truck, so I break away from the newspeople and jump into the driver's seat. Aimee has the key in the ignition. I fire up the Ford and drop it into reverse before the news team can recover. As we roar out of the driveway, I see Benji jumping into the air, throwing up a victory fist, while Gramps holds the curtain open and laughs.

AIMEE

We don't say much on the way over other than how relieved we are that the news van isn't following us. That's not normal for us. There's this big ball of dread inside me, filling up the pit of my stomach, tugging at me every time I breathe. Chris is dead.

"I've been doing ridiculous things lately," I say as Alan turns onto the bridge. He doesn't say anything, so I go on. "I mean, going alone to the hospital didn't seem ridiculous at the time, but it was, I guess. You go through your life figuring there's certain things you can do that are safe. You can take a walk. You can kayak. You can just be by yourself in your house, but that's not the way it is. If I were watching my life as a movie, I'd be all, 'Dork! Do not kayak alone! Do not go into the woods alone!'" I pause. "I don't want to be the damsel in distress."

"You aren't." He seems so confident.

I rest my fist on his thigh. "I'm not?"

"No, you aren't. Technically, I guess Courtney is."

"And you're the knight errant who's going to save her."

"No," he says. "*We* are the knight errant who's going to save her."

"Maybe . . ."

"No 'maybe' about it. Instead of thinking of it as putting yourself in harm's way by going to the hospital and going kayaking, maybe you should think of those acts as tests of courage. That's what you'd think if it was me doing it. You'd think I was brave. You wouldn't think, 'Oh, Alan is being a damsel.'"

"Sure I would," I tease. I know, though, that he's right. Why is it when women do something brave, we think it's something dangerous? And when a guy does something dangerous, we think it's brave?

I'm about to ask Alan this when he goes, "You saved one of those guys, Aimee. Yeah, he sucks. But you saved him. You know it."

"Chris died."

"You couldn't have stopped that."

"How do you know?"

"I know." He says it as if it's absolute knowledge.

"I wish I did. I wish I knew." I swallow hard. "I know you hate him, but I'm worried about Blake."

"I know." He pulls the truck onto their road. It bumps along. I close my eyes.

Alan's voice steadies me. "It must have been hell out there, huh?"

I open my eyes and stare up at Court's familiar, cozy house. "It was."

Alan switches off the car and turns to face me. He kisses my forehead soft and sweet, which is not what you expect from such a big guy, such a football-player kind of guy, and I can't help it. I tilt my head up. He doesn't pull his lips away from my skin; instead he trails them softly down my nose. It's a light grazing touch. My skin feels like it swells to meet his lips, wishing he would press against me. He kisses the tip of my nose the way a brother would. I do not want him to be my brother.

"Aimee . . ." His voice comes out husky and low and very unbrotherlike.

My hands grab the side of his face and I pull him to the proper angle because I can't wait anymore, can't hope for him to make the first move. So I kiss him. My lips touch his lips. My breath meets his breath. And we grab at each other. His hands clutch the fabric of my coat and my hands cling to his face, holding him there, because I'm so afraid of letting him go, of having him drift away.

There is enough light coming through the truck windows that I can see the tiny lines in the skin by his eyes, the place where his eyebrows stop. When he opens his eyes, the brown of them makes me smile and laugh, surprised and happy.

"I kissed you," I say, breaking away, but not going too far. My hands fall into my lap.

"Yeah," he says.

I punch his arm. "That's all you have to say? 'Yeah'?"

"Hell yeah?" he teases, then hops out of the truck. I manage to scurry across the seat, open my door, and jump out before he can open the door for me. Landing on my leg hurts a little bit. Still, I gloat.

"Ha!" I point at him.

He fake clutches his heart. "How will my macho masculine self survive?"

"Shut up." I bop my hip into him. He drapes an arm around my shoulder and we head toward the house, but then I stop at the last second. "I'm scared."

"Of the house? It'll be okay. I've smudged it. And I'll be right here."

"No," I explain. "Not of the house. Of your mom."

He lets go of me. "My mom?"

I nod, kind of fiercely.

"You look like a little kid when you do that," he says.

I shrug.

"And now you're shrugging?" He cracks up.

"Not funny."

"No? But I'll tell you what *is* funny: you being scared of my mom." He gets that gigantic smile he gets.

"Like you weren't scared of my dad?" I grab the doorknob and start to turn it, but then it jerks open and Alan's mom (I mean, I think it must be Alan's mom) is standing there, a superhuge look of happy planted on her face.

"So," she says, and I catch a lot of tired in her eyes. "You must be Aimee. Oh, what a cute girl you are, all that red hair."

She hustles me inside, not giving me a second to answer. Instead, she just keeps talking and talking and talking. I catch phrases like "Oh, I am so glad that Alan has found someone." And "Courtney says such good things about you." And "I heard you were a good student. I hope that rubs off on—"

Seriously, it's a frenzy of mom-talk, and finally Alan goes

up to her and puts his hand gently over her mouth. "Mom. Breathe."

She grabs his wrist and pulls his hand away. "I can't breathe with your hand on my face." She adjusts her shirt and then her hair. Some wood chips sprinkle out like overlarge pieces of dandruff, and she says, "I guess I was talking your head off, wasn't I?"

"I do that all the time when I'm nervous. Not that you're nervous." I cringe.

"Oh, she's making excuses for me. She *is* nice." Ms. Parson bends down to pick some wood chips off the rug. I squat down and help her. They are tiny beige chips in a carpet of red. It's amazing to think they were once part of a living tree. That poor tree. "She's really nice. You don't have to help, Aimee."

"Yep. Yep. She's nice." Alan shakes his head like it's all too much and too awkward to deal with.

"It's good to meet you, Ms. Parson," I say, and extend my hand even though I'm still squatting.

She shakes it.

"It's the mill work," she apologizes and stands up. "It's giving me blisters. My hands haven't toughened up yet."

I stand up, too. "I'm so sorry. I hope I didn't squeeze too tight."

"Not at all," she says while Alan turns her hands over and inspects them. There are new blisters on the pads underneath each of her fingers where they join the palm, but as we watch the redness starts to fade. I've healed her.

She cocks her head like a puppy.

"How strange." Her voice goes serious and quiet. "I can tell you're a good girl, Aimee. You'll be good to him, right?"

"I will," I say. "I promise."

255

She drops her hand and the moment is gone. "You two go on and talk. As long as no police cars or principals show up, I'll be happy. What a day."

Alan hugs her. "You're a trooper, mom."

"Yeah, right . . ." She laughs.

Alan leads me up the stairs. "My room is up here."

"Next to Court's, right?"

"Oh, yeah, I forgot you've been here before."

"Only about a million times," I say.

"Keep the door open!" Ms. Parson yells up the stairs.

"Mom!" Alan turns bright red. He closes his eyes and breathes deeply for a second. "Sorry . . ."

He motions to the guestroom that Court's mom used to do quilt projects in. It smells tangy and sweet. I sniff. "That's sage."

Alan nods to some herb stuff by the bookcase. "I was burning it."

I step a little farther inside. It's already a very boy room. There are posters featuring some rock bands that I have no clue about. Clothes are strewn in one corner. There's a bed, a stereo on a shelf above the bed, a bed, a rug by the bed, a bed . . .

I look away from the bed.

There's nowhere else to sit though, except the floor.

He plops himself down on the bed. There's a little smudge of something black by his ear. "Come on, Red. It's okay. I'm not going to bite."

"It's just . . ." I sit next to him, stiff and annoying, probably. "It's just . . . There's a lot going on, and today was—I felt like I couldn't do anything, like I couldn't do enough, you know?"

"Yeah. I know."

We're quiet for a moment. Then I say, "I'm tired of worrying about everything."

He grabs my hand. "Me, too. It'd be nice if we could just like each other instead of . . . instead of . . ."

"Instead of being warriors in the battle for Courtney's soul? Instead of being star-crossed lovers kicked out of school, beaten up by Blake's posse, questioned by police, and hounded by reporters?"

"You make it all sound so glamorous." He pokes me in the side with his finger. "Loosen up, Red. We'll take care of this."

"You're only sounding confident because you think I expect you to sound confident." I breathe in and look at him. "You don't need to be confident. It's okay to be human. It's okay to be scared."

He brushes the hair off my forehead. His big hand holds the hair there. "Like you were scared in the river?"

I nod.

"Tell me what happened," he says.

So, I do.

I'm pretty much through my story when my cell phone rings. I check out the display name even though I recognize the ringtone. "It's my dad." I snap it open. "Hey, Dad!"

"Hey, sweetie." He sounds preoccupied, even though *he* called *me*. "How are things over there?"

"Okay. I met Alan's mom. She's nice," I say. Alan gives me a cheesy thumbs-up. I give it back. He shifts closer and behind me, his arm around my waist. I lean back.

"So what are you doing?" my dad asks.

"We're just hanging out." I cough.

"Uh-huh. Good, good." He sounds like he sounds when I call him up at work and he's talking to me and simultaneously reading interoffice memos or e-mail. "Look, honey—there are more reporters here now."

"More reporters? Why?"

"I don't know. Slow news day, I guess, and it doesn't help that I'm your father: *Hospital CEO's daughter saves boy who beat up her boyfriend the same day.*"

I pull in a breath. "Oh. You know about that."

"The whole town knows about it now, Aimee."

"They jumped him, Dad. He's not a jerk. I swear." When I say it, Alan's arm stiffens a little bit.

"Blake's missing."

I can barely manage to say the words. "I heard."

"I just . . . Can you sleep over there tonight? Sleep in Courtney's room, maybe?"

"You want me to sleep here?" My stomach lurches. "What if something happens and I'm not there?"

"Aimee, nothing is going to happen. I have things under control. There's just no way I can get you back into the house without these reporters getting some shots. There are way too many now. Even Alan's football moves won't be able to do much."

"Fine."

"Fine?" he prods.

I meet Alan's eyes. "I'll ask if I can stay."

* * *

The women of the house bustle all around.

"We'll put you in Court's room," Court's mom says. "She's got one more night at the hospital. She'll be fine with you sleeping in her bed."

"Yeah. I know . . . It's just weird to sleep in it without her." Alan is giving me an odd look. "Whenever we have sleepovers we share the bed. Courtney *always* kicks me."

"And then complains that Aimee hogs the covers," Mrs. Tucker explains, smiling sweetly. She hands me some of Court's teddy-bear pj's. They are going to be way too short.

"Which I don't," I insist. "Alan. Stop looking so amused."

"I'm not amused," he says, backing up.

"Right." I hold the pj's to my face and sniff in the good fabric-softener scent of them. "Has the news said anything about Blake? Is he still missing?"

"No word." Mrs. Tucker leans against the wall right by Court's poster of Miley Cyrus, which she put up in a snarky way, not because she's a fan. At one sleepover we painted fangs on Miley's face with pink nail polish. Mrs. Tucker taps the poster. "Remember when you did this?"

"We had a monster Miley-hate on," I explain. "We were thirteen or something."

That's when all of it gets me. We will never be thirteen-year-old happy again. We will never *not* know about possession and evil. Chris Paquette will be dead forever. Mr. Tucker will be dead forever, and Blake . . . I don't know if he's dead, too.

I try to smoosh all the worry and fear down into my stomach so I can seem strong. I hustle them out of the room so they don't think I'm weak. Alan's got these worry lines showing up around his eyes, but I just peck his cheek.

"Good night," I whisper, and then shut the door behind him.

It's only when I'm all alone in Court's room that I press my fingers into my eyelids and let the sadness overwhelm me.

I don't know how we're ever going to beat this.

· 22 ·
ALAN

I can't sleep. I can't even pretend to sleep. Part of it is nervousness. What kind of supernatural craziness might happen tonight? But, of course, that's only part of it. A small part, really. Aimee is there, right across the hall, in my cousin's bed. Wearing those cute teddy-bear pajamas.

I shouldn't think about that. But it takes my mind off my stomach. It's been about twelve hours since I ate anything, and that was just a few bites of school lunch. Just a doughnut before that. It's been, what—about thirty hours since I had a real meal. My stomach growls in acknowledgment of that fact.

All I can think about is hunger and Aimee in a bed across the hall.

Is she asleep? Is she lying awake thinking about me? What is she thinking? Is she thinking about sneaking into my room like I'm thinking about sneaking into hers? *Into Courtney's room,* I correct myself. What if I went?

I can almost feel her hair against my hands, smell it against my cheek. Her eyes. It would be so intense to look into those eyes while . . .

I throw the covers off. The air in the room is cold. Too cold. Even for late fall in Maine, I think. My whole body breaks out in goose bumps. I grab an old pair of gray sweatpants off the foot of my bed, then pull on a Sooners sweatshirt and turn on the reading lamp.

"Great Spirit, protect this house. Protect Courtney's family. Deliver us from this evil spirit. Send it back where it came from." I repeat this over and over as I light the sage incense. The smell doesn't come fast enough. I reach for one of the sage bundles.

It flies away from me, slamming into a wall and exploding out of its binding so that the individual stalks scatter and rain down around the room.

I can feel him.

The shadow stands in the corner by my closet. It's huge and thick, completely cold and evil. It waits across the room from me. The cold rolls from it to me like waves, like the current of an icy river. Its head nearly reaches the ceiling. How can he be so strong? He's drawing all this energy off of my cousin, and I hate him for it.

The river of ice slams into me again. I stagger back, reaching behind me to try to steady myself. I almost knock over the incense. The shape takes a step toward me, and suddenly I'm scared. Maybe I can't do this. Maybe I can't win.

The sound of an angry cat rips through the night. This isn't in my mind. This isn't even outside. For just a moment I see her: Onawa, bright and shimmering, wild and beautiful with bared fangs and burning green eyes, stands between me and the River Man.

The black shape screeches and vanishes with a loud *pop* that leaves the room smelling of sulfur and rot. Onawa turns to look at me, her face set, her eyes warning me.

And that's when I realize it: I am just a tool here. I'm just a tool in a battle that's so much bigger than me and Aimee and Courtney.

The moment I realize this, she's gone, and my bedroom door flies open. Aimee is in the room first, with Mom and Aunt Lisa right behind her. Aimee runs at me, throwing her arms around me as she hits me with all her force. I'm still unnerved by what I've just seen, and I stagger under her fear and fall onto the bed, my own arms wrapped around her.

"Alan!" Aimee sobs.

"Alan, what in God's name is going on in here?" Mom demands.

"What was that, Alan?" Aunt Lisa's face spasms with worry.

It takes a minute before I whisper, "I'm okay. I'm all right."

Still, Aimee won't let me up. She won't move. I look at the older women. Their eyes are fixed on me.

"What's that smell?" Aunt Lisa asks.

"Incense," I say, glancing at the burning cone.

"No, not that." She sniffs again, then wrinkles her nose. "It's like a rotten piece of steak or something."

"I don't know," I lie.

"Alan, what was that noise?" Mom asks. "It sounded like a lion."

"It was me." I *hate* lying. Even worse, I hate lies that sound

263

lame. "I had a dream, and . . ." I try to look embarrassed before finishing. "I guess I might have screamed when I woke up. Sorry."

"That was you?" Aunt Lisa asks, wrapping her arms around herself. Mom looks just as skeptical as Aunt Lisa does.

"Yeah. I'm sorry. I probably sounded like a little girl, huh?"

"No, Alan, it sounded like a mountain lion," Mom says.

"Well, it wasn't. I mean, I'm not keeping a mountain lion in my room. I swear it. Look under the bed."

Why is Aimee still holding me like I'm going to evaporate?

"Don't be a smart-ass, Alan," Mom warns.

"Come on, Holly," Aunt Lisa says. "He had a dream and screamed. I'm sure our big football star is embarrassed enough about that. Go back to bed."

Mom's face concedes, but then she finds a new cause as she looks from my face to Aimee, wrapped around me like a winter coat. She starts to say something, but Aunt Lisa stops her again. "They're fine. Aimee's a good girl, and Alan's a good boy. Trust them."

"They're on the bed," Mom argues.

"Alan," Aunt Lisa asks, "do you promise your mother you'll behave yourself?"

"Yeah. It'll be a while before I'll be going back to sleep."

"It isn't sleeping she's worried about."

My face burns scarlet, and that makes both women smile. "I promise," I say. Then they leave us, but I note that Mom leaves my bedroom door open a crack. I'm sure she leaves hers open enough to hear if I close mine.

"I'm so scared, Alan," Aimee whispers. "I had a dream, too. The River Man had you. He was here and he had you by the wrists, just like he had Chris, and he was dragging you down and down and down to a dark place, and you couldn't get away."

She sobs again, and I hold her tighter. I wonder if I should tell her what really happened. Not now, I decide. She doesn't need to know right now. She's upset enough. My stomach growls. Courtney will be home in the morning. Then Aunt Lisa will join Mom at work for a shift and a half.

"It'll be okay," I whisper back to Aimee, my face pressed into her beautiful red hair. "I love you." The words just come out. Now, the feel of her on me, the smell of her, the strength of her arms around me . . . I can't help but say it.

"It's because we might die. You're saying that because one of us might die." Her voice trembles with some sort of emotion that I can't recognize, and I don't know how much of what she's saying is true. I know it's crazy to care so much about someone so quickly, but I can't imagine her not here, can't imagine not being with her—and there's no other word for that than love, is there? I want her to be safe. I want her to be with me. I want to be with her. It's all like some crap country song, but she's like a ball of sunshine when I'm with her—even when things suck. That's got to be love.

"It isn't just that," I say. "It's not just because we might die."

"But that's part of it."

"Maybe. But there's no other word that even comes close to describing how you make me feel, Red. Nothing."

She finally looks up, her big green eyes wet and shining, but there's a happy gleam in there, too.

"Really?" she asks.

"Yes, really," I promise. "I've never felt like this before."

265

"Me, either," she says, looking awkward for a second. She shivers. "Wow, I'm cold."

Despite the door being open a crack, we get into my bed, under the warm blankets, and she curls up against me, her hand on my chest, her leg thrown over mine. I can't believe I told her I loved her. I can't believe I said that. It was too soon, way too soon. I've totally blown it.

She clears her throat. I wait for her to tell me how crazy I'm being, for her to echo my every single insecurity.

"I love you, too," she says slowly, thoughtfully. "Nobody can die. None of us can die."

Then there's a long silence, and I'm thinking she must be just about asleep, until she says, "You didn't have a dream, did you? He was here. And Onawa was here, too."

She looks up at me. She's so close to sleep that I could almost believe she's talking in her sleep, but I know better. I kiss her lips. Her mouth is so warm and her smell is so strong and feminine. I let my head fall back onto the pillow.

"Yes," I admit. "But we're okay. Sleep, Red. We have a big day ahead of us."

I can hear Mom and Aunt Lisa talking about us when I open my eyes. It's morning and they're in the hallway outside my bedroom.

"You saw how they're sleeping," Mom is arguing.

"That doesn't mean they did anything," Aunt Lisa says. "And even if they did, can you really hold it against them? They're seventeen years old."

"That's too young."

"Holly, maybe they did, maybe they didn't. I don't think they did, but either way, he's your son and Aimee is one of the nicest girls you'll ever meet."

"Your mom hates me now," Aimee whispers.

"No, she doesn't," I whisper back, wishing she could have slept through this. "She's thinking about what her life was like before she met my dad."

Mom is saying, "Still, right here, in this house, with us in the same hallway. I can't believe—"

"Mom!" I call. "We *did not* have sex. We just got cold, then fell asleep. Please chill out. I promise Aimee is as pure right now as she was when she walked through the front door yesterday."

Aunt Lisa laughs. Mom doesn't say anything.

Aimee whispers, "Unfortunately," and smiles up at me, almost making me laugh.

Mom pushes the door open and gives us a critical look. "In my day, boys and girls didn't sleep like that unless they'd had sex first."

"That was the Stone Age, Mom. Or the eighties, or whatever. Kids today aren't animals. We can control ourselves."

She tries to give me her angry stare, where she presses her lips together real hard and a line forms between her eyes, but she slips and smiles just a bit.

Aunt Lisa is wiping tears off her cheeks. "Come on, Holly. We're going to be late getting you to work."

"You two . . . ," Mom says, looking at me and Aimee as Aimee tries to scurry out of the bed.

"Mom, I promised to behave. It wasn't easy. I mean, she couldn't help herself. She was all over this hunk of Navajo

267

manhood, and I had to keep telling her I'd promised not to let her violate me. Eventually she wore herself out and fell asleep."

"You are a horrible liar," Aimee says, but she winks at me with the eye Mom can't see from her angle.

"Alan, I'm taking your mom to work, then picking up Courtney. She slept through the night without incident, they said, so she can come home, but we have to watch over her. You'll help with that? Maybe Aimee can stay a while, too?"

"Sure, Mrs. Tucker," Aimee says. "I'll stay. Dad said I could miss school today because of . . ." Her face suddenly falls as she remembers the boy in the river.

"Okay. Thank you," Aunt Lisa says. "I'll bring Court home, then I have to go to work. You want me to bring you all something to eat? Courtney's already texted me to say she wants a cheeseburger."

"I'll just have some fruit," Aimee says. "You still have oranges, right?"

"Of course," Aunt Lisa says. "We always have fruit for you, Aim."

"Fruit for me, too," I say. My stomach growls again, and I think how sweet it would be to bite into a nice juicy orange. Or a banana. Yeah. A banana. But not now.

"Make sure he eats, Aimee," Mom says. "I don't believe he did last night." She gives me a stern look, and I don't answer. How do moms know these things?

"I will, Ms. Parson," Aimee says.

"And . . . you two behave," Mom says. She gives us another worried cocking of her eyebrows, then leaves.

★ ★ ★

Sitting at the table in the kitchen, Aimee's trying to peel an orange with her bare hands. Little bits of peel come off in dime-sized pieces. I put my hand over her hand holding the orange and lift it so I can kiss her fingers while I stand next to her. The smell of the orange is overwhelming.

I. Am. So. Hungry.

I take the orange out of her hand and go to the kitchen counter, pluck a knife from a rack and twirl it automatically, then slice the orange into quarters and peel the pulp off the skin.

"A knife-twirler, too," she comments. "There's just no end to the things you can do with those hands."

I put the orange quarters into a little bowl and place the bowl on the table in front of her. "Nope."

I sit down beside her and sip from my glass of water. She actually bites into the orange pieces and sucks the juice out, like a vampire, before eating the pulp. It makes me smile, and that makes her self-conscious, but she doesn't stop.

"What do we have to do?" she asks.

"Sweat lodge. You'll have to stay here with Courtney, so I'll build it myself."

"In the woods? By yourself?" Her face crinkles up with concern.

"Yeah. I'll be okay."

"That's what I thought yesterday, too," she says.

She has a point. I stand up and go to the kitchen window and look out over the backyard to the woods beyond. On the other side of that slope is the river. "I could go back there, just over the hill. Build it there."

"Can't you do it in the backyard? We have the privacy fence," she argues. "I don't want you to go into the woods."

"I'd still have to go into the woods to cut some branches to use as the frame for the lodge," I explain. "Unless you have an answer for that, too."

"I guess not."

"All right. That's what we'll do. I bought a saw. I'll cut some saplings and bring them back to the yard."

She comes to stand behind me, putting her arms around my waist. "You'll be safe?" she asks. "Should I come with you?"

"I'll be okay," I tell her. "I promise. One of us needs to be in the house to listen for Courtney coming home. If Mom and Aunt Lisa can't find us in the house, they'll see what we're doing in the backyard, and then they'll never leave us to finish it. Holler at me as soon as you see them. Okay?"

"Holler?" she teases, grinning at me. Then she mocks my drawl, saying, "You ain't in Oklahoma no more."

I have to admit that I'm surprised cutting the saplings goes without incident. Why? Is he gathering his strength? Does the River Man know we're about to fight? Does he know Courtney is on her way home? I think about all these things as I cut down about a dozen small, flexible trees and haul them to our back fence, where I heave them into the yard.

I'm in the backyard stripping limbs off the saplings when I hear Aunt Lisa's SUV roll in. I run inside to join Aimee as we welcome Courtney home. Aunt Lisa turns her over to us, hugging her repeatedly, then hugging us and hugging Court again before she leaves for work.

"You would not believe the tempers flaring at the mill," she says through the window before she backs out. "Fights galore. I don't even want to go back there."

But she does. As soon as she leaves, Aimee and I quickly tell Courtney the plan. "Now that your mom's gone for the day, I'm going to use some of your firewood to start a small fire in the backyard so I can heat the stones," I say.

Aimee nods, all business.

"We need to move everything out of Court's room. Everything but the bed."

"Why?" Courtney looks skeptical.

"This thing has attacked us with windstorms twice. It's the debris that hurts. He threw the sage across the room last night, a picture frame before—I don't want there to be anything he can throw."

Aimee stands on tiptoes and kisses me quickly, then takes Courtney by the hand. "Let's go," she says, and pulls her toward the stairs.

I'm really nervous about the fire. I dig a shallow pit in Aunt Lisa's backyard behind the shed, bank the dirt up around the pit, then dump a load of firewood on top of some old newspaper I balled up for kindling. The fire starts easily enough, and feels good in the cold morning air. There isn't much smoke, and the sudden bursts of breeze pretty well break it up before it can look too bad to the neighbors.

I dig another pit about four feet from the fire, bank it with the loose dirt, then sharpen ends of saplings and stab them into the ground in a circle around the new pit. I bend them over, lash them together with the twine I got from Craft

Barn, wipe the sweat off my face, then use a short-handled shovel to arrange my granite stones in the embers of the fire pit. I add some more wood to keep the fire going, then return to my developing frame, planting, bending, lashing.

With the dome finally in place, I check my fire again, add some wood, then ask the girls to come help me put the tarp over the frame. It takes some stretching here and some folding there, plus adding a few new holes for twine so we can tie it to the frame, but after about twenty minutes we get the thing covered with the heavy canvas.

"How do you get in it?" Courtney asks.

"Easy enough." I twirl the knife over my fingers, winking at Aimee while I do it, then cut a slit in the tarp facing the fire, where I left enough space in the frame that I can crawl through it. At the bottom of the slit I cut to each side so the flaps will stay open while I bring in the hot rocks.

"Is this it?" Aimee asks. "It's ready?"

"It's ready."

"Mom's going to freak when she sees what you've done back here," Court says.

"Probably. But I'll fix it. Let's go inside for a minute." I lead them into the house. They've moved Courtney's furniture into the upstairs hallway and stripped her walls of posters. "We need to take the light fixture off the ceiling, too," I say. "Court, will you take care of that? Aimee, I need your help in my room."

In my bedroom I toss the sage and sweetgrass bundles onto the bed, then take Aimee by the hands and look into her earnest green eyes. "I don't know what's going to happen today," I tell her.

"You think he's getting ready, don't you?" she asks.

Nodding, I tell her, "Yeah. I think we'll win, but . . . I don't know. I don't know what it might mean if we lose."

"I know." She says it, but she has no voice, and I know she's seeing Chris Paquette with his gashed wrist, missing arm and leg, and bloated face. Still, I think she's only thinking of the bodily harm, the end of life. Could there be worse? I don't know, so I decide not to say anything.

"I'll be in the sweat lodge for two or three hours."

"Should we do anything else?"

"Keep her calm. I don't know if . . . if we should tie her to the bed."

Her face shows her shock. "Do you think we need to? It seems so wrong—like, I don't know . . . like it's violating her or something."

"I don't know, Aim. I've never done this before. I'm just thinking of what happened before, at school."

"Okay. Yeah, I understand. I'll do it. I don't think she'll like it."

"No, she won't. Be gentle. Put some padding on her wrists and ankles, but tie her tight over those. There's rope in the shed. Come on and I'll get it for you." I pick up my sweetgrass and sage and lead her out of my room.

Stupidly, we go downstairs and outside without checking on Courtney. I find the white cotton rope and cut off four three-foot pieces for Aimee. We kiss again and she starts to leave, but I grab at her hand and pull her back.

"Remember, Red, I love you," I tell her.

"And I love you."

There's no kiss this time. We just look into each other's eyes and mean what we say. Then she goes into the house.

I fold back the flaps of my sweat lodge and, using the short-handled shovel, lift the rocks out of the fire, carry them through the opening in the lodge, and drop them into the new pit. When all the rocks are inside, I put out the fire with dirt from around the pit, filling in the hole as much as I can in a short time, then I look around to make sure no one is watching.

There doesn't seem to be any neighbor peeking through knotholes in the fence, so I strip off my Anthrax T-shirt, boots, socks, and jeans. One more look, then I add my underwear to the pile and quickly crawl through the hole in my lodge. It's already hot. I grab my sweetgrass and sage, then pull the flaps closed.

Sitting cross-legged between the closed door and the hot stones, I close my eyes and whisper, "Great Spirit, I put myself in your hands. Onawa, guide me to know what I need to do. Great Spirit, help us all."

I throw a bundle of sweetgrass onto the stones, where the dried leaves begin to blacken and curl while giving off thin tendrils of sweet smoke.

I'm sweating. I don't feel hungry anymore.

I close my eyes and focus on my breathing, looking for my spirit guide, searching the darkness within me.

AIMEE

The house is cold when I go back inside. It's probably as different from the sweat lodge heat as I can imagine. Alan is going to
be naked in there. I will not imagine that. Nope. No. Not
imagining. I turn up the thermostat that's on the wall by the
couch. The furnace kicks in. That's when I realize it: the house
is supernaturally cold.

For a second I think about going back outside and getting
Alan, but he has to do the ceremony. That means I have to deal
with the house, with Courtney. Hopefully, there is nothing to
deal with.

"Aimee."

I jump about twenty feet into the air. It's just Courtney,
though. She's at the top of the stairs, waiting.

"Hey." I wave at her. "You scared me."

"Are you coming upstairs?" she asks.

"Yeah. Sorry. I was turning the heat up, and—"

"Come on," she interrupts. She steps down the hall, out of sight.

My flesh gets all goose bumpy. I rub my arms and head up the stairs after her. My gut tells me things are not good. Things are all wrong, in fact. I take the steps two at a time. Court's standing at the end of the hallway. It smells up here.

My gut told me right.

It's that same horrible rotting smell. I cover my mouth and nose with my hand, but it's not enough. I gag.

"Aimee . . ." Her voice is both a whimper and whisper. A plea. Everything in my body shakes when I see her. She's trembling. She looks terribly small and so easy to break.

"Courtney? Honey?"

"Aimee . . . he's . . . he's here." She shivers.

I rush down the hall. "I know. I know. It's okay. It's going to be okay."

My words are hopeless promises out in the middle of the hall. They drift there for a moment, then flit away to nothing.

I grab her by the arms. Her sores are coming back.

"Is my face . . . ?" she asks.

I put my hand against her cheek. "I'll heal you in a sec, okay?"

"Okay." She is almost floppy, like a stuffed animal standing there. There's no fight in her. She's already given in.

"Court, honey, you need to fight him. I don't know how. I don't know what it's like, the stuff going on inside you right now, but you have to fight him."

"I'm trying."

"I know, sweetie. I know." I hope Alan's ceremony is going well, and I hope it's going quickly. I remember what it was like in school when Court threw Alan across the cafeteria. "I'm going to tie you up. Just in case."

That gets her attention. Her head snaps up straight and she stares at me, totally confused. "You're going to what?"

"Tie you up. Okay?" I show her the rope. "I have to. In case he—"

"In case he takes me over?" she interrupts. Her face pales. It makes the sores stand out even more.

The smell increases.

Something in my skin prickles.

He's here. I can feel him.

The evil of him permeates everything. It's a shadow behind me, filling the air. It's not just a smell; it's a presence, a weight against my soul.

I don't know what to use for padding, but I have to do something so the rope doesn't chafe Court's skin too badly. I rip off my shoes and drop them on the floor. Then I go for my socks. "I'm sorry if they smell."

She half chokes, half laughs. "It's not as bad as him. But you could just wait until we get in my bedroom and get some of my clean socks out of the closet."

"True." I wrap the socks around Court's wrists. "But I'm afraid to wait."

"You're shaking," she says.

"So are you."

Her voice is suddenly strong, but it's still her voice. "Tie me tight, Aimee. I don't want to hurt you."

Our eyes meet for a second. "I don't want to hurt you, either," I say.

The house shudders. Court's body jerks. I wrap the rope

around her wrists and secure them together with a square knot. Her body jerks again and I catch her as she falls. I was going to tie her to the bed, but I don't think there's time.

"He's close," she whispers. Her eyes fill with fear. "He's—"

Something smacks me in the back. Pain ripples through me. I shove Court down the hallway wall. "Into your room. Quick."

We run across the wood floor, slipping on the rug, trying to get away. Pictures are flying off the wall. Glass shatters. A picture frame jabs Court in the face. She is screaming. I'm grabbing her around the waist and pulling her into the room. Another picture hits me in the shoulder.

I slam the door. It shudders and groans. I throw myself against it.

"Aimee!" Courtney hunkers in the corner. Her hands are tied in front of her. Her eyes frantically search for something. "I don't want him! I don't want him, Aimee!"

"Fight him."

"I can't!"

"Fight him!" I order.

The door wobbles more behind me. I brace myself, trying to keep it shut. The wood splinters a little. Pieces of it pierce my skin. I groan. It's such a losing fight.

"Aimee!" Court curls up in a ball. Her hands scratch at her face.

The door is still. He's here. I scurry toward her and try to pull her hands away from her cheeks. Deep gashes mar her skin. Blood drips. She resists me, pulling. No, that's wrong. *He* resists.

"Hello, crazy whore . . . Just like your mother," she says. It's not her voice. It's *his* voice: low and evil.

Anger swells up in me. Not fear, anger. "Let her go."

Her eyes narrow. She laughs.

I'm yanking at Court's hands, trying to pull them away. Court kicks out. Her feet make contact with my hip and my stomach. It's powerful. I stagger back and hit the wall. All the wind rushes out of me.

She smiles and stands up. "You can't fight me." She pulls at her wrists, increasing the tension on the rope. "Even with this on, I can kill you."

I swallow hard, staggering up. I imagine white light. I imagine how much I love Alan, how much I love Courtney, how much I loved my mom. This—this is what killed my mom. Anger fills me. Anger at the pain and the loss.

He makes Court laugh. He makes Court smile and take a step toward me. "You could have saved him, you know? The one I took."

"Chris Paquette," I whisper.

"You could have saved him if you went in the water, but you didn't. You were too afraid." Another step closer.

I pull myself up, pressing my back into the door for support and balance. I point at him. "Shut up."

Another step closer.

Another smile.

I don't move. "No."

Despair shimmies through my blood. That's what he wants: despair. I won't give it to him. Instead I look for light— the white light. My hands. My power. I helped Court before. I can do it again. I lift my palms, pointing them toward her. I focus. White light. Healing. Love. My voice is more powerful than I expect. "Get out of my friend."

He says nothing.

279

"I can make it hard for you. I can fight you, make you weak." I focus all my thoughts on healing, on surrounding Courtney with the white light. My body shakes from the strain. I know I can't last long, but I know I have to. It'll help Alan. It'll help Courtney. It has to. But it costs. Magic? Power? It doesn't come cheap.

Court's body jumps back a little. "Stop it!"

I don't say anything. Focus. I just focus.

"I said, *STOP IT!*" she orders.

The door behind me is breaking apart. A piece of it flings into me. The wood stakes itself into my arm. The pain is intense. Still, I don't even rip it out. I keep my hands outstretched.

"DO NOT PROVOKE ME!" Courtney/the River Man screams.

My hands shake from the force, from the power. My heart rate is up to five hundred beats a minute or something. I can feel the power welling inside me, focusing, but at the same time it drains me.

It's worth it. It's worth it to save Court.

"Courtney! Fight him!"

He makes her laugh.

"I love you, Courtney!" I scream. She looks up at me, and for a second it's her eyes I see again. "I love you!" I scream. "Help me! Mom! Help me!"

I don't know why I yell for her, for my mother, but I do. And then it's like hands are on my shoulders. The smell of vanilla is in the room with us.

"Fight him!" I insist. "Help me fight him."

Wood and plaster squeals. Court shudders, collapses on the floor next to her fluffy blue rug, then gasps. The house shakes.

I am falling down, too, dead tired. The smell of vanilla is growing fainter.

"Mom," I whisper. "Mom . . ."

But nobody answers.

· 24 ·
ALAN

I am not in my body. I am not in the sweat lodge. I am not in the physical world.

It's a strange feeling to be outside your body, but there I am, standing in a dark space that seems to be filled with movement I can't see. It's like being blind and standing in the middle of a busy interstate with more highways running above and below me.

There is little I can do to prepare you.

I spin around, and there is Onawa. At first, just her green eyes show, but then her tawny, sleek body materializes in the darkness. She is huge, much larger than the cougars in the zoo back in OKC. Her head is level with my chest. Is she actually speaking to me?

It is not for you to decide your cousin's fate.

Her mouth doesn't move. It's more like her words are put directly into my head, but there's no doubt the words are coming from her.

"Is it up to her?" I ask.

It is up to the one who made you, who made her, who made everything that is.

"How . . ."

You simply ask, Spirit Warrior.

"Why do you call me that?"

He is attacking her now.

I feel the panic take hold of me for a moment. Panic, I've found, causes the astral consciousness to retreat to the physical body, ending the psychic experience. Onawa calms me, though.

Be at peace, Spirit Warrior. Look into my eyes.

I do. I focus completely on her huge green eyes, so fierce and wild, but at the same time calming and wise.

The Healer will buy you time.

"Healer? Aimee?"

She is not alone. Her allies are weak, but together they will prevail for a while. You must be prepared to return to them.

"Tell me."

Your body will be purified by heat, but will your mind be pure?

I can only look at her.

You must put aside your arrogance, Spirit Warrior. It is not you who will free your cousin.

"The Great Spirit. Through me?"

You are learning. This dark spirit will attack you. It will know things about you. It will say things that are true and things that are not true. It will speak of things that have happened and things that may happen. You must ignore it. You will not speak to the dark spirit except to command it to leave.

"I understand," I say.

If you do, you will find your destiny today, Spirit Warrior.

"Alan?"

The new voice is female, soft and weak. I turn away from Onawa to find a woman standing next to me. She is nearly transparent, and the form I see is like an old lady's scarf being pulled by the wind. She is literally ragged and rippling around the edges.

She looks so familiar. Then I realize who she is: Aimee's mom.

"She needs you, Alan," the ghostly woman says. "Please help my baby. He's coming back. He shouldn't be here . . ." The wind rips her to shreds, and she flutters away into the world of unseen traffic.

Sit on my back, Spirit Warrior.

"What?" I don't get it. Onawa is speaking to me now. Okay. But . . . did she just tell me to get on her back?

I must take you somewhere. Sit on my back.

"Where?"

She doesn't answer. She only looks at me with those huge, patient green eyes. In a daze, I throw a leg over Onawa's back and grab hold of her neck. Where is she taking me? She leaps forward, and I can feel her muscles tensing and relaxing as she races through the darkness that has no floor, ceiling, or walls, moving faster than I ever could, moving faster than sound, faster than the night.

There's a tunnel of light ahead and we race toward it. The round doorway grows bigger and bigger, and then we explode through it and into light.

We have left the Spirit World, but we are still spirits. Now, however, we are standing in a familiar location in the physical world. I look at my body sitting cross-legged in the sweat lodge. My hair is damp and hanging over my glistening shoulders. Sweat runs off my body. The air is humid. I slide off Onawa's back and stand over my body. Somehow, as a spirit, I can stand in the low-roofed sweat lodge; Onawa, while still seeming huge, also fits in the low structure.

Enter your flesh, focus your mind on the Great Spirit, and go to meet your enemy. Your cousin and the Healer need you now.

Onawa fades away like Aimee's mother did back in the dark place. I give my body one more look, wondering for a minute how I'm supposed to do this, then just jump at it as if I'm making a tackle.

I fall over on my side, suddenly heavy with flesh and muscle and bone. I push myself up and sweat runs into my eyes. I wipe it away and get to my knees. Reaching outside the flap of the lodge, I grab my clothes and pull them on.

"I'm coming, Aimee. Hold on . . ."

It looks like an Oklahoma tornado has torn through the hallway upstairs. There's not a picture frame left on the wall. The furniture Aimee and Courtney moved from Court's bedroom is shattered into hundreds of pieces. Courtney's clothes are torn and strewn up and down the hallway. Along both walls are deep scratches that dig all the way through the plaster. Worse, though, is the sight of Court's bedroom door. It's gone. Only a few jagged splinters hang on the brass hinges in the doorframe. Pieces of the door are in the hallway, and I know there will be a lot more inside.

I want to run. I want to run to Aimee.

But I can't. I walk slowly. I remain calm. I remain focused.

"He's coming back, Aimee. He's coming back! He—" Courtney seems to choke on her own voice. Then another voice speaks, a deep, cracked, evil voice. His voice. "Come on, you bastard boy. Come meet your destiny."

I step into the doorway. It's a shocking scene and shakes me to the core, but somehow I keep my composure. Courtney is tied to the posts of her bed. There are socks wrapped around her wrists to keep the ropes from chafing. She's still wearing her shoes and socks, white pieces of rope knotted around her ankles.

"We've been waiting for you, boy," Courtney says with the demon's voice.

Where's Aimee? For a moment I can't find her.

"She's got a boo-boo." The thing on the bed cackles at its own joke. Aimee—my Aimee—is slumped against the wall, a long splintery piece of wood protruding from her right arm, just a few inches below the shoulder. Her face is pale and drained, and she's so weak. I kneel beside her and take the hand of her injured arm. Her green eyes meet mine.

"We collapsed on the floor. He lost energy for a bit and I only barely got her tied to the bed, and then . . ." She trails off as if speaking all that so rapidly wore her out.

"I met your mother, Aimee."

Her eyes light just a little.

"This will hurt. Go clean it, then wrap it in a towel, okay? We'll get you to the hospital when this is over."

She gives the slightest nod, and I take the splinter in my left hand, steadying her arm with my right. "Great Spirit, let it be your will this doesn't hurt her too much."

Slow and steady, I pull the shard of wood from her arm. Her beautiful, tired face winces, scrunching up in pain, and then the splinter is out. I toss it aside. Her arm is bleeding, but the blood is not spurting. No major veins or arteries were hit. I guide her out of the room. I watch as she stumbles into the bathroom, then I turn to Courtney.

"Impressive," the thing on the bed says. "But you won't pull me out of this girl like you pulled the splinter out of your whore."

"No, I won't," I answer.

Do not speak to it! Onawa's voice roars through my head.

"Courtney! I know you can hear me. You have to fight this thing. Fight him, Courtney. You told me you want this evil spirit to leave you alone. Fight him now."

He growls something inarticulate and inhuman as I take a step toward the bed. Courtney's body begins thrashing wildly, and I'm afraid for a minute that the ropes won't hold, that the wooden bedposts will break off, that I won't be strong enough.

"*GET AWAY!*"

I reach for her.

"Please don't, Alan."

I stop. The voice is Courtney's—almost. I study her face for a minute. It's a raw, red mess of leaking sores. Her eyes burn with a feverish light, and she smiles a wicked, evil smile that isn't hers at all.

My fingertips make contact with her side. Her mouth opens wide, wide, wider than it should ever open, and she makes a sound that no human could possibly make. It's a low-pitched shriek that builds and builds, thudding at my brain like a jack-hammer. The River Man makes her turn away from me. Her arms strain against the ropes. I sit on the bed and press my left hand to her back, under her heart.

I close my eyes and focus.

You are a tool of one who is greater.

"Great Spirit, if it is your will, send this dark spirit out of my cousin. Fill me and use me to do your will."

Keep praying.

The thing growls like a caged, angry bear.

I repeat my prayer.

The thing speaks again. "You can't fight me. You are nothing. Your father left because he knew you would be worthless."

"Shut up!" I scream at the thing.

Do not speak to it!

The River Man laughs at me, a low, rumbling chuckle that is very out of place coming from my little female cousin.

"Do you know the things she used to do with Blake?" he asks.

"Great Spirit, I am weak," I call out. "I can't do this. You have to do it. If it is your will, send this dark spirit out of my cousin. Fill me and use me to do your will!"

The River Man screams again. I repeat the prayer, saying it over and over while the thing inside my cousin thrashes and fights me. Again and again I say it, until the words run together. No, they are not running together. I am speaking another language.

It's the language from my Navajo CDs.

It is the language of my ancestors.

Of my father.

My hand is cold where it's touching Courtney's back, as if something is crawling from her flesh into mine.

Bring it to us.

I'm not sure what Onawa means at first, but then I remember the dark place with all the spirits moving through it. Slowly I close my hand, keeping the fist pressed against Courtney's back. The cold spreads up my arm like ice, freezing my blood. I know if I open my eyes I will see my skin turning hard and blue.

Bring it to us now.

I concentrate on remembering that dark place where I spoke with Onawa. Then I am suddenly traveling. I am outside of my body again, but I'm not alone.

The River Man is there, in my grasp, struggling against me. He is a slippery shadow, squirming like a snake. He looks at me with black eyes that are somehow even blacker than the shadow that is his body.

"Don't do it, boy," he says in a soft, hissing voice. "Anything you want, I can give it to you. Football. I can make you the best ever. The best of anything. I can make you a king of men."

I never stop moving somehow. I'm not walking. It's more like a fast glide, kind of like flying, but not in a stretched-out Superman way. I don't answer the beast in my hand.

He stretches himself out again, then coils his long, clammy body around my arm until his face is near my ear. "Anything you want, Alan. Anything."

My mind betrays me. I think of Oklahoma, of football, of Aimee sitting in the stands of Memorial Stadium in Norman, cheering for me as I score touchdowns for the Oklahoma Sooners.

"Yesss," the River Man hisses. "Even that. Just say you want me. It will be yours."

Where is Onawa? Why won't she speak to me?

"She's left you. She is afraid, Alan. She made you fight me, but she's afraid to help you. She knows I'm too strong."

I stop moving. I search the darkness, looking for Onawa's glowing green eyes. What kind of spirit guide abandons her charge when he needs her most?

"She is useless. Useless and weak, Alan. Together, though, we are strong. Take me back. Let's go back."

He's pulling at me, dragging me back the way we came, back toward Courtney.

"No!" I manage to pull back. My arm is so cold. The freezing sensation has moved up to my shoulder, spreading across my chest, moving toward my heart. I know if it gets to my heart, the River Man will have me, too. "No." My voice is weak.

The River Man chuckles again. We begin sliding back toward Courtney.

"Onawa . . . where are you?" I beg. "Aimee . . ."

Suddenly a blast of heat bursts within me. It's like a sun has exploded inside me, burning me in a good way, driving the cold out of my chest.

"I'm here, Alan."

It's Aimee's voice, but she isn't here. Not here in the dark place. She's back in Courtney's bedroom.

She's put her healing hands on my body, adding her strength to mine.

"Great Spirit! I bring you this dark thing that you made for reasons I can't know," I yell into the darkness. "If it is your will, take it away from me and my family and friends and never let it bother this place again."

And there, finally, standing before me with her beautiful glowing eyes, is Onawa, my spirit guide. Her cougar mouth is smiling at me.

You have done well, Spirit Warrior, she says. *Give him to me.* She opens her mouth, and it's like her head splits apart. Between her teeth is only light, a light so bright it should be blinding, but somehow it isn't.

I reach forward. The River Man is still in my fist, but he's fighting, squirming and screaming and cursing and trying to make promises he can't keep. I push my fist between Onawa's long, sharp teeth, into her throat as far as I can reach, until my shoulder is pressed against her muzzle.

Inside her body I can see the River Man, a thing of writhing shadow, expanding around my arm, confined within Onawa. He glares at me, spitting and cursing, and then I release him and pull my arm free. Onawa closes her mouth.

The Great Spirit is pleased with you, but now the dark spirits will plague you until you go to join your ancestors.

"Who are my ancestors?" I ask. "Who is my father?"

There will come a time for that answer, Spirit Warrior. For now, know that it is not a man's ancestors who define who the man is. It is what he does for himself.

I'm so tired. I feel so weak.

Onawa is still talking. *Every man has a destiny, Spirit Warrior—but each man must decide if he will accept it.*

I feel like I'm falling. I reach forward and my hand finds Onawa's head. I lean against her. Sag against her, really.

Your body is near death. The dark one's poison was very deep.

"I'm dying?"

Look behind me.

I somehow find the strength to raise my head. I see a light, like the mouth of a tunnel, behind Onawa. "What is it?" I ask.

The next world. It is where spirits go when the flesh dies.

When the flesh . . . dies?

We move slowly toward the light.

· 25 ·
AIMEE

All my life I've wanted to save people, to be a hero kind of person. All my life I've wished that I could've stopped my mom from going out to that river, that I could've kept her alive.

But I failed.

The moment I step back into the bedroom and smell the decay, I realize I've failed again. I never should have left him alone to fight. I never should have tried to find gauze to take care of my arm.

"Alan!" I yell his name like that will help, like it is magic or a prayer.

But his name is just a name, and my yelling it doesn't keep him from being collapsed on the bed with the thing that's taken over Courtney. His hand is beneath her back. His other arm is thrown sideways, parallel to her leg. He's breathing, but only just. His mouth twitches. He's fighting him. He's fighting the River Man somehow.

I run to him, to them. The entire house shakes. The floor seems to buck. The walls sway. He's trying to make it fall on us, I think. He's trying to ruin it all.

When I get to the bed, Court's eyes flash open. It is not Court inside them. It's something wicked. It is something that is so evil it could never understand the light.

Court's mouth moves and says one word: "Mine."

Anger surges inside me. "Oh, no way, baby. Not on my watch."

It almost makes me laugh. *Not on my watch.*

I lunge forward, placing my hands on Alan's broad back. He doesn't move. Something in the hallway crashes to the floor. The studs in the walls creak.

"Alan." I say his name, trying to make it into something magic. But that's not how it works. The something magic is in me. I am so tired, but I will myself to focus. My hands tingle with power. It's the power of light. I whisper the words, "I'm here, Alan."

He doesn't move.

I push the panic away. I force the pain away. Pieces of door are slamming toward us again, whirling around us. One strikes Alan in the shoulder. One hits me in the leg. I keep focused. The light surges. My hands shake with it. It's draining me, draining everything from me, and I don't care. I just want Alan back. I don't want to fail again. Something shifts in the room. Courtney's eyes soften, fluttering closed as if she's exhausted. It still smells rank—like feces and death, but something is gone. Alan stops moving.

He's gone.

I turn him over, check for a heartbeat. Nothing. No pulse. His chest isn't moving.

"Aim?" Court's voice comes from the bed, weak and scared.

"I'm here, Court," I say. I put both hands on Alan's chest. "Stay with me. Please, please, stay with me."

I shove all the power I have toward him. Hopefully it isn't too late. He can't die. He can't. He can't die.

Every single cell of me pushes light to him, begging God that he doesn't die.

"Please," I plead. "Please . . ."

There's nothing. He doesn't move. The lump in my throat widens so that I can't swallow. I refuse to look away. I grab his head. My fingers lace into his hair and I whisper his name.

He gasps and opens his eyes. They are his eyes, just his, nobody else's. Blinking hard, he smiles.

"Aimee?" he whispers. He grabs my hair like he's making sure I'm real.

I smile. I'm so weak from saving him that it's hard for me to not fall on top of him, but I don't. My hands are shaking as they move to his face.

"You came back?" I ask, matching his whisper with my own.

"For you." He wets his lips. His voice is hoarse, like he's been yelling. "For you."

I lean down. Our lips touch and it is sweet, so sweet.

Courtney croaks in a kind of laryngitis-style voice, "Guys. Could you stop making out and untie me because . . . you know . . . it's a little on the weird side of kinky, the whole tied-up thing. And . . . I . . . ?"

I laugh and pull away from Alan. I'm tired from bringing

Alan back, but just seeing Courtney there rejuvenates me a little. Her face is clear. Her hair's a total mess, but her eyes are Courtney eyes, kind, a little sarcastic, but good.

"Oh," I say, and start working at the knots on her hands. My arm hurts from the movement, but I don't care. "Oh, Court, you're so beautiful."

"Beautiful?" She shakes her head. I free one hand and start working on the other. "Think we should take a pic?"

"And put you in for prom queen?" I get the other hand free and help her sit up. "Yes."

Alan struggles to sit up, too.

"You," I order. "Stay there. You just died."

Court had been working on her foot bindings, but her fingers stop. "Alan died? You died?" Her quivering hand covers her mouth.

Alan nods slowly. The deep, distant gaze of his eyes leaves her face and focuses on me. "Aimee saved me."

That's when it hits me. I did. I saved him. Me.

We are all too messed up and tired to clean anything more than our wounds. We sort of stumble down the stairs and sit together on the couch. I take the middle. Alan's arm rests around my shoulders, but it's almost a dead weight. He's so tired. Court and I are in pretty much the same boat.

We sit there and stare at the TV. It's not even on, but we stare at the black, blank screen like it's some fascinating blockbuster epic.

"We should clean upstairs," Alan says. He runs his free hand across his eyes. "Your mom will go insane when she sees it. My mom, too."

"Clean?" Court snorts. She rests her head against my shoulder. "There are claw marks in the walls. My bed is kindling. I don't suppose either of you can magically poof it all back to normal."

I wiggle my fingers. "No special poof powers."

She groans. "Some kind of healer you are."

We sit.

"Do you think we're in shock?" I finally ask.

Alan nods.

We sit some more.

"Do you think he's really gone?" Court shudders. "Is he gone for good?"

We both wait for Alan to answer. He hauls in a deep breath. His entire chest moves with it. "He's gone."

"And you know this for a fact?" Court prods.

"I know it," he insists.

Our eyes meet. There's so much pain in there, but there's strength, too.

"I'm so sorry." Court's voice is a half sob. "I'm so sorry. I just wanted my dad, you know. I wanted him back so bad. I just wanted . . ."

I wrap my arms around her. She crumples into them and cries.

The house is so silent, except for the sound of regret and of mourning and of pain and loss, and that's the way it is supposed to be. Alan leans toward us and wraps his arms around both of us. For a second I imagine my mom smiling at me. Alan and I did what she couldn't do. We protected us.

"It's okay," I whisper into Court's hair. "It's all okay now. It's okay."

After a minute Court lifts her head. She sniffs and rubs at her nose. "What happened with that stupid Cheeto? Did they sell it yet?"

I wipe the tears off her cheeks. "The bidding's up to $1,200."

"You're not serious," Alan says.

"Man." Court flops back against the armrest. "This world is so freaking weird."

· 26 ·
ALAN

"You really have changed." Mom reaches over and touches my hair when she says it. This is unusual for Mom; she's not much of a toucher, really. But since she came home that day and found the three of us sitting on Aunt Lisa's couch, things have been a little strange. Not that they weren't strange before.

The hair Mom touches is gray. I am a seventeen-year-old half-Navajo boy with streaks of gray hair at both temples. I guess that comes from traveling in the Spirit World. From dying and coming back.

"We all change, Mom," I tell her. "It's part of life."

"Says the boy who fought so hard to stay in Oklahoma," she teases as her hand drops to her side. Her hands slide around and she hooks her thumbs in her back pockets; a strange look comes over her face. "I'm sorry I dragged you away from home."

"Home is where you can scratch no matter where it itches" I grin, and she shakes her head. "There's also that other saying, you know." I look through the open front door to where Aimee and Benji are cleaning paintbrushes in the yard.

"What saying is that?" Mom asks.

"Home is where the heart is."

She laughs at me then. "We only had to travel halfway across the country to find a girl good enough for my boy."

"I think there were other reasons," I say. "But Aimee is a definite perk."

"Talking in riddles again?"

I smile at her, but I know it's kind of a sad smile. "It's the new me."

It's Sunday afternoon, more than two weeks after the battle with the River Man. A lot has changed. I went to my first New England funeral, for Chris Paquette, and I'd be happy never to go to another one again.

Blake was picked up on U.S. Highway 1 about ten miles north of town the day after the battle with the River Man. An older couple on their way to the coast saw him stumble out of the woods and collapse beside the highway. They brought him into town and left him at the hospital, where he was treated for hypothermia and questioned by the police. Blake didn't know anything about Chris's death. The news was pretty hard on him. After our fight, he'd gone home, he said. That's the last thing he remembers until he woke up facedown in the woods beside the river.

"It was like a shadow had been sucked out of my head," he'd said in a newspaper article printed a couple of days after he was found.

Today, the house is full of the smell of fresh paint. The

upstairs hallway has new Sheetrock, put in yesterday, and today it is painted, all with the help of Aimee and her menfolk. Courtney has new furniture, though most of it came from a secondhand store in Bangor. She calls it retro-chic, and I honestly don't know if she's trying to make the best of sleeping on a used bed or if she really thinks it's cool.

Gramps and Mr. Avery come down the steps. Gramps is grinning at me. "Women love a gray-haired man," he jokes, running a hand over his own head.

I laugh. "Thanks again for all your help," I say.

"I don't mind," Gramps says. "But you know Benji's price."

"I know." I grin and look back out the door. Benji and Courtney are using the brushes to throw water at each other now. The sky is overcast and the TV weatherman says it'll snow tonight. "Dinner and a movie with me and Aimee. And a new football."

"He'll expect some kissing on the date," Gramps says. "That way he can tell on her. And you have to teach him how to throw the football like Tom Brady."

"Well, if I must," I agree. "I suppose that's a pretty good trade for the $1,567.43 you guys got for a Cheeto with boobs."

Yes, that's how much they got for the Marilyn Monroe Cheeto. It was Benji's idea to give the money to Aunt Lisa to help pay for fixing her house.

Benji may be the only one besides me, Aimee, and Courtney who truly believed our story about what happened in Aunt Lisa's house that day. Maybe Gramps does; he's hard to read. But nobody really argued with us, either, so maybe I'm just not giving them enough credit. Maybe they sense a change in the house. In the town. Maybe they're just glad the dreams are gone and Courtney is back to normal.

Gramps and Mr. Avery move away, going outside. Aunt Lisa walks out of Courtney's room upstairs and smiles at me as she comes down. A stair above me, she's my height. She stops there and puts her arms around my shoulders.

"Thank you," she whispers into my ear. Maybe she *does* believe. She leaves me and goes outside with the others.

It's just me and Mom, alone in the house, watching everyone else outside. Mom comes over, pulling a folded paper out of her back pocket. Even before she hands it over to me I see the University of Oklahoma logo on it. "This came for you yesterday," she says. "You were busy, and . . ." She sighs. "It's from the athletic director's office."

"Oh." I unfold the cream-colored sealed envelope. There's a stamp from where it was forwarded from our old Oklahoma City address. I look at the red OU logo in the return address corner. I don't open it. I just look at it.

"Alan?"

"Yeah, Mom?" Her eyes are watering a little. "What's wrong?"

"You look just like your father," she says.

I put my arm around her and hug her so tight her back pops. I release her just a little as I say, "I know, Mom. Sometimes Fate puts us right where we need to be, and we don't realize it until later."

She hugs me back, then steps away. Now the tears are running down her cheeks, but she's smiling.

She says it again. "You really have changed."

· 27 ·
AIMEE

Things slowly become a new kind of normal. The footsteps in our house go away, but occasionally I still smell vanilla. My dad doesn't get cranky when Benji or I mention it. Instead he smiles, and sometimes he'll even say, "It's nice to know she's still around."

And it is.

My mom may not have succeeded in stopping the River Man, but she lost her life trying to keep her family safe. We think the painted rock and the ruined painting were done by her, not him; she was trying to warn us, to keep us safe still.

I used to be embarrassed by my mom, but now I know what she is—she's a hero. I can only hope that I'll use my gifts half as bravely as she did. I only hope that I can figure out exactly what my gifts can do. I will. I'm sure.

Sometimes I write her little notes and drop them into the river, which is sort of silly, I know. They say things like "I love you" or "Thank you" or "Look for Court's dad." They are small pieces of paper, and the tide takes them, wetting them and heavying them before they finally sink below the water. It might be silly, but I think she reads them.

The most recent one I sent was just this morning. Benji was off at swim practice with Gramps, and I walked down to the river with my dad. The water was smooth and beautiful. You couldn't tell that people died in it. You couldn't tell that something wicked lurked inside it. We took out the kayaks and when we were just about a quarter mile toward the bay, he said, "You seem stronger now, Aimee."

"I think I'm liking who I am," I said, and stopped paddling for a second, just letting the tide slowly take me. "It sounds cheesy and maybe egotistical, but I like the parts of me that are Mom, the weird healing-dreaming parts."

"I like those parts, too," he said.

And I know he wasn't lying.

I put the big yellow paddle back into the water and we pushed toward Eagle Point. That's where I dropped the last note. The river took it. Water pulled it away and under until it became just a speck of white paper, and then just a memory. Once it was gone, a seal head popped up and it reminded me of her—those huge eyes.

"What did it say?" my dad asked.

I swallowed. "It said, 'Thank you for being my mom. I am so proud to be your daughter.'"

"She would be proud of you," he said. His voice broke, and he obviously tried to save himself from being all emotional by splashing me with water. It tasted of ocean salt.

I splashed him back for a second, and then I couldn't help it. I asked, "Are you? Are you proud of me?"

"I am, but it doesn't matter."

"It doesn't?"

"No. What matters is that you're proud of yourself."

Acknowledgments

Carrie and Steve would like to thank Jeaniene Frost and Melissa Marr for introducing them, as well as Edward Necarsulmer IV at MacIntosh & Otis Literary Agency and Michelle Nagler and Margaret Miller at Bloomsbury for believing in this project.

From Carrie:
Thanks to Jackie Shriver, Karin Raymond, Chris LaSalle, Dave Lafleur, Dave Stoker, and Joe Tullgern for helping me make it through all the scary that happened before college. Thanks to my favorite knight, Edward Necarsulmer, Lori Bartlett, Marie Overlock, Alice Dow, Kelly R., Laura Hamor, Amilie Bacon, Jennifer Osborn, Jim Willis, Emily Ciciotte, Betty Morse, Lew Barnard, Melodye Shore, Deb Shapiro, Fans of Awesomeness, and Shaun Farrar for helping me make it through all the scariness of now.

From Steve:
Thanks to Gayleen Rabakukk and Paul White for keeping me going when writing was more frustration than fun. Thanks to Edward Necarsulmer for taking on Carrie's friend. Thanks to Ms. Dragoun for not having me arrested when I wrote my first horror story in tenth grade, and to Dr. Gladys Lewis for showing me that literature is more than individual books. Thanks, also, to the students, staff, and my fellow faculty members at Western Heights High School. And in memory of Wilda Walker, who introduced me to creative writing and became a friend.